LUST AND LADY SAXON

Charles helped me to my room and I collapsed across the bed. I giggled, feeling drunk and silly – and very naughty.

'You'll have to undress me, Charles,' I said. 'I feel as weak as a kitten.'

He hesitated. 'If you're trying to seduce me, Diana, you may regret it in the morning.'

'But I can't manage by myself,' I said and he reached for the zip at the back of my dress. He drew it off over my coiled auburn hair and the tresses came loose and fell to my shoulders. He was staring at my overfilled brassiere. I struggled to unclip it myself and threw the flimsy garment aside, shaking my breasts and enjoying the sudden freedom from restriction.

'And now the rest,' I said to him.

'It will be my pleasure,' Charles whispered softly . . .

Lust and Lady Saxon

Lesley Asquith

HEADLINE
DELTA

First published in 1995
by HEADLINE BOOK PUBLISHING

A HEADLINE DELTA paperback

10 9 8 7 6 5 4 3 2 1

ISBN 0 7472 4762 5

Typeset by CBS, Felixstowe, Suffolk

Printed and bound in Great Britain by
Cox & Wyman Ltd, Reading, Berks

HEADLINE BOOK PUBLISHING
A division of Hodder Headline PLC
338 Euston Road
London NW1 3BH

Lust and Lady Saxon

Chapter One
ITALY

'I adore your breasts,' murmured the Italian, staring across the table as if intent on eating me alive. Possessor of a large and shapely bosom, I'd heard much the same phrased in different ways since I was a teenager and my breasts had first attracted men's covetous glances. Basically they all wanted to bare my ample tits and fondle and suck them.

Liberal amounts of champagne had relaxed my host and I, firing up his lustful nature and making me feel wickedly wanton.

'Such perfection, such magnificent mounds,' my dinner companion continued, warming to the subject of my bosom. He kissed his fingertips. 'Those glorious nipples, they threaten to pierce your gown. I wish to worship them with my lips, Lady Saxon. Shame on your absent husband for neglecting such beauty.'

'Signor Giotti—' I began, trying to maintain a straight face at his flowery speech. He interrupted me, taking my hands in his.

'Romeo, please,' he insisted, stroking my palms suggestively. He had been well named, I had to admit, trying to extricate my hands. His heavily accented English was no doubt well practised in seducing susceptible females, even if it was a little outrageous for a first date. Do remember you are with a married woman, sir! I should have told him, but I've always enjoyed flirtatious rogues.

I had accepted Count Giotti's invitation to dinner because I'd been left alone in a strange city. It was hard to resist. The restaurant he suggested was the best and therefore the most expensive in town. And he was my husband's immediate superior, a figurehead, perhaps, but one whose position and influence could further my Harry's United Nations' career. I didn't know he would ply me with wine and come on strong. And I had resolved to play the faithful wife while on my own.

'Romeo, then,' I agreed to call him. 'If as you claim my husband is neglecting me, it's because you sent him off to Thailand before we were even settled in Rome. I shall suspect an ulterior motive if you insist on saying such things to me.' While gently admonishing him I smiled to show I was not too angry at his forwardness. I had never been averse to being flattered by good-looking men, which he undoubtedly was with his dark Latin macho features. I speculated that he was at least a good ten years younger than myself, which is always a strong temptation for an older woman.

'With his record in developing nations,' Romeo Giotti pointed out smoothly, recapturing my hands and continuing to fondle them, 'Harry was the ideal man to send on this fact-finding mission. The Thai government wanted him and he was delighted to go.' His dark eyes glowed with wicked intent. 'And I was delighted to send him.'

I'll just bet you were, I thought, recognising undisguised lust in his dark eyes and on his handsome aristocratic face. This was the look of a randy male intent on seduction. He had wined, dined and flattered me opulently all evening with the one object in mind.

'Don't ogle my bosom so obviously,' I chided him in a low voice, drawing together the loose neck of my evening gown. I knew I was revealing inches of creamy cleavage. Of course, we well-endowed women do wear low-cut dresses to attract attention and show off our wares, even if we pretend it is not so. 'People at the next table can see you staring.'

'They are Italian and would not expect me to do otherwise,' he said, dismissing my protest. 'More champagne, Lady Saxon. Or shall I see you safely home?'

Safety had nothing to do with it. As an uninhibited woman by nature who considered a sexual adventure one of life's gifts, I still did not want Giotti to think the wife of one of his senior executives could be charmed into an affair so easily after a first evening together.

'I shall order a taxi to take me to my apartment,' I said as if meaning it, seeing him shake him head. Of course, apparent reluctance on the part of a female marked out for seduction is added zest to a man like Giotti. He snapped his fingers and a waiter appeared as if by magic, hovering and bowing low to enquire what Count Giotti desired.

He desired me, of course, and even the waiter with his smirk in my direction was aware of it. He had no doubt seen Giotti lead off many women to be ravished so I determined that this lady was not for being laid. Stuff you too, I thought, poking out my tongue in a defiant gesture at the waiter, making him recoil.

I wasn't overly impressed by the knowledge that my ardent lothario was a count. I was the youngest daughter of a quarry labourer, brought up in a Scottish cottage by proud parents. My life since running away from home at sixteen had been full and adventurous, satisfyingly sexual, and I'd mixed with both the highest and lowest born. I stood to allow the waiter

3

to adjust my wrap about my shoulders, noting that he regarded me with due respect.

I was escorted outside to a gleaming black limousine. A uniformed chauffeur stood at attention, holding open the rear door for me to enter. A tall and handsome young Italian stallion, he too could not disguise a grin of approval at his master's choice.

In the fresh air I found the champagne made me feel tipsy. Much as I regularly needed a good servicing from a lusty male, again I resolved the confident Giotti was going to be out of luck. The chauffeur steadied my arm as I made to get into the car. As he did so, I felt a hand sidle over my buttock cheeks, lingering as if to savour the rounds through the smooth silk of my gown. Both moons were squeezed and patted as if being assessed for size and shape.

As ever, such an advance, appreciative and entirely unexpected, sent a flow of sensations coursing through my lower stomach to my sex. I was half-inside the car and therefore ideally positioned to be fondled. The hand then ventured between the cleft of my cheeks. I felt groping fingers at my rear-directed bulge, pressing to the target through both the silk of my gown and briefs. So much for my determination, I reprimanded myself, not only allowing the liberty but rotating my bottom back against the hand. I found the will to draw away only at the thought that Giotti was so sure of me he'd begun his campaign at the pavement.

Yet looking out I saw him yards away, engaged in tipping the top-hatted commissionaire at the restaurant door, while the young chauffeur stood by pleased with himself. 'You, it was *you*,' I said perplexed, but wry amusement at his cheek forcing a smile. 'You were feeling my bum, you naughty boy. Shame on you. And did you enjoy it?'

'Si, signorina,' the boy agreed appreciatively. He added

in English, speaking quietly as his master approached, 'I should like very much that we continue. May I call on you?'

The very idea was intriguing, of course. He was handsome and athletic, a ready-to-hand toy boy who could supply my needs while Harry was away. But I had no chance to answer him for Giotti was joining me in the rear of the car.

'We must go topless,' he announced. 'Riccardo, operate the roof mechanism. Let us see the stars; this night is too romantic to be shut out.' The roof of the car folded back and indeed the Roman night was bright with stars. 'Do you feel romantic, my dear, on such a pleasant night?' he enquired in a smooth voice, taking my hands in his again. 'This is Rome, after all.'

'You'd better take me home,' I insisted.

'To *my* home,' he said. 'I want to show you my villa.'

Riccardo drove slowly to negotiate the night traffic. In the soft-leathered luxury of the Rolls-Royce, Giotti leaned close, his shoulder to mine, now stroking my arm sensuously. The man is really trying, I thought, not averse to a fling with him, yet wary of his absolute discretion if I allowed him even a one-night session. I had no wish for it to become common knowledge that Harry's wife was so easily obtainable in his absence. I removed his hand. 'I'm not interested,' I said.

For a moment I thought he would believe me, shrugging and smiling as if accepting my wish to be unmolested. He captured my hands again a moment later, however, to resume the assault. '*Cara mio*,' he said in his best seductive voice. 'You are *bellissimo*, so very beautiful. Is there no chance?'

'I'm a married woman,' I reminded him.

'Yes, regarding that,' he began slyly, stroking my palms seductively as if to transmit his passion to me, 'I have to inform you that your husband *volunteered* to be sent to Thailand and leave you so alone. He pleaded that there was so much his expertise could do to improve life for the peasant farmers there.'

'Good for Harry,' I said to show my approval. 'How like him.'

'Most wives would not agree,' Giotti said, pursuing the topic. 'His brief was to be stationed here in Rome, accompanied by you, given a luxury apartment in this most beautiful city. Instead he chose to rough it in some jungle. I agreed that he should go. The Food and Agricultural Organisation of the United Nations have every confidence his reports and submissions will be of great value.'

I could have told him that, my husband being an acknowledged authority in the field of irrigation and added crop production for developing countries. Harry had received a knighthood for his work in Africa and had made an official lady out of me. Never happy tied to an office, he sought to be in the field where he could do most good. If Giotti had brought up the subject of me having to fend for myself in a strange city as yet another ploy to further his more immediate goal, fucking his colleague's wife, he would have to do better. I should have known, dealing with such a smooth operator.

'How would you like to live in Thailand with your husband?' was his next gambit. 'Bangkok is a beautiful city. Wonderful night life and restaurants. The most beautiful beaches along the coast. You would love it there—' One of his hands left mine and he used the back of his fingers to idly stroke my bare shoulder. 'Think about it, my dear.'

'Harry's assignment is a temporary one,' I said. 'He's due back when his findings are completed.'

'I could suggest his posting be for at least a year or even two,' Giotti smiled deviously. 'That's what your husband requested.' The rest was left unsaid as my neck was stroked gently. I saw his eyes look greedily down the neck of my gown, no doubt picturing the unseen rounds of my breasts, desiring to have them free and unfettered for his pleasure. Such lewd and obvious intent invariably made them swell to a tightness; my nipples tingled, anticipating loving attention. 'Think of it,' he repeated. 'You could leave quite soon.'

'And as Harry's head of department you would recommend that – in certain circumstances?' I suggested, giving him ten out of ten for effort. With my ear lobe now being fondled between his thumb and forefinger I felt more inclined to let him have his way with me. I was intrigued to discover if his sexual prowess matched his impassioned words. Sleeping with such a scheming and attractive seducer might be very satisfying, and if it enabled my husband to get exactly the job he wanted, so much the better. 'I'd do whatever is necessary to let Harry work in Thailand,' I added as innocently as possible. 'I mean to go out there to join him. I'd be so grateful if you could help.'

'Just how grateful, Lady Saxon?' Giotti answered, leaning to kiss my neck and cheek lingeringly. 'You know I find you a most attractive woman, so hard to resist. Let me show you how much.'

'Diana,' I said weakly, my amusement at his tactics and my act as the loyal wife overwhelmed by a sudden surge of arousal which gripped my lower belly and lubricated my sex as his hand slipped down inside my gown. He cupped both breasts as if testing their mass and weight, his fondling unhurried and expert. 'You'd better call me Diana if you insist on doing that,' I moaned softly, his thumb flicking my taut nipples.

His mouth descended on mine, wet and open, a warm tongue probing as my arms automatically went around his neck. As our lips parted I gasped out that I didn't mean this to happen, hadn't meant it to start. His mouth twisted in a cruel grin of triumph, no doubt congratulating himself on the seduction of a respectable married woman. 'It's not right,' I protested feebly. 'But you *make* me want to—'

I imagine no more thrilling words can be uttered to inflame an already randy male. '*Si, si, cara mio*,' Giotti exulted, reverting to his native tongue. 'Such breasts, such firm flesh, they're so big, so adorable. Please, please, I must, must—'

He drew them out from the neck of my gown, his mouth seeking and sucking avidly on his near-side nipple while grasping the neighbour breast. Highly sensitive to fingers and lips I cradled his head, giving out low moans of unstinted pleasure, switching him to the unattended nipple which grew elongated and stiffer as he sucked. My hand sought his lap and discovered an engorged stalk standing bolt upright from his trousers, throbbing hot in my grasp.

'You want it, don't you?' he grunted, pushing me back along the seat, clawing up my long gown in haste, bundling it above my waist to reveal my thighs. My briefs tore in his urgency to remove them, then his face was between my thighs, his mouth at my source of pleasure, tonguing me to a climax that had me thrusting my sex violently against him while I cried out in relief.

'Fuck me now, fuck me!' I demanded, the only appropriate thing to say for what I wanted badly. But Giotti was sitting up, drying his mouth and his slackened penis with a silk handkerchief. 'Drive on, Riccardo,' he ordered his chauffeur, and I noted that the car had stopped and the young driver had turned with his arm across the seat to observe all that had taken place. He grinned at me as I sat up and straightened my dress.

'Yes, drive me home,' I ordered, playing the distressed wife. 'I think quite enough has happened for tonight.'

Much as Giotti pleaded that I should go spend the night at his villa and much as I had a wilful desire to do so, my decision to be taken to my apartment was a deliberate one. I didn't want Giotti to think I was too available, one who couldn't help herself being seduced against her better nature. Withholding something from him would ensure he kept his word on my husband being allowed to stay in Thailand and my joining him – and it would make the Italian all the keener to have more of me. He kissed my hand as I left the car at my apartment, saying he would send his chauffeur to collect me in the morning and that we must spend more time together. Why not tonight? he added, making a last plea.

'Then I shall arrange something special,' I was told as he accepted my refusal. 'You like sailing? We'll go to the nearby port of Ostra where my yacht is moored. Let me make your short stay in Italy memorable before you leave for Bangkok.'

'I'll come if you promise I get to join my husband,' I said, leaving him to think that over.

In my bedroom I undressed, standing naked before my mirror. I was pleased with my figure. My breasts were firm and uptilted, the nipples still sharply pointed from the ardent attention they'd received. My sex was loose and oily from the tonguing I'd received, a demanding itch within it. I showered and soaped between my thighs, my fingers lingering, entering, until I leaned back against the tiled wall of the cubicle and gave myself relief. All in all, I had to admit, my introduction to Italy gave promise of an interesting stay.

Chapter Two
ENGLAND

Weak as I confess I am at resisting temptation of a sexual nature, I never *sought* to give my husband any reason for being dissatisfied with me as a loving wife. My aim has always been to ensure his continued pleasure in having me and I have striven to further his career ambitions in every way – and I do mean every way. For my part I am blissfully content with our married life. I was happy even in the early years when Harry was at university studying civil engineering. Debts mounted no matter how frugally we lived but I did without and scrimped and saved to make our little home comfortable.

We lived in an attic flat in Oxford with a sloping roof and a kitchen that doubled as a bathroom, which was all we could afford. My independent husband refused financial help from his wealthy father, working at nights and weekends between studying, earning extra income as a barman or a labourer on building sites. Our first baby had arrived due to the enthusiastic lovemaking we thrived on, but I too earned useful sums typing addresses on envelopes at home for a mail-order firm. We didn't even own a radio but our great pleasure was in the time we could spend together and especially in bed. I determined to stay truly faithful and was

11

a demanding young wife in one respect only – sex.

If Harry was too tired returning from late-night work or I was asleep when he came in, I could rouse more than his interest by my special method of waking him the next morning. With the covers drawn back he would get a rousing early call with me bending over his midriff, taking his beautiful penis in my fingers and sucking the slackness to iron-hard erection. He would often pretend to sleep on, enjoying the attention, so I would straddle his loins and impale myself on the stalk I had encouraged to stiffen in my mouth, riding him to a lovely come. At other times he'd roll me over to penetrate my cunt and fuck me strenuously. We always used such words to heighten the lewdness between us. My awakening him in this way never failed to lead to a torrid session until our infant son, Peter, awoke across the room in his cot demanding his early-morning feed of my abundant breast milk.

Being me, though I had the best intentions of remaining a loyal and dutiful wife, I could not pretend that other men held no further attraction for me. I have always enjoyed being admired and experiencing the thrill of having sex with someone new but I was determined to set my mind against weakening. There were many offers, young mothers in the bloom of youth always arouse a lech in certain men. The butcher where I shopped for the cheapest cuts of meat was mesmerised by my milk-swollen breasts whenever I entered his premises. His hand would linger on mine when he gave me change. At home I'd find sausages or a small joint of beef had been slipped into my basket, secretly wrapped with my purchase. But he was fat and middle-aged with a suspicious wife behind the counter, and his bait was withdrawn when, over a period of time, I gave him no encouragement. At least we dined better while it lasted.

Also an offer in return for sexual favours at this time was

the waiving of weekly payments due on the bed Harry and I slept in. Lamont's was an old-established family business. Their customers invariably bought their goods on the hire-purchase system, known more generally in those post-war days as 'on tick' or 'the never-never'. Just as rent collectors called house-to-house to get weekly payments, so firms like Lamont's ensured they got their instalments by sending out so-called tally-men. My weekly visitor was a Lamont called Nigel.

He was young, shy and, after his first knock on my door, quite infatuated with me. I made tea when he arrived so he began to bring biscuits or a cake from a nearby baker's shop. One afternoon, as I was seeing him off at the door, he suddenly kissed me. Then, as his lips left mine he turned bright red and stuttered out an apology. He stumbled backwards, about to go headlong down the steep attic stairs, when I grabbed him to prevent his fall. Holding him close, my breasts to his chest and our bodies pressed together, our next kiss was more deliberate and longer. As it lingered, my mouth opened to accept his probing tongue. On the plump mound at the fork of my thighs I felt a growing hardness stretch directly against my cleft.

Nigel leapt apart, blurting out another apology before bolting down the stairway. I closed the door and leaned against it, trembling and weak at the knees. My feelings were a mixture of strong arousal and relief that Nigel had not continued kissing me or pressing his hardness to my palpitating sex. If he had, and then led me indoors to the bed beside which my baby slept for his afternoon nap, I would not have found the will to resist. To compensate, my thoughts whirling in my great excitement, I fell on the bed, my hands clawing up my dress.

Legs stretched wide apart, I put my hand inside my cotton

knickers and onto the raised bulge of my pussy, the crisp hairs surrounding swollen outer lips, parted and ripe for self-pleasuring. I gave a low moan as my middle finger entered, sliding up easily in the juicy oil lubricating my inner folds. My clitty was a hard prominence, tingling at my touch and my pelvis lifted as I gave myself over to the tremors rippling my whole being, convulsing my stomach, transmitting gasp-making sensations to my breasts and nipples.

An intuition that I was not alone suddenly stilled my hand. My wildly rolling eyes focused on my husband standing before me. 'Go on, Diana,' he urged in a strange low voice, 'Don't stop now. I love to see you masturbating. Go on and finish, give yourself a lovely come.' He sat down alongside me on the bed, a hand roving over my breasts. 'What brought this on? Were you thinking of me? Have I been neglecting you?'

He had not been neglecting me, with my appetite for sex I never allowed that. As for thinking of him, it was with a rush of guilt I remembered I had been fantasising about Nigel Lamont fucking me across the bed. 'I don't know what made me want to,' I lied. 'The feeling just came over me. Fuck me, Harry. Now you're here, I don't need to do this.'

'I want you to,' he said, excitement making him sound hoarse. 'It's a wonderful sight for a man to see a girl bringing herself off. But I haven't time to fuck you now, I'm only here for a moment to pick up some lecture notes. You're almost there, love. Go on—' He stood to look directly down on me, eyes alight. 'Let me see you come.'

'You mean devil,' I moaned, much too far advanced in arousing myself to prevent my hand from continuing. 'I'll make you pay for this later.' And with my husband watching my every move, my excitement mounted until my cries were so loud that Harry put his hand over my mouth to avoid waking the baby. A better way of stifling my noisy pleasure occurred to me. I twisted my face from his cupped hand. 'Give me your cock,' I urged him. 'Use my mouth. Fill it. Let me suck you.'

My offer was too hard to resist. Harry leaned forward over my face, undoing his fly and bringing out his thick stalk stiffened by viewing his wife in the act of masturbating. He fed it to my lips and I craned my neck to get as much of it as I could, all the while fingering myself to a frenzy. The lewdness of my behaviour had my lower torso convulsing agitatedly, my bottom thumping the bed in my final spasms while my jaw worked. Then Harry stifled a long groan, knees jerking as he saturated my throat with repeated spurts of his come.

'You take a lot out of me,' he teased me as we recovered. 'Wouldn't change you for the world, even if you take so much keeping up with. But I'll do it. I wouldn't want anyone else doing my job.'

'I'd never let anyone else have me,' I promised, but after Harry had left my mind wandered back to Nigel's sweet kisses. Forget it, I ordered myself, he's just a naive boy who got carried away in the heat of the moment. In fact he was just a year or two younger than myself.

All the same I found myself looking forward to his next visit, but for the following month he did not appear. Then one day while I was shopping, we met face to face in the street.

'Where have you been, Nigel?' I said to him, blocking his escape with my baby's pram as I saw his young face redden and he tried to walk on with an embarrassed nod of recognition. 'You haven't been for your weekly payments and it's mounting up—' It was ten old shillings a week and, although I had put it aside, the temptation to spend it at times had been hard to resist. 'I'm on my way home now, so come with me and you'll get your money.'

'I'd better not,' he mumbled nervously. 'I am rather busy.'

Silly boy, I thought. All this over a kiss or two. 'You've been avoiding me,' I admonished him sternly, enjoying his discomfort as females do with an impressionable subject. 'I don't want to fall behind with my payments. No argument, I want you to come and get the instalment book marked up to date. I can't afford to get into debt.'

'You're not in debt, Mrs Saxon,' Nigel informed me, almost wringing his hands in his anguish. 'I haven't called because, because of my inexcusable behaviour last visit,' he blurted out, 'but I've marked up the payments every week. I did it because I wanted to, to help you – I paid it as my way of apologising.'

That would mean the two whole pounds I'd saved in my piggy bank was mine, my calculating thrifty little housewife's mind calculated. What's more, seeing Nigel fidgeting about before me, knowing the spell he was under, made me desire to torment him further. Of course it was unfair and playing with fire, but the devil in me prodded me to proceed.

He escorted me home at my bidding and stayed for coffee. He sat opposite me, holding his cup and saucer awkwardly, only mumbling as I tried to ask him about himself. He wasn't going into the family business, I discovered, he was at an art college, and his great interest was photography. It was like drawing teeth, as they say. I had Peter on my lap getting hungry, and the wicked impulse I'd had before returned. Should I feed him before this youth? 'It's time for Peter to be fed,' I found myself saying, trembling at the thought that I'd be uncovering my breasts with Nigel so close before me. 'You don't mind, do you?'

'I'll go if you wish—' he began, starting to rise, but I

ordered him to finish his coffee, unbuttoning my blouse and unclipping the front catch of my nursing bra. His eyes widened as I brought out one hugely swollen teat and fed the nipple to Peter's eager lips. The thrill that swept through my sex and into my lower belly was like the surge leading up to an orgasm. My blouse fell open and fully revealed my other breast, milk-laden with the nipple thickened.

'I've never seen anything so beautiful,' Nigel suddenly said in a voice full of reverence. 'I wish I had my camera here to capture it. A portrait of mother and baby. That would win the diploma at my club's exhibition.'

'Bring your camera next time you come,' I said, my voice strangely hoarse. 'I wouldn't mind you photographing Peter being fed. I'd like a copy to keep myself—' I moved Peter over to my other breast. 'Don't wait until next payment day, come any day at this time.'

'I'd pay you, of course,' Nigel offered. 'We pay all our life models at the camera club. We're always looking for suitable models.' His voice hesitated. 'It's nude modelling, so I don't suppose you'd do that.'

Again my calculating mind went to work. I'd always enjoyed the thought of posing naked. 'How much do you pay?' I asked. 'Not that I suppose I would even be suitable,' I added coyly.

'Oh, you'd be suitable,' Nigel enthused. 'The best model we would ever have had. You're beautiful, perfect! I mean it would be purely art studies, nothing salacious. Some of us photograph, some draw or paint, it's all in the nature of capturing the female form. We pay three pounds an hour.'

Peter had fallen asleep at my breast, gorged with my milk. I went through to the curtained-off bedroom space, tucking him in his cot for his afternoon nap. While turning to leave him, the strongest urge swept over me to have Nigel see me

17

naked, a desire I was unable to resist. I undressed, standing
before the long mirror on the door of our wardrobe to consider
myself. It was all there that a man could want, what my
husband loved to see and admire: the full thrusting orbs of
my breasts with their pink uptilted nipples, the curve of my
full hips, a flat belly descending to the hair-surmounted
prominence at the join of my thighs, and the twin rounds of
my creamy buttocks. Three pounds an hour, I thought, I was
worth that.

'Would I do?' I asked Nigel, trying to control my
excitement as I emerged from behind the curtain. He stood
bolt upright from his chair as if he had been given an electric
shock. I saw the bulge grow and thrust out the front of his
trousers as he regarded me with a wild eager light in his eyes.

'Would I be suitable to pose at your club?' I repeated,
turning around slowly to let him see me from all perspectives,
lifting my arms to raise my breasts.

When a girl's got no clothes on before an admiring young
man it's difficult not to think of sex. Nigel came close,
mouth agape with his delight, reaching a hand out to my
breast before hastily withdrawing it.

'Feel them if you want, Nigel,' I offered in a voice weak
with arousal. 'I want you to. Kiss me like you did before. I
keep thinking about that time. Every time I do it makes my
tummy tingle. Take off your clothes and make love to me. No
one will ever know, it will be our secret.'

For a long moment he stared at me as if unbelieving of his
luck, then he held me fiercely, hurting my full breasts against
his jacket, kissing my mouth as if to swallow me, his erection
jerking to my crotch, his hands down my back and cupping
my bottom cheeks. 'Oh, God, God,' he moaned suddenly,
'I've come, come! It was too much. What will you think of
me?'

'That you've never been with a woman before,' I said, amused but frustrated too. 'Was it the first?' He nodded with his head hung so I kissed him fondly, reassuring him as I began to loosen his tie. 'There's no hurry. Undress now, Nigel, and we'll lie on the couch just to pet for a while. You'll soon be ready again I'm sure, then you'll see how nice it can be.'

I went into the kitchen which also contained our bathtub, rinsing my flannel in warm water from the kettle and returning to find Nigel standing naked and ashamed, his cock limp against his thigh. Again I kissed him to reassure him that all would be well and made him lie back on the couch. I gently washed his penis, fondling it as I dabbed it with the face cloth, admiring its size and the youthful whiteness of his skin. And I would be its first, I thought lewdly, and he would never forget this time and the naughty young married woman who let him.

Nigel groaned pleasurably and what youth wouldn't? I felt the warmth and throb return in my handling, washing, dabbing, his organ filling and stretching nobly. 'Oh, this is heaven, it's what I have dreamed of,' he sighed. 'Dear, darling Mrs Saxon, how can I ever thank you?' His penis reared, so desirable in my grasp that I had to lower my mouth over it, sucking and feeling it lengthen to its full potential. 'That's lovely,' he croaked. 'I've always wanted a girl to do that to me. How can I thank you?'

The best and obvious way, considering the state I'd worked myself into, was to start thinking of myself. I crawled forward over him, my knees either side of his waist, holding his stalk upright. With a groan of satisfaction I directed it to the parted lips of my sex and thrust down to impale myself on him to the hilt. From then on, I really didn't care about Nigel's part in it, squirming and rising and falling over him in an increasing frenzy with my breasts flying as I came and came – twice, thrice, then a fourth shattering time until I fell forward over him, steaming. I realised his thrusting up at me had ceased and he had climaxed inside me.

'You'd better leave, Nigel,' I said then, realising what I had instigated. 'I know it shouldn't have happened, but it did. I blame myself, just don't ever mention it to a soul.'

'I'd never do that,' Nigel said, rising to dress. 'Mrs Saxon, it was the most wonderful thing that's ever happened to me. Word of honour, no one will ever hear it from me. I'm just glad it happened.'

I went to wash myself, wondering if what was said about nursing mothers not being able to be made pregnant was a medical fact or an old wives' tale. Whatever, Harry had me often and without taking precautions, so I couldn't afford to worry about it. Still naked, I saw Nigel to the door, kissing him and saying again it had just been one of those things that had got out of control.

'You will still consider being a model at our art class?' he said. 'It will be extra income and I'm sure you'll be much in demand.'

'Right now I'll have to think about it,' I told him, but my mind was already made up. The money in our present circumstances would be vital and I could think of no easier way of earning it. When Peter woke up I went out with him and used the two pounds I'd not had to pay to Nigel to buy a bottle of wine and lamb chops for dinner that night. I laid the table and had a candle burning and all ready to serve up when Harry came home.

'I don't know how you manage so well, my love,' he said as we toasted ourselves in raised glasses. 'My great worry is that money is so short while I'm studying to graduate. You do wonders. One day I promise I'll make up for this time.'

'You can make up for it when we go to bed tonight,' I teased him. 'At least fucking is free, and that's what we like best. We're really lucky, aren't we?' I was thinking too how lucky I was to have two lovers in one day. Naughty as it had been, the session with the virginal Nigel had been a lovely change of partners, and was Harry any the worse for my lapse if he wasn't to know of it? I thought not.

Chapter Three
ITALY

I slept well after giving myself relief, awakening bright-eyed and bushy-tailed as the saying goes – which is certainly true if it refers to the abundant thatch of dark chestnut hair that curls over my mound and surrounds my vaginal lips. Rising and stretching, my breasts lifted, the nipples still a deeper shade of red from Giotti's ardent sucking, I smiled at the memory, recalling that it had all been in a good cause, as I liked to think. A stay in exotic Thailand with my husband was an exciting prospect, worth adultery in the line of duty – or so I reckoned.

After all, what the eye doesn't see the heart doesn't grieve over, so some randy philosopher once said. Probably some over-sexed female like me, I have to confess. But Harry was none the wiser, far away as he was. I could not for the life of me consider it harmful to find someone else attractive enough to have sex with them – provided there's no other involvement but the physical. If you fall in love – which I admit is sometimes hard to avoid – obsession or jealousy creeps in and that's when trouble starts. I never sought that in my affairs, being truly a happily married woman, even if a sexually adventurous one.

After all, a fuck is a fuck and not the end of the world. I'm sure that Giotti would have had me in his limousine had he not got so engrossed in eating me out so, bringing me off on his tongue and shooting off in his excitement. Turning down his invitation to spend the night with him would keep him on the boil, I knew. No doubt that day he would expect to go all the way with me, but I intended to make him work for that privilege. I would play the dutiful wife again, shocked at what I had been weak enough to allow the night before. I smiled at my deviousness, touching my nipples which were still tender. Giotti and his chauffeur were quite a pair. I thought of the handsome hunk who had brazenly fondled my bottom as I made to enter the car. Now there was a young stud to turn an older woman's head.

My thoughts were distracted by a repeated buzzing of the intercom on the wall of the apartment's lounge. Naked, I went through from the kitchen to press the answer button, forgetting I was in Italy and enquiring in my Scots-accented English who was calling. Think or speak of the devil, they say.

'Riccardo Scalesi here, Count Giotti's chauffeur,' a voice came back. 'I'm here to collect you, Lady Saxon. Last night you agreed to spend today with him, remember?'

'It's a bit early, isn't it?' I queried, glancing at an ornate gilt wall clock and noting it was barely eight. 'I'm not dressed yet.'

'That is how I imagine you,' I heard him reply. 'The way I have thought of you since last evening.'

'Well, you're out of luck, young man,' I told him severely while admiring his nerve. 'I'll press this thing here to open the front door. You will wait in the foyer until I'm ready to come down.'

The apartment building boasted a security door of unbreakable glass that could be opened to admit visitors by pressing a second button on the intercom. It also had a luxuriously carpeted foyer with comfortable chairs and potted plants where visitors could wait. There were lifts to the apartments above the ground floor, which contained modern shops selling *haute couture* fashions, wildly expensive perfume and jewellery. It was a million times removed from the humble cottage I'd been brought up in.

'I'd prefer to come up and talk to you,' the determined chauffeur said emphatically. I had already pressed the button to open the door by then, so it was too late to keep him at bay. Keeping my door locked would foil him, I decided, wondering why I found myself in such situations so frequently. Then he added calmly, 'Don't consider not letting me in. I shall ring your door and knock loudly until people in other apartments complain of the noise.'

I slipped on a dressing gown and passed a brush over my hair, aware my hand trembled. No young randy hound could take me for granted, I determined. Nevertheless I felt an unsolicited flutter of arousal in the pit of my stomach, transmitting its sensations to my sex, breasts and nipples. No you mustn't, I resolved. It was bad enough that the master had set out to seduce me – he at least could be used. His servant acting as if I were a push-over was too much. I could imagine how every lurid detail of his intended conquest of me would be related with relish to others of the count's staff. My reputation while in Rome would ensure a fine scandal. I resolved, trying somewhat vainly to ignore the pulsing between my thighs, that I would put Riccardo firmly in his place right away.

I wrapped the dressing gown tightly about me as if a defensive measure, wishing the thin silken material was thicker and not so figure-hugging. Answering the door, I found my caller lolling against the door frame in jeans and a casual open-necked shirt, thick black hair curling up from his chest to his throat, about which hung a thick gold chain and a ruby pendant. The tight tailored jeans he wore emphasised the impressive bulge at his crotch. He held out a large bouquet of delicate yellow roses which I refused to accept. If he expected a delighted feminine exclamation of 'For me!' he was sadly mistaken. He merely shrugged, strolling in arrogantly, his eyes undoubtedly undressing me.

'Good morning, Lady Saxon,' he said. 'How attractive a woman is in the morning when she has just risen. Especially a beauty like yourself. We Latins appreciate a well-fleshed lady.'

'Do come in,' I said sarcastically. 'Don't wait for anything like an invitation.' It was wasted on him. He unwrapped the foil paper around the bouquet to reveal that they stood in a tall, milky-white vase of the finest glass. Looking around, he placed it on a round table, arranging the blooms, glancing at me for my approval.

'Flowers *and* a vase,' I mused. 'Big deal. Did the count send his boy with these to impress me?'

'I'm nobody's boy,' he informed me curtly, his features changing, darkening his Mediterranean face as if a shadow had passed across it. He could be a dangerous and aggressive young thug, I could see, a chill shivering down my back as he regarded me.

He advanced on me, a hand reaching out to fondle my cheek and I was too fearful to resist. 'The flowers are from me, and the vase,' he said, menacingly near, his cologne strong. 'It is the best Venetian glass. Giotti won't miss it. I take what I like.'

'You think that includes me?' I said, trying not to let him intimidate me. 'If your master is expecting me, you will wait here while I shower and make myself ready. Do you hear that? Wait here in the lounge.'

'You think he's my master? I've no master,' the young man said levelly. 'You think I'm just a goddam chauffeur? I'm his paid minder, bodyguard, and no servant.' His fingers smoothed my lips. 'You have a nice mouth. I like everything about you.'

'Let me get ready,' I said.

'No hurry,' he answered casually. 'Giotti won't expect you until later. The Villa Appia at eleven so he said. I took it upon myself to call earlier, to spend time with you.' His hand went down from my mouth, fingering the silk at the neck of my robe, drawing it aside to reveal the upper slopes of my breasts, rising and falling in my breathless state. 'You sure got the tits, lady,' he said. 'I could go to town on those babies. How about it?'

'No, no, certainly not,' I protested, trying to remain calm but a strange excitement, a mixture of fear and unease, made my voice tremble. 'Leave me alone, please. I'm not that kind of woman.'

'Oh yeah?' he laughed aggressively. 'You broads all are when given the chance. So you didn't enjoy my touching up that fine ass you got last night, or Giotti sucking out your pussy until you were going bananas on his tongue. I was there, remember, I saw it happen.'

'Stop that right now,' I said, swallowing hard to force myself to appear in command of the situation. I took hold of his hand to prevent him opening my robe wider. 'What a charming way you have of putting things.'

'American-Italian-English,' Riccardo said, laughing, and ignoring my sarcasm. 'I was sent to stay with an uncle in Brooklyn when I was twelve. You ever heard of the Mafia? I was with the mob till they deported me. Come on now, open up, let me see those big tits. I know you want me to.'

'Don't you dare!' I screamed, with my hand still gripping his as he jerked at the neck of my robe, pulling it apart as far down as my waist, baring my breasts completely. I used my free right hand to smack his face as hard as I could. He did not stagger back or flinch, immediately returning my slap, stinging my cheek.

'I'm Sicilian,' he swore. 'No one screws me about, especially a bitch who pretends she don't want it. One look at you last night and I saw you were built to be a good lay.' With both my wrists gripped in his strong hands, he forced my arms behind my back, making the slippery silk robe slide to the floor and leaving me naked. The action made my back arch, thrusting my breasts forwards and upwards, tilting my nipples. His lewd stare lowered to my breasts, his tongue licked around his lips as if in anticipation.

'Just look at them,' he ordered sternly. 'They're bigger with excitement, and your nipples are hard too. You can't fool me, they give you away. And what tits! Have they ever been fucked by a big stiff dick? You'd love that.'

'Maybe I would, with the right man,' I screamed. 'I'll tell Count Giotti all about this, you bastard.'

'So inform him,' Riccardo laughed. 'Inform your husband too while you're at it, Lady Saxon. Or maybe I should! He'd love to learn all that's been happening since he left you alone in Rome. Relax and give out, and no one will ever be the wiser. Look, I'm not going to kill you, just fuck you.'

'If I could be sure of that,' I moaned, his mouth sucking strongly on a nipple, drawing in the flesh of the breast and aureole with his suction. Switching to the other nipple, he gave it little nips and bites which sent sensations coursing down to palpitate in my sex. He began to nuzzle my breasts, moving his head purposefully from side to side, his nose and mouth burrowing into the divide to set each big boob swinging apart, slapping his cheeks. Next I was carried across the room and laid out on an inlaid dining table, my back pressed to the smooth rosewood top and legs hanging over with my bottom intentionally positioned at the table's edge. I imagined the sight I must have presented to him: thighs parted widely by his hands and my cunt thrusting forward, tilted at the perfect angle for mouthing or being put to the cock.

Looking down between my splayed breasts I saw for myself the raised bulge with its bush. I shuddered as the itch in my sex grew of its own accord, the outer lips thickening and parting, opening like a flower. I felt my lubricating juices flowing. Riccardo was fully aware of my rising arousal, he could not help but be, by the ease with which a probing finger entered me, bringing a stifled moan from my lips along with my protests.

'You young beast,' I managed to grind out as my throes mounted. 'I don't want this. Leave me alone, damn you. This is the same as rape.'

'Not in my book,' my tormentor laughed. 'You're getting your kicks by making out you don't want it, lady. You don't fool me. Look at your ass working and your fanny juiced up at the thought of a young stud doing all this to you. You like to pretend you're being taken against your will. I've worked on married bitches like you before. It's what you dream of.'

He was right, of course. Many women felt guilt at being taken in this way – usually by someone other than their husband – and their protests ease their consciences while invariably adding to the lewdness of the participants. In my case, although these facts were significant, the thought that a tough young hoodlum had arrived at my apartment especially early to have me so blatantly, subdued my other feelings.

I sat up defiantly, pushing him away. 'Out!' I shouted.

'How can you think I'd allow you to fuck me is beyond belief. For a start it would take a real man, not a boy. You will leave now and wait for me in the foyer.'

'This gets better and better,' Riccardo said calmly, starting to get out of his few clothes directly before me. 'You protest too much, lady, and you're dying for it. I'll show you who's a real man, and you'll thank me after. Look at this to whet your appetite.'

This, as he said boastfully, was the massive erection he revealed as he shucked off his jeans to pose naked almost between my legs. I had to admit he was a splendid specimen of young manhood – narrow-waisted but with shoulders, biceps and thighs developed, undoubtedly, by weight-lifting and regular work-outs.

'You're beautiful,' I had to gasp.

'And I always deliver,' he promised cockily. 'My women know just what they've had. Let your hair down, lady, and enjoy. It's the name of the game while your old man's out of the picture. Giotti sure as hell intends to screw you before the day is out, and you'll let him just to get to Thailand with your husband. So let's start the day with a bang, to get you in the mood.'

'I said it would take more than you,' I felt bound to say, not intending to inflate his already boosted ego. All the same my eyes could not tear themselves away from the size and beauty of his magnificent prick. It reared massively, the girth and length of dimensions that would stretch a woman's cunt to the utmost. He took my hand, noting my amazed look, clasping my fingers around the smooth hot stalk. I could barely encompass it.

'Tell me what you think of that,' he said. 'I want to hear you say what a lovely big dick you've got in your hand. And how you'd like it in your mouth, between your tits, up your cunt and even in your ass.' His right hand took hold of my chin, squeezing as if to apply greater pressure. 'Come on,' he threatened. 'Talk!'

'It is an exceptional one,' I managed to say, as in truth it was. 'I'm sure it has delighted every woman that's ever tried it.' His grip on my jaw slackened, the hand dropping to fondle both my breasts, the centre of his palm circling over the hardness of my aroused nipples. The stalk I held seemed to thicken and stretch even more in my clasp, its pulsating warmth spreading through my being to vibrate in my sex.

'What kind of ladylike spiel is that?' he laughed. '"It is an exceptional one!" Jeez, you've got hold of a prize dong that has fucked Vegas showgirls and movie stars. Lady, I'm doing you a favour.'

'Less talk then,' I said, my resolve weakening, curious now to try his monster shaft although still intent on appearing reluctant and pretending that this was not my usual behaviour. 'You seem determined to have me, so go on, get it over with.'

'Have you? Get it over with?' Riccardo scoffed. 'You mean *fuck* you, so say it out of those ladylike lips.'

'So fuck me,' I mumbled, agreeing.

'Rub up my dick,' he ordered. 'Get the feel of it.' I complied, feeling the outer skin slide over the iron-hardness, increasing my strokes as the urge grew in me. 'Don't worry that you'll finish me off that way, I never come until I want to – when you're pooped out and begging me to stop. Now say what I told you to.'

'It's a lovely big beautiful prick,' I said. Saying and hearing lewd words during sex play always helplessly heightened my arousal, made my insides turn to jelly. 'Oh, yes I want it,' I said, giving the cock in my grip a tighter squeeze and rubbing it more enthusiastically. 'You young thug, I didn't mean this to happen, but so help me, now you've made me want to. Oh God,' I added sorrowfully to increase the salaciousness of my being taken, and also I well knew to increase his delight, 'if my poor husband could see the pair of us – heard me saying I wanted another man's stiff prick in my mouth, between my tits, hard up my cunt and even in my bottom. Oh God, you're an animal, what have you done to me?'

'I'm just bringing out what's been inside you all the time, waiting to be let loose,' Riccardo preened himself, certain his seduction had been all of his making. I could, of course, have told him he was but the latest in a long line of sexual athletes and that I was actually enjoying playing the seduced wife.

I would play the part to the hilt, I decided. It made me lewd. He would doubly enjoy believing he had made a respectable married woman helpless to resist his macho approach and the outsized cock of which he was so proud. 'No one must ever know of this, Riccardo,' I begged. 'Do what you will with me, I can't stop you, only let it be our secret.'

I saw his eyes light up with excitement at my plea, felt the tremble in the hand that played with my breasts. Yes, I'd enjoy him fucking me, but I was determined to deflate his massive ego as well as his big cock before we'd finished. He would come all right, whatever he said about never doing so until he wanted, and the one who would be pooped out begging to stop would not be me. In the matter of lasting out, the woman has been gifted with more suitable equipment than any male.

He pulled me forward, nudging his prick up my stomach until the stem forced a passage between my breasts and nestled tightly in my cleave, held between the full firm orbs, hot to my chest. 'Press those big teats together,' I was ordered curtly, 'so I can fuck 'em.'

As I did so, pushing inwards with my palms, he began a rocking movement with his thighs, in effect sliding his full length up and down against rounded tit flesh. His hand slid between my thighs, a curled finger increasing my agitation, making my initial climax moments away unless I fought against it. He was no beginner at arousing a woman, I had to admit, and I stifled groans of the utmost pleasure at his double assault. He sensed me fighting against surrendering so early in the bout, gauging my subdued shuddering, the tensing of my body, the gritted teeth. I suffered erotic agony.

'Let yourself go, bitch,' he exulted in my face. 'Give yourself over to good honest lust for once in your life. I'm fucking your tits and fingering your cunt, so come, come. Let me hear the groans and see your body jerk off. Your old man isn't here now. Does he ever use those great boobs as a cunt? I'll bet he don't! See, my knob's now sticking up from out between your tits, so give it a suck. Let it all hang out. *Come*, you slut.'

I couldn't remember a sex partner with so much to say before and I found it erotically pleasing to be ordered about so determinedly. Peering hard over my nose at the stalk shunting up and down in my breast cleavage I saw the glistening bulbous helmet of Riccardo's prick thrusting out begging for a mouth. 'Suck it, you bitch!' I was ordered, even as my chin tucked in voluntarily and I sucked greedily. 'You learn quick, lady,' he said, no doubt considering me the genteel type who had never stooped to such depraved behaviour before. 'I'll make a goddamned good cocksucker of you!'

In the battle of wills I was determined to win, there was no doubt the first round was going to the strong young chauffeur. Sucking on a big dick, the rest of its great length fucking my ever-sensitive breasts, with an expert fingering of my engorged clitoris making my lower half writhe in ecstasy, I gurgled out my pleasure through a mouthful of cock, bucking like a wild mare from the hips. The strength of my climax made me sag back on the table, still shuddering from long wracking spasms, while Riccardo regarded me with triumph in his dark Sicilian eyes.

'Oh God, God,' was all I could utter. 'God help me, I'm drained! Oh, young man, I could be your mother—'

He stood over me, running both hands over my steaming body from my heaving breasts down to the curve of my thigh and my palpitating cunt. 'You're a fine lady,' he said, his tone gentler now. 'With a body like you got there's a fortune waiting for you in a joint like Las Vegas as a high-class whore or stripper. I wanted you the minute I saw you. I bet your old man never made you like it so much or come like that, eh?' he added proudly. 'He never screwed your tits or made you suck his dick I bet.'

'No, never,' I said languidly, just to please him. 'It was heaven, I've never known I could come like that,' I lied. 'But I think you'd better let me shower and dress now. It must be time to leave.'

'With this dong I've got on me?' Riccardo laughed. 'I came to fuck you with it, lady, so you can say you've had the biggest and best there is. Did your husband ever eat out your snatch? I do it better than Giotti.'

'I'll bet you do,' I agreed sweetly, recovered and not averse to allowing such a brash young man to continue what he thought of as tutoring me in the finer points of sexuality. He must have thought my Harry a complete jerk. To keep him going I added shyly, 'He would never do that – lick me out – although I've wanted him to.'

'Heh!' Riccardo said scornfully. 'What a dumbo you married. You got a terrific box between your legs; hairy as a Sicilian whore and plump as a ripe peach. Say, you're not such a stuck-up bitch as I thought, lady. Just never been taught. You want a real licking out, you got it. Then I intend to fuck you good.'

'Oh, yes please,' I said, sounding grateful, watching him lower his face between my thighs. 'Just this once, so that I'll always remember it.'

'You tell me what it's like, lady,' I heard him mutter a moment before his tongue flicked over the outer lips of my pussy. 'Tell me, I like to hear.'

It was easy to do that, lost in the deep pleasure of his tongue curling and flicking inside my cunt, circling my clitty, making me sigh and moan, and arch my back. I held his head, drawing it closer between my thighs, moving my pelvis up and down to match the bobbing of his head. 'It's absolute heaven,' I cried. 'Oh, clean me out, darling, lick my cunt nice and clean. Tongue-fuck me, Riccardo, make me come again. I want to come on your mouth. Tongue-fuck me!'

That it was appreciated I could tell by the increased tonguing I received, and the quickening thrusts he made with his face pressed to my cunt. My intention had been to reduce him to a quivering mass of excitement but now all I wanted was his continuing pleasuring of my body. My groans, grunts and whispers were entirely spontaneous as his long tongue flicked and searched out every nook and cranny of my pussy. My buttocks rotated in corkscrewing motions as I pressed his mouth and nose to my inflamed cunt. I came, shaken to the core by the power of the sudden climax, and begged him to *fuck me, fuck me, my darling!*

'Please,' I moaned. 'I need your prick so badly! Fuck me, Riccardo—'

'Damn right,' Riccardo agreed, lifting his face, sodden from nose to chin with the copious flow of my juices. He bent over me and we kissed long and deeply, a lover's kiss I was unable to resist. I hugged his hot torso close, flattening my tits into his chest, muttering my profuse delight and praising his prowess at pleasuring me so delightfully. I couldn't help myself, even if a small warning voice within reminded me such ardour should be reserved for a loving husband and not a casual bed-partner.

'My darling, my darling,' I called him ardently as I kissed his mouth, chin, chest and nipples. He was magnificent, I had to admit – rugged, handsome and virile. This was lust pure and simple, surely, and nothing else. I couldn't possibly be falling for someone so flashy and vulgar and *young* – not with my Harry only days gone from my side.

'Oh, love me, love me, my darling,' I heard myself beg – which is not usually my style. '*Love* me,' I repeated.

My appealing had an immediate effect on the young man. He became gentler at once, his hand caressing my face, looking tenderly into my eyes, nodding as if in agreement with the sudden change in our situation.

'You're so beautiful,' he whispered. 'It's never been like this for me before—' and he kissed me lingeringly. I returned the kiss eagerly, my arms around him, shifting my position under him and curling my legs around the small of his back, wanting him as much as any woman could.

'Please, Riccardo,' I implored him like a love-sick girl. I felt the head of his iron-hard shaft force apart my outer lips and then inch after inch of solid flesh slid up my cunt. I felt filled to overflowing and unusually aware of the shape and size of the great member invading me so delightfully. We both lay still for long moments, savouring the joy of being joined together. 'Now make love to me, darling boy,' I commanded.

'I want to more than ever before,' Riccardo said, his flanks starting to move against the first lifting of my hips. His great prick shunted slowly at the initial thrusts, going in to the hilt to make me arch my back and gasp, then withdrawing to the very tip, making me heave to get it back, every lovely inch, my hands hauling his tight young muscled buttocks hard to me. Pure unadulterated lust reared its licentious head, increasing the frenzy of our coupling. Our bellies slapped loudly together, our thrusts quickened and we shouted out as we fucked so strenuously.

'Shove it up, all of it, fuck me rigid!' I heard myself cry as Riccardo's big weapon serviced me. 'You can fuck me any time, fuck me with that lovely monster prick, you horny young ram. Go on, go on, harder, deeper!' He had to cling to me, such was my humping up and down against his crotch in wild undulations that threatened to unseat him.

How many times I came with that huge shunting engine pummelling my cunt was impossible to gauge. My climaxes overlapped until I felt my vulva and anus one mass of heaving spasms. On top of me, I heard Riccardo croak out words in Italian, his flanks jerking uncontrollably in a shuddering orgasm, as he shot his come far up inside me. When he rolled aside it was to lie with heaving shoulders, muttering into the hard table top before sliding down to sit with his back against one of the table's legs.

'That,' I told him, still struggling to regain my breath, 'is what is known in my country as a good old table-ender. I thank you, young man. I do think, however, we should cool it a little if we do this in future. For a moment there I almost lost my head. Do you know what I mean?'

I looked down over the table's edge to see Riccardo nodding thoughtfully. 'I guess so,' he said almost regretfully and my sentimental heart skipped a beat. I offered my hand which he took and gave a fond squeeze. 'Yeah, too much,' he agreed. 'It's not my scene to fall for a dame, not me.' He glanced up, smiling and suddenly looking very young. 'Even with you. That was the best fuck I ever knew. Did I hear you mention something about if ever we do this again in future?'

He had proved such an exceptional lover that I smiled and nodded. 'If it's entirely our secret,' I promised, looking at his splendid body and unable to contain a wicked thought. 'Like right now if you wish. This table is so hard – wouldn't it be comfier on a nice soft bed?'

He leapt to his feet, leading me by the hand through to the unmade bed where I'd slept alone, wishing my husband was beside me. Laying me back, he kissed my mouth, breasts and nipples, then ran his tongue down from between my cleavage and over my stomach to the fork of my thighs. To return the compliment I twisted around, my buttocks over his face in the classic 69 position, to admire his cock and suck on its sweetness. I was taken from the rear at our second coupling, on elbows and knees, while Riccardo grasped my breasts as leverage and brought me off beautifully with his belly slapping against my bottom cheeks. We had barely finished, lying side by side in the sweet aftermath of good fucking when my bedside telephone rang.

'Lady Saxon?' enquired Count Giotti's voice down the line. 'Has my chauffeur arrived yet to drive you here? I told him to be at your apartment by ten-thirty. It's past eleven now. You do intend to see me today as promised?'

'If you keep *your* promise,' I said. 'As for Riccardo coming here,' I suppressed a sly chuckle, 'the young man arrived very promptly, he certainly came. I'm to blame.' I bent my head and exchanged a kiss with a grinning Riccardo. 'We'll be there as soon as I'm ready. I slept late.'

'Then I'll look forward to your arrival,' Giotti said unctuously. 'A party has been organised for you on my yacht. I guarantee you'll have a wonderful time. Until we meet then—'

Beside me, Riccardo sat frowning. He had heard the conversation and did not like the sound of it. 'I know the kind of parties he organises,' he said darkly. 'Refuse, if you don't want to go.'

'I think I know what you mean,' I said, intrigued by the thought. 'Would it matter after what we've been doing this morning?'

'You don't know what a nice lady like you will be letting yourself in for,' I was warned. 'Anything goes on that boat of his. Drink, drugs if you're into that scene, all leading to one hell of an orgy like you've never seen. Giotti's got estates in Sicily, an industrial plant, vineyards, a fishing fleet, even a goddamned football team. So just say the word and I'll go back and tell him to go to hell—'

'How sweet of you,' I said, kissing him again. I didn't add that I had been to orgies and the thought of finding out what Giotti had arranged to further corrupt a colleague's wife appealed to me. 'What clothes do you think I should wear for a trip to sea?' I asked. 'What is the usual—?'

'Not a damned thing,' Riccardo said sullenly. 'Not a stitch, once his kind of party gets swinging.'

'Will you be there?' I asked, trying to appear anxious that I'd have a protector. 'I'd like that.'

'Sure,' he admitted. 'With my prize dong I'm the star performer. No doubt once they think they've got you softened up, a real lady and new to the scene, they'll want to see me fuck you.'

'Would that be so terrible?' I laughed. 'Come on, let's have a shower together. I can look after myself, don't worry.

Whatever happens, remember I'm only doing this for my husband's sake.'

'Yeah,' Riccardo said eagerly. 'Poor bastard, but a lucky one at that, I guess. I never met a wife like you.'

I took that as a compliment.

Chapter Four
ENGLAND

I stood in the entrance hall of the imposing Victorian building and studied the notice board. Camera Club in Room Ten on the second floor, I read and mounted the stairs with my tummy a-flutter. In the studio were men of all ages ranging from seventeen to seventy. Cameras of varying size and expense were much in evidence, slung about necks, lovingly nursed in hands, even set-up on tripods.

Nigel Lamont approached me excitedly, and introduced a tall handsome man of indeterminate age with grey hair. 'This is Mr Gerard Manley, photographic tutor *par excellence,*' he said and beamed at me proudly. Manley shook my hand casually, giving no hint of whether or not he approved of me.

'Miss or Mrs Saxon?' the suave tutor enquired, eyeing my poor coat and well-worn best dress. He was sartorially elegant in a checked shirt, Paisley cravat knotted at the neck, cavalry twill slacks and suede laceless shoes. I did not take to him at first sight, his arrogance and aloofness put me off. But I needed the job.

He took my elbow lightly between finger and thumb, and led me through the throng of students to a small private room attached to the studio. The way all eyes followed my progress showed more than an artistic interest in my figure – at the age of twenty-two I was in full bloom and I knew I curved in all the right places. The thought that I would be posing completely naked all evening before that lot sent little tremors pulsing through my lower stomach.

'Mrs Saxon, of course,' Gerard Manley said as he closed the door behind us. 'You're a young married woman, I now recall Nigel Lamont telling me. You do realise this work entails art studies – the nude figure? Is your husband fully aware of that fact?'

'Certainly,' I lied. Harry was at home engrossed in studying, with baby Peter tucked up for the night. Now I no longer breastfed him I took a weekly night off in the ninepenny seats at the cinema – which is where my unsuspecting hubby thought I was that evening. My reason for not informing him I was going to pose nude for money was purely to enable me to save a secret nest-egg. I wanted to take my two loved ones on our first holiday and to show Peter the seaside. 'My husband is aware,' I said.

'Good,' Manley intoned. 'In that case, there's no problem. Now, let me see you undressed. Use that cupboard if you want to hang up your things or fold your clothes over a chair if you prefer.' He made no attempt to move, parking his arse on the edge of a table and waiting expectantly. 'You're not shy, I trust?' he said almost disdainfully. 'My dear girl, your unclothed charms are going to be viewed and photographed from *every* angle, and I do mean every angle. I hope you aren't having second thoughts.'

'I'm here, aren't I?' I said as defiantly as I dared, the job and the money still in my mind. Much as I would have liked to tell him where to go I could not afford to annoy him. I did not relish his overbearing attitude. He was a cold and arrogant jumped-up snob, I decided, and no gentleman if he insisted on remaining while I undressed. 'Do you intend to stay?' I asked.

'My dear,' he said wearily, 'I have seen more naked females than you can imagine in my work. Also I'm a naturist – a nudist to you – I spend my holidays and weekends at venues where nature-lovers gather. Besides, I'll be seeing all of you for the next two hours. Does your modesty object to my being present while you disrobe? I need to assess your body so I can judge how best to pose you in the studio.'

I strongly suspected he just wanted to watch me undress, but the fact that he was keeping me on to model made my spirits lift. Anyway, he would be only one in a long line of men who had witnessed me taking my clothes off before. I need the money, I reminded myself, removing my coat and preparing to slip out of my dress. Manley walked to the tall cupboard, opening its door to full width, indicating with a flourish of his arm that I could undress behind it. 'Thanks, but no thanks,' I said. 'After all, you want to see the goods—'

He gave a short laugh, showing for the first time a little animation. 'Well said, I like your spirit. Naked and unashamed is what we should all be.' He did not take his eyes off me as I shed my dress and I was glad I was wearing my prettiest bra and briefs.

'You're quite a beauty, aren't you?' he said. 'Obviously you're in it for the money. What does your husband do?'

'He's a student,' I said, hanging my bra over the back of a chair and feeling his cold eyes on my breasts. I stepped out of my panties and placed them with my other clothes, standing back and holding my arms out wide to my sides. 'There,' I offered. 'That's as much as anyone can see of me. Do you approve, Mr Manley, sir?'

He gave another of his short sarcastic laughs. 'You'll be wasted on that bunch of would-be photographers in there,' he said acidly, jerking his noble head in the direction of the studio. 'You're too good by far for them. I suspect some of 'em don't even put film in their cameras.'

He eased his backside off the edge of the table and approached me, studying my thrusting boobs and well-furred pubic mound. He walked behind me, muttering his thoughts. 'What a gorgeous bottom,' he said. 'I think that the female posterior is the most perfect of all God's creations. A student, is he? The lucky fellow,' he said, referring to my Harry. 'So you do need the money. Oh, I'll use you, never fear.'

'I'd be more than grateful,' I said, but I realised he was more than pleased with me. 'You can use me as much as you like, if you pay me.' It was not a suitable choice of words, I realised as soon as I'd spoken. I saw his mouth tighten.

'You can rest assured,' he said, smiling faintly. 'Breasts, large and quite delightfully shaped; buttocks enticingly rounded, quite splendidly cheeky; all limbs shapely and figure beautifully proportioned. As a photographer of the human form I find you voluptuous and utterly enchanting.' His fingers lightly brushed the curves of my bottom. From behind, his hands came around to lift my breasts and let them fall.

'Ripe, firm and full, and delightfully heavy,' he announced, while a tremor shook my body at his touch. He came back to face me, staring down at the fork of my thighs, and the plump forested bulge of my *mons*. 'Such excellent colouring for photographing too, that rich burnished chestnut of your hair.' The back of his hand swept up over the prominence of my sex, making me jump back. He caught my arm and steadied me, unperturbed.

'Look but don't touch,' I told him, my trembling increasing, making my voice strange. 'Photographs only, that was the deal.'

'A good deal for us both,' he said meaningfully. 'I can get

you all the work you want, if you co-operate. Need the money, do you, young Mrs Saxon?' he reminded me again, sounding pleased it was so. 'We shall discuss future business after class. Now, are you going through like that? Models experienced in this work bring a dressing gown.'

I hadn't realised, of course, so I had to follow Gerard Manley into the studio with every eye devouring my body. Thereafter I posed in many different positions: standing, reclining, sitting cross-legged and in other configurations considered arty or classic. Manley circulated among his class, advising them on shadow and perspective in his laid-back way, apparently good at his profession. During a short rest period I went back into the little room to sip a coffee Nigel brought me. I didn't care that I was naked before him, I felt as if I'd been nude all my life.

'What do you think of Mr Manley?' Nigel enthused. 'He really is a top lensman. His pictures have won awards and been in magazines everywhere. Here, I've got my mum's car tonight, Diana. Would you like a lift home after the class?'

'It will save me a walk,' I agreed. And get me home earlier to Harry as well, who would be treated to the fish and chips we could rarely afford seeing as how I expected to be paid. Then, after posing all evening with men ogling my private parts, which had left me in need of a good going over, my husband could return my kindness by making love to me. The second hour of posing seemed longer than the first but, in time, the class packed away their equipment and departed. 'I'll wait for you outside,' Nigel called to me as I went back into the side room to get dressed. His fellow students regarded him with awe.

In the room Gerard Manley sat at the table counting out silver coins and banknotes into three separate groups. 'Our night's takings,' he said. 'Twenty students at two quid a head makes a tidy forty pounds. Two pounds an hour for the let of this so-called studio and six for your modelling fee leaves thirty notes. Quite reasonable, you think?'

I thought what thirty whole pounds could do to ease my house-keeping budget – new clothes for baby Peter, overdue shoes for my husband, a few bills cleared. As if mesmerised by the money divided up on the little table I did not begin to get dressed. It seemed quite natural to stand there without a stitch and talk.

'It's more than quite reasonable to me, Mr Manley,' I told him naively. 'Six pounds is an absolute Godsend to me at present. I hope you'll want to employ me again.' I gave him a hopeful, friendly smile, cringing inside pathetically, but it was all to ensure a source of income.

He glanced up from the money, an amused smile on his arrogant face. 'Count on it, if you're flexible,' he said, a hidden meaning behind his offer. His eyes lowered slowly from my face to my breasts to my sex, and remained fixed on my prominent split with its thick growth of hair. 'You're very photogenic as well as beautifully developed. My class members drooled over you. They will return for more of you. However, this kind of lolly,' and here he swept his hand across the arranged takings, 'is peanuts. Peanuts to what you could earn sticking with me, young woman.'

The sweep of his hand moved on until it stopped between the fork of my legs, palm upwards, long artistic fingers almost idly stroking the lips of my curved mound. I drew in a sharp breath, surprised and excited by the sudden uninvited fondling. Before I was able to protest, his middle finger had slipped inside me, titillating me slowly and deliberately, moistening the folds of my inner flesh. He found the responsive nub of my clitoris with an expert touch, making me flinch and stifle a moan.

46

'So, what kind of girl are you?' Manley enquired unflatteringly. 'Do anything for money? I need to know.'

'You shouldn't do that,' I whimpered. 'Please, don't, you mustn't.'

'You like it,' he stated flatly. 'In fact, you love it.' He rose from his chair with a curled finger still probing me, turning me around until I faced the table. Only then did he release me, the hand that had toyed with my inner sex now roved across my bottom cheeks, insinuating between their deep divide. To my relief the searching finger re-entered my oiled cleft easily. I was now with my thighs pressed against the table's edge, pushed forward over it so that my breasts drooped from my chest, hanging like twin bells. The hand in my cleave stroked away at my rear-pointing groove, the wrist tight between my parted cheeks. 'What magnificent buttocks,' Manley declared, sounding as cool, calm and collected as ever, while I was flinching and gritting my teeth to contain utterances of forced pleasure. 'I've always been a bottom man myself and you, my girl, tempt me greatly to do wicked things with yours.'

'No, no,' I pleaded. 'Oh, what are you doing now?'

'This,' he said. 'Inserting my thumb up your delightful little bum hole.' I had felt his thumb straightening while his finger stimulated my pulsating cunt and had sensed the upward push against my tight rear orifice. I gurgled my reaction as the thumb's pressure made the closed serrated ring 'give' and allow its full penetration. My rear was invaded while the other opening so close by worked itself into a mounting frenzy on the sustained fingering. My bottom quivered, jerked, tilted, all of which increased my agitation. I fought the urgent surge that made me want to surrender and compressed my stomach muscles to wantonly continue the highly indecent sensations coursing through my whole lower regions. I writhed agonizingly from the waist down.

'What about young Nigel?' Gerard Manley enquired at that moment. 'I'm interested. What does he mean to you, that boy? You're a highly sexed individual, I can see that. Is he your lover? A married woman's bit on the side?'

Despite my excruciating arousal, I felt I had been humiliated more than enough, or perhaps that erotic feeling of sweet pain and pleasure at my humbling increased my fervour. It was as if I had to be submissive to this hateful man and suffer his insults and indignities.

'Please,' I begged pitiously. 'Don't say that about Nigel and me. It's not true.' I drew in my breath, teetering on the verge of being brought off mightily, but his hand suddenly stilled. 'Do go on!' I urged. 'You're the only one I've let do things to me apart from my husband. It's not true – Nigel hasn't had me.' I was lying for my reputation.

'Hasn't he?' Manley said snidely, no doubt amused by my low moans and desire to be finished off satisfactorily. 'The truth now, girl. He showed me some very revealing photos he'd taken of you in your flat. Don't tell me he didn't want more?'

He had, of course, and the photo session had ended that day with Nigel and I fucking. It was hard not to want to after flouncing about naked before him and the poor boy so randy that his bulging trouser front had been obvious. 'I only posed for him,' I pleaded in my agony. 'Why do you do this to me? You like to hurt me. You've no right to imagine he made love to me.'

'I don't imagine,' he said, enjoying my discomfort. 'It was what Nigel led me to believe. Of course, if you want me to continue giving you the pleasuring you so obviously require, I want to know the truth. Nigel's been fucking you, hasn't he?' His thumb up my behind was like a short stubby prick and I began to move my bottom to enhance the feel of it, clenching my cunt muscles too, hoping his fingering would resume. He slapped my bum hard to stop me.

'There's more where that came from,' he warned. 'It would be my pleasure to smack some truth out of that perfect bottom. If I don't hear you admit you have cuckolded your young husband with Nigel, you can dress and leave here now. I'll have nothing more to do with you, no modelling, no money.'

I began to howl, wondering what had come over me. Usually I was a strong and assertive girl who could stand up for herself. Manley, of course, was a sadist. He had coldly calculated I was fair game for his blatant sexual abuse and the interrogation he enjoyed inflicting on a victim. Yet somehow I found it exciting too, going along willingly even though apparently in abject misery.

'All right,' I sobbed, 'I admit it. Nigel has fucked me, I let him. He fucked me, now you fuck me too.'

'So we understand each other,' he said bluntly. In my position bent over the table I looked over my shoulder to see him unbuckling his belt with his free hand, pushing down his trousers and underpants to his knees and revealing a good-sized prick standing out rigidly from a thick pubic bush and tightened balls. 'Relax now,' he warned. 'I don't know if you've ever had it this way but I've never done it to a woman yet that didn't get to like it.' He closed on me, his hands parting my buttock cheeks. 'Told you I was a bottom man,' he reminded me, for once some excitement in his voice. 'This way there's no chance of getting you pregnant, remember? Brace yourself, Mrs Saxon.'

He would not be the first in that particular orifice but I was not about to tell him that. It would also, I felt, spoil his lewd pleasure in supposing he was fucking a virgin bottom. I was aware of his lubricating my anus with saliva and felt the nudge of his bulbous knot at my hole.

'It's so big and I'm so tight there,' I said nervously. 'I don't think I'll like it – oh, I feel it pushing in! Oh, oh, it's not nice, it's not right. Even my husband doesn't do that to me—'

My chosen words could not have had more effect and I heard his short cry of delight. He eased up more of his stiff stalk very carefully, then paused with several inches embedded up my behind. Tentatively moving my bottom against him, I began to enjoy the feel of the cylinder of hard flesh filling my back passage. I groaned, my bottom motions increasing. 'Beast, beast,' the words came out in low grunts. 'You're up my bum, fucking my arse.'

'Nearly there, relax your anus for my full length,' Manley coaxed. 'Groan all you want, girl, it increases both our pleasure.' His belly was now pressed to my tilted tail and my passage fully plugged by his every inch. It was as hot as a poker and seemingly up to my stomach. 'Well done,' he said, hands parting my cheeks for even deeper access in my divided buttocks. 'We're going to get on very well, I'll make you lots of money. Now I'm going to fuck your sweet little bum hole. Yes, yes, you're a natural, just made to bugger with that delightful arse you've got.'

He rose on his tip-toes, his hips thrusting. The sliding of his iron-hard rod up and down my tight rectal channel made my bowels churn, my back dip and buttocks rise to accept his every inch.

'You're made to bum-fuck,' he said, his voice thick with lust. 'Say you love my prong up there, girl – tell me how nice it is for you!'

Words were hardly necessary for I was groaning out my pleasure, my breathing had quickened into gasps and my bottom shamelessly bumped and rotated hard against his belly in my throes.

All the same, obscenities uttered while so erotically aroused add even more lewdness to no matter how licentious the sexual act already engaged in. 'Yes, yes, bugger me!' I implored him wantonly. 'I just love it, love it – fuck my bottom faster! It's filling me up, splitting me, it's heaven. Keep fucking me there—!'

'You divine bitch!' Manley croaked hoarsely, shafting away ardently, his hands now around me to grip my breasts tight in his cupped palms, pulling me back to meet his thrusts. 'It was ordained that we should meet, that I would have this delightful bottom hole. I shall drain my balls in it, drench your very vitals. Take that and that! I come, COME! Aaaaagh!'

I came off deliciously with him at the same time, too engrossed in the explosive power of an unstoppable climax that coursed through my bottom, belly and pelvis like an electric current to notice that my thighs were bumping painfully against the table's edge. I slumped forward, feeling Manley's tribute leaking from a bottom hole still pulsating, opening and closing like a fish's mouth, as he withdrew his limp dick. I remained where I was, too done in to move for long minutes while I sensed him going to a washbasin set in a corner of the room and tidying himself up. He was fully dressed and looking his old arrogant self when I arose to clean myself up. He sat back in his chair to watch me and said nothing until I had dressed.

'I didn't mean things to go that far,' I said, trying to appear contrite. 'But it happened and I couldn't help getting aroused. You took advantage of me, Mr Manley. I hope you don't think that I'm usually that kind of girl – to let you—'

'Rubbish,' he said sternly. 'You were ready for it and you

enjoyed it. It was an exciting episode in your hard-up, mundane little housewife's life. Be thankful it happened and count it as an experience. It's like masturbation, harmless if you don't worry about it or have feelings of shame afterwards. Take the guilt out of sex, girl, and you'll enjoy it as it should be, a marvellous gift.'

Hard-up I might be but my life was anything but mundane and I'd never had guilt about enjoying sex. I just wanted him to think that. 'You did mean what you said about my making more money as your model?' I thought to remind him. To make doubly sure, I added as reticently as I could, 'I suppose it will also mean you'll want to – want to – do what you did to me tonight?'

'Very likely. I can't resist such a perfect bottom,' Manley admitted calmly. He turned to the money now scattered over the table from the shaking it had received during our strenuous bout. 'Here's your six pounds for tonight's modelling, plus four to make it ten, a little bonus for your compliance, shall we say? That's ten pounds, not bad for a few hours work. More than some men earn in a week.'

'Thank you, sir,' I said, laying my gratitude on thick and heavy and surprising myself to find I got a curious thrill out of being so subservient to this creep. I put the money in my shoulder bag, saying it was time to leave.

'Of course, your dear husband will be waiting for you,' he could not resist saying. 'We'll talk of the plans I have for you at next week's class. Don't worry, I'll find you plenty of well-paid work. You're a beautiful girl, I'll say that. A horny little piece, too.'

'You made me that way, Mr Manley,' I said, pretending to be ashamed of the lapse. He nodded as if in full agreement, even shaking my hand as I left.

Going downstairs to the street, where Nigel was still

waiting, I hugged my shoulder bag to my side to assure myself there really was ten whole pounds in it. As for my submissiveness to Gerard Manley, I supposed his aloof and pretentious manner had intrigued me. It was not the usual chat-up and flattering method used by other men to get their way with me. I had allowed him to use and abuse me in the basest way, like a slave would her master, but I had enjoyed the feeling more than I cared to admit. It had made a change to let someone else take charge. In my other role as wife, mother and penny-pinching homemaker, the responsibility was constant. Manley made me feel I had nothing to worry about while I was with him. All I had to do was relax and let him see to everything. If that meant being submissive, it was a relief. I liked the feeling.

So help me, I was looking forward to our next meeting already.

Chapter Five
ITALY

Count Giotti's palatial yacht *Sophia* ploughed a leisurely course southwards in the startlingly blue Tyrrhenian Sea towards the exotic isles of Ischia and Capri. Waiters in crisp white jackets hovered behind the seven guests aboard, including myself, ready to serve us at the snap of a finger. We sat in a horseshoe formation on cushioned loungers, four assorted females and three males getting to know each other in the first hour of a luxury private cruise. The calm ocean reflected the bright sun in flashes and sparkles, the receding coast of Italy a greyish blue in the heat haze. It was all very sumptuously enjoyable.

Giotti circulated, making sure we had every comfort, oozing charm to ensure we all became more than friendly. I could guess why, looking at my companions. The men studied us females like predators, almost licking their lips in anticipation, a quartet of opulent and essentially highly successful bodies in their various pursuits. These men, I had learned, were in film-producing, oil tankers, banking and publishing, though their main pursuit at that moment was undoubtedly having their lusts catered to while at sea.

Joe Giovanni, a Hollywood mogul who had brought with him his latest starlet, a dumb-blonde Marilyn Monroe lookalike, seemed fascinated by my breasts. His eyes were glued to them as he ignored his escort and engaged me in a one-sided conversation all about himself. Even when flattering me on my looks and waving his huge cigar, it was to say he should have put me in movies. 'How come I missed you,' he said, 'a fine English actress?'

He must have got me mixed up with someone else and I was not about to enlighten him, feeling it practical to adopt a discreet anonymity in such company. On meeting Giotti that morning I had learned for the first time he'd arranged a sea cruise and that I was included among other interesting guests. I could guess just what he meant by interesting but before I had a chance to say I couldn't possibly be away from Rome for a week in case my husband called, he snidely said he had a surprise for me. The telephone rang in the ornate room hung with priceless renaissance paintings where he was pressing a third martini on me. With a smug look on his handsome face, he indicated that I answer it.

'Diana, is that you?' Harry's delighted voice replied as I answered the call. 'Count Giotti said you'd be there. Has he told you the good news, that you'll be joining me here in Bangkok? I can't wait to see you. He's arranged that I stay here for a long tour. Good for him. We've been too long apart and you'll know why!'

'I've missed it too,' I laughed with him. 'When can I join you? It's got me all of a flutter thinking about being with you again.'

'Horny, you mean,' my husband teased. 'It's the same for me, not sleeping beside that lush body of yours, my darling. You'll love Bangkok, it's a wild city full of marvellous temples, waterway markets, night clubs and excellent restaurants. A brothel and massage parlour in just about every street too. Of course I've avoided them but the girls here are so beautiful it's made it very hard for me – or rather very hard for *you* when you arrive!' He made kissing sounds into the phone. 'Just wait till I get you here. We were not made to do without each other, were we, my love? I'm sure it's been as difficult for you there alone in Rome.'

'Very difficult, very lonely,' I had lied, even as I felt Giotti's hand purposefully unbuttoning the front of my dress and slipping inside to cup my left breast while his other hand reached for the division of my thighs, curving over my plump mound and giving it suggestive squeezes.

'So when can I join you, Harry?' I repeated. To show Giotti he was annoying me, I pushed my bottom against him as if to thrust him away. He gave me a lewd grin and held me tighter. My bottom pushing against him merely made things worse. The cleave of my bum met the upright stalk of a rigid erection bulging his white linen yachting trouser front. It nestled there, a hard cylinder pressed in the comfortable groove through my light dress. A moment later he began moving his hips against the rounds of my cheeks.

'I've already arranged a nice apartment for us,' Harry's voice began, 'but I'm off upcountry today for a work project. I'll be away about a week, but it will take that long for you to get any injections and book your flight.'

The first injection I was obviously going to get was one from Giotti as I felt him drawing up the skirt of my dress over my hips and tucking the hem into the belt at my waist. 'Leave all the details to Giotti,' my husband continued. 'He's evidently got a way of making things happen at the centre of things.' I could have told Harry that, my panties were already down to my ankles, my breasts lolling out over my bra and thrusting from my open dress, with Giotti's other hand now up to the wrist between my rear cleavage and two fingers squelching noisily inside *my* centre of things.

'He's an Italian,' Harry laughed down the line from Bangkok. 'He works about as often as Santa Claus and I thought I'd be stuck in his office in Rome doing all his work for him. For some reason he gave me the Thailand post, for which I'm truly grateful. I wonder what came up to change his mind?'

Came up was exactly the right choice of words as I felt the plum head of Giotti's mighty erection nudge my outer lips and press home its full engorged length up my channel. I had to stifle a gasp and try to act as normal while being fucked with a large stiff prick. Giotti uttered low growls in his lustful pleasure, withdrawing his hardness to the tip and easing forward until it became an agony for me to control my desire to meet his thrusts. I had parted my feet to allow him better access to my rear. Now I reached back with my free hand to pull apart my buttock cheeks for his deeper penetration, all the while holding the telephone receiver and bending forward over the little table with my bum tilting higher at each lunge.

'I'll leave all the ins and outs to the count then,' I thought it apt to say, suppressing a gasp as his thrusts continued. 'I mean seeing to my travel arrangements, dear. He wants me to join a party of his friends on his boat but I'd much rather be with you.'

'So he told me earlier,' Harry said. 'I think it's a great way to pass the days until you join me. Go ahead, enjoy a millionaire's cruise. You'll more than hold your own with any of 'em. Just don't do anything I wouldn't do,' he laughed. 'I'm being a good boy, saving it all for you. See you in a week or so, my love.'

'Goodbye,' I said throatily, 'I love you.' I hoped the husky croak of my voice would be interpreted by Harry as wifely emotion.

Giotti took the telephone from my hand and tossed it aside. He took hold of my breasts, his shafting now more urgent and vigorous, my own reaction matching his thrusts as I helplessly gurgled out my delight. His belly thrashed against my bottom, the knob of his plunging dick nudging up to my cervix, sending spasms coursing through my belly. I urged him on, ordering him in my shameless throes to 'fuck me, fuck me harder, don't you dare come yet' and other wanton entreaties. Then we were shuddering and jerking together, my cunt pulsating and gripping, churning in a continuing climatic convulsion as he shot his load up me in drenching spurts.

I came to rather dazedly with Riccardo beside us replacing the telephone and announcing the car was ready to take us to Lido de Roma and the yacht. I gave him an embarrassed smile as I adjusted my dress but his return look was grim, the displeasure of a young man who was jealously inclined. Obviously he thought I was above such wanton behaviour with any other but him. His mouth formed the word 'Whore' as he turned away. And fuck you too, I thought angrily. You weren't above having me and you don't own me. Magnificent young specimen though he was, and such a good sex partner, could it be that a strong love-hate relationship was forming between us? I fought down the feeling, thankful that in a week or so I would be far away.

Later, newly arrived on the yacht and shown to the luxurious cabin I was to use during the cruise, Riccardo tapped on my door and entered as I was dressing after a shower. Still in chauffeur's uniform, he stared at me. The next instant we were in each other's arms, kissing passionately. 'My darling,' I heard myself say. 'Darling!'

As our mouths parted, a warning voice within told me that I was acting like a besotted schoolgirl and, at my age, feelings for this magnificent young man were foolish in the extreme. 'No, no,' I begged, trying to prise him from my arms as his lips sought mine again. 'We agreed, Ricky. I'm married and you are just a boy. We can't possibly.'

'Possibly what?' he said darkly. 'Love each other already? I don't want to, but I do. Goddam it. I watched Giotti fucking you. You went along with it, you loved it.'

'He forced me,' I pleaded, 'you must have known. He took me while I was talking to my husband. I couldn't help myself.' I pressed kisses to his lips. 'I wished it was you. I would sooner spend this next week in Rome with just the two of us.' I felt his massive cock erect and iron-hard against my crotch. 'Take me now if you want me,' I offered him. 'It's only you I really care about.'

Riccardo shook his head sadly. 'Oh, I'll be fucking you soon enough,' he said grimly. 'That's what I do on these trips, entertain the guests with my outsized dong, give sex shows for Giotti's rich and famous guests. I fuck wives and girlfriends for the amusement of their sugar-daddies and you'll be expected to play along. For once I don't like it. That's how I feel about you. Dumb, isn't it? Fancy you and me being stuck on each other.'

'It's impossible,' I agreed, unable to stop kissing him. 'I'm sure I'll never forget you.'

'You make it worse,' he laughed bitterly. 'Me a goddamn chauffeur and you a lady. The wrong people at the wrong time, I guess. Just don't let these bastards aboard make you do anything you don't want to.'

'I can't say I'll mind you using that outsized dong on me,' I said mischievously. 'We are a pair, aren't we? At least I can look forward to that. Whenever we get the chance.'

'You're one hell of a lady,' Riccardo said with a grin. 'I only came on the boss's instructions to tell you to help yourself to the clothes in the wardrobe. He also told me to say he wants you on deck to show off to his guests. Got to go, a menial like me has work to do, taking luggage to the cabins.'

'You'll never be menial,' I told him fondly, seeing him off with a last long kiss.

The evening sun was still high and hot and the *Sophia* was at anchor. People were swimming over the side. I looked in my wardrobe for a swimming costume. It was filled with all sorts of expensive clothes, from sportswear to evening dresses, including shoes and sheer lingerie. Giotti left nothing to chance, it seemed, there was even a selection of bikinis. I was undressed and considering an electric-blue two-piece when a tap sounded at my door and the Marilyn Monroe lookalike put her head around the door. 'Come in,' I said. 'If I recall rightly, you are Darleen Delancy. Is that your right name?'

The pretty thing laughed, making me warm to her. 'Hell, no, it's what Mr Giovanni decided for my film career. Crazy, isn't it? Do I look like a Darleen?'

'What's in a name?' I laughed with her, 'as long as you get what you're after. I'm just plain Diana Mackenzie.' I had made Giotti promise that he would not tell the other guests that I was Lady Diana Saxon.

The girl advanced, looking at me admiringly and I realised I stood before her naked. 'That's a real name,' she said, reverence in her voice. 'Mr Giovanni says you're a famous stage actress back in England. That's what I want to do more than anything, become a real actress. He hasn't used me in one of his films yet, only screwed me lots of times. How else can a girl get on?'

'True,' I said, declining to laugh at her honesty. 'Haven't we all? What stars have been created on the well-known casting couch! Us girls have to use what weapons we've got.' I held up the bikini. 'I'm longing for a swim, the sea looks so inviting. Do you think this will fit my ample curves?'

'I think your body is beautiful,' she said unreservedly. 'You're the loveliest woman on this boat. I heard the men discussing you; Mr Giovanni thinks you're gorgeous. He sent me down to ask you to join us. I don't think,' she added, hesitating, 'that you'll need the bikini. They expect us to swim naked—' I was about to say tough luck for them then, for I'd be wearing the bikini, when she pleaded with me. 'Would you mind? I'll be expected to go naked. I'd feel kinda cheap if we go up with only me like that.'

'Then what the hell,' I said. 'I really prefer skinny-dipping. Throw off your clothes, Darleen, and we'll go on deck together naked and unashamed. I've got a feeling we won't be wearing much more than a smile this trip anyway. What about our other two female companions? The darkly beautiful Italian woman and that slightly overweight girl with her. I took it they were mother and daughter—' We looked at each other and giggled. 'Surely not?' I said. 'Not on this kind of voyage, with that pack of lecherous hounds on board!'

'I've done many a thing,' Darleen admitted, smiling with me. 'Been a street hooker in goddam Gary, Indiana; a call-girl in New York; a stripper in a joint in Atlantic City and given head to every agent in Hollywood, but never with my mother around! What else can they be here for?'

It would be interesting finding out, I decided, watching Darleen disrobe and thinking that, whatever her past, she still looked youthful and fresh. Her skin was of a smooth, ivory whiteness, her body and limbs rounded and perfectly proportioned and her curvaceous figure cried out to be made love to. I was enchanted with it, feeling an immediate desire as I did at times when strongly attracted to another of my own sex. Her tits were bigger than average, with protruding pinkish nipples slightly above centre on each breast, begging for a suckling. Her hip flared and led down to shapely legs and calves, tiny feet, and between her strong thighs nestled a plumpish bulge with a light covering of wispy fair hair, surrounding a neat split quim with inrolling lips. It looked like a little girl's cunt, almost unused.

'Don't look at me like that,' she teased, pleased with my reaction as I advanced to her saying breathlessly how lovely she was. I reached out both hands to cup her breasts. As I pressed my palms to the hardening nipples, I felt the shudder go through her body. I could not resist stroking her mound, getting a response as her hips moved to my fondling.

'Do you like girls?' she breathed questioningly as our bodies closed together, breast to breast, pubic mounds starting a slow grind together deliciously. 'I can be that way too. It's what I am,' she admitted as our mouths fused and tongues probed. 'I fuck men but I love women. It's so good.'

'Oh, yes, it *is* so good,' I moaned softly against the scarlet cupid-bow lips of her sweet mouth. The heat in our naked bodies rose dramatically as we strained against each other, her nipples hard as flints against mine, our cunt mounds rubbing together ever faster. With the kisses and close hugging, plus Riccardo's hard erection lingering in my mind to make me aroused, this entirely unexpected bout of torrid female lovemaking had me coming off almost at once, shuddering from head to toes, grasping at Darleen to prevent myself collapsing to my knees. She came too, holding me for support in our standing position, giving out barely suppressed whimpers and cries and buffeting her plump little cunt to mine feverishly as our climaxes coincided.

We still clung together, glued by the perspiration that

bathed our naked flesh from the strenuously uninhibited coupling sticking us together. I was so turned on. 'When I first saw you,' Darleen said reverently, 'I wanted at once to be like you, so beautiful and serene.' She kissed my lips tenderly, fondly. 'You're a real lady. I watched the way you weren't impressed by those sleaze-ball rich bastards up on deck. You know they'll want to screw us every which way on this trip? They'll put on porno movies and shows to get 'em going. Don't you mind that?'

I could not help but return her kiss. 'I have my reasons too,' I said, hugging her. 'We'll see it through together.' I did not add that, to my mind, a sea-going orgy seemed a very pleasant diversion to pass the time until I joined my husband. And if we had to put on a lesbian show, at least it would be no pretend act with the gorgeous body of Darleen as a partner. Then too there was Riccardo and his lovely prick that gave me such pleasure. He had already said his prime duty on board was to entertain and amuse the guests with his amazing sexual prowess. As for being observed while fucking and performing lewd acts before an audience, I had always found it increased *my* wanton arousal tremendously – as I suspect it would many a woman if she would only admit it. I have always considered it a tribute to myself and even to my husband that so many men desire to fuck me.

'I suppose we'd better show ourselves on deck,' Darleen said wistfully. 'Me, I'd sooner stay down here with you. Your breasts are so lovely, you know,' she added, pecking kisses to my round and taut nipples. 'I think I'm falling in love with you. Is that really dumb of me? I can't help it. Kiss me,' the impassioned girl pleaded. 'Say you like me!'

'You're lovely, beautiful, so sweet,' I could not resist telling her, quite charmed and thrilled by her naive confession. Our lips met again lingeringly, tongues entwining, our bare flesh pressed together as if in helpless desire to fuse our bodies as one.

'Sure, go on, tell the horny little bitch you like her,' said a derisive voice from the cabin doorway. 'I can see you do from here.' Darleen and I turned in shocked surprise to see the matronly Italian woman standing before us, the eyes that regarded us filled with disdain. We drew apart hastily. 'The guests are getting impatient, wondering why you two have been so long,' she continued imperiously, as if she were addressing the paid help. 'Get up on deck now! Make your kind of sex in your own time in future.'

'You can tell them we'll come up when we're good and ready,' I said, cold with fury. 'That is, if we decide to appear at all.'

'Please, Diana,' Darleen begged me in a nervous little voice. 'Don't make waves. My future depends on pleasing those guys.'

'I suggest you remember that,' Daniella Siracusa said smugly. 'You obviously haven't been invited for your intellect, either of you. You're here for your own benefit, you need Count Giotti and his friends. Here to perform and your personal feelings don't come into it. Now, both you dirty bitches report on deck. At least you are already stripped for the pleasure of the guests.'

'And just who the hell are you?' I demanded. 'Why are you here? Do you screw like the rest of us or do you just bring along fat young virgins?'

Her reply was a look that could have killed and a swinging slap to my breasts that made me reel back. I went back at her at once, clawing in fury, my breasts stinging and smarting from her blow. She was no weakling, holding me at arm's length despite my strength. She was a formidable woman of buxom proportions, ripely mature. I had thought, when first being introduced to her, that she would no doubt appeal to men with a taste for a voluptuous figure. As it was, she wrestled me down to the bed, holding my wrists, her knee pressed to my stomach. I was laid out like that, gasping with exertion and anger, when Count Giotti appeared in the cabin with his three greatly interested male guests.

'What the devil is going on?' he said, highly amused at my plight. 'We could hear the commotion up on deck. Daniella, is it entirely necessary to pinion Diana like that? What has she done?'

'Let me up! Get that fat bitch off me,' I howled in my humiliation. 'I didn't come on this trip to take orders from her.'

'I can't have mutinous conduct on my yacht,' Giotti laughed. 'I must say, my dear Diana, you look delicious when angry and completely nude.'

'And such great tits on her,' Joe Giovanni said enthusiastically. 'See the way they heave when she's mad. She obviously annoyed Daniella, so let's hear the evidence against her. Let's put her on trial.'

'Yes, with suitable punishment if found guilty of mutiny,' said the thin little banker eagerly. 'State your case, Daniella.'

'Get that big-arsed cow off me!' I yelled, rested enough to put up a struggle again. Giotti tut-tutted, eyeing me with evil intent, no doubt delighted at the unrehearsed entertainment I was providing for his guests.

'Let me up,' I demanded again.

'We can't do that,' Giotti said with a grin. 'You would obviously be a hostile witness or whatever the term is and not let Daniella give her evidence without having to hold you down. As you evidently don't intend to co-operate, we shall have to bind your wrists and ankles to the bed. Riccardo!' he called and I caught a glimpse of his chauffeur lurking in the doorway. 'Bring the silk cords. We have a lady here who will not behave.'

Whatever Riccardo's stated feelings for me, he obeyed his master, his eyes avoiding mine as he and Daniella bound my wrists and ankles to the four corners of the cabin's bed. I was spreadeagled on the sheets with my arms and legs making an 'X' of my body. The silk cords were drawn tight and allowed little movement although they were not painful. A pillow was slipped under my bottom, raising my crotch to present my cunt with its split mound and thatch of dark auburn hair to ogling eyes. In such situations I find it impossible to prevent a certain degree of arousal, and I felt the first flutterings in my lower belly and quim.

'I came down to get Darleen and this woman to join us on deck,' Daniella began with malice in her voice. 'I found them making heated lesbian love – locked together rubbing at each other in a fury of lust. They didn't notice me, they were so engrossed.'

'It's none of your bloody business,' I spat out at her.

'But entirely selfish behaviour, nonetheless,' Giotti, taking on the role of judge, said in mock severity. 'None of us have any objection to you and Darleen making out. Your crime is that you did it in secret, not allowing us the benefit of enjoying the spectacle. Go on, Daniella, having disturbed the lovers, what happened then?'

'She was insulting to me and refused to join your guests as I requested her to do. Then she attacked me, as you witnessed.'

'That is not all true,' I began, but Giotti ignored my protest, shaking his head at my supposed conduct.

'Diana is with us on this trip,' he said to his guests, 'because I arranged something for her husband's benefit. But it's not too late to change my mind about the favour. Madam,' he said, looking me in the eye in pretend gravity, 'the punishment I've decided you merit is for a good dozen strokes of the belt on your delightful bottom. Then, to compensate poor Daniella for your inexcusable behaviour to her while merely obeying an instruction from me to invite you on deck, you will pleasure her in any way she thinks fit. So that you give her complete satisfaction we will all witness the punishment.'

'You're disgusting beasts,' I told the gathered assembly. 'All I want to do is to join my husband. Giotti assured me.'

'And you will, my dear,' Giotti promised suavely, 'provided you take your punishment and behave as I expect for the rest of our little cruise. I've decided to have you across my knee for the first part of your sentence. Nothing is more ignoble or humbling for a proud woman to be treated like a naughty young girl. Do you agree to allow that sensibly, Diana?' He began to untie my bonds.

'What choice have I got?' I mumbled as I rose to my feet, all eyes taking in the bounce of my breasts and flounce of my buttocks in getting off the bed. Giotti wanted me draped across his lap for the pleasure of my naked body close to his, my buttocks with its tight cleft directly under his gaze. The thought of it, all those avid male eyes watching, had my pussy steaming. Obediently I lay across Giotti's knees, seeing Darleen looking at me with pained sorrow in her eyes. My tits hung down as I positioned myself. Then my twin cheeks were being smoothed by a light touch, fingers lingering and two hands drawing apart the deep cleave to show my rear-hanging bulge with the crisp surrounding hair and curled lips and, adjacent to it, the crinkled pucker of my nether hole. Despite unsought-for feelings of excitement I cringed at the utter indignity and humiliation of being so wantonly displayed.

'That's one fine ass,' opined Constantine Stavros, the plump little Greek tanker fleet owner, peering down closely into the parting of my raised buttock cheeks. 'Does she take the cock up there, you think, Romeo? Who is this woman anyway? She's not the usual paid performer, I would say.'

'Maybe not,' the know-all Joe Giovanni chipped in, 'but that looks like a well-fucked cunt to me even if Daniella caught her making out with my girl. Guess she's a switch-hitter, likes it with both sexes. Who cares, as long as she saves a piece of ass for me.'

Giotti added to my growing mortification by patting my bottom as one does an obedient pet dog who pleases his master. 'Diana is an exceptionally beautiful lady and we are most fortunate to have her grace us with her presence on this occasion. Constantine is right in his assumption, she is no paid performer but a dutiful wife who has fallen into bad company – us!'

'How perfectly stimulating for us,' said the shifty banker. 'I hope this is her first fall from grace. Has she known only her husband? I'd like to think we are about to introduce her to much more interesting experiences.

'The woman's a whore,' snapped Daniella viciously. 'Constantine is a fool to think she doesn't fuck with others, dutiful wife or not!'

'True, I must admit,' Giotti said chuckling hurtfully. 'I have to reveal I've already had the pleasure, and a most memorable fuck she is. It was just this morning, while she was talking to her husband—'

'You bastard!' I shouted. 'Tell them it was all your doing, while I was on the phone.'

'Get on with punishing her, Romeo,' urged the buxom Daniella. From my position draped naked across Giotti's knees I saw the Italian woman's clothes being shed on the thick pile of the cabin's carpet. 'Thrash the arrogance out of the bitch, let her know she's just like the rest of us on this cruise.'

I tried to rear up at her in my anger, shouting other insults while Giotti held me down with a firm grip on my neck.

'Behave, Diana!' he roared and brought down the leather belt across my squirming bum with a crack like thunder. Three or four more stinging blows striped my cheeks and I howled out, uncaring of any loss of dignity. Howled out first in fury and hurt pride, then I sobbed for mercy as the smart in my bottom grew as hot as fire, my cheeks clenching to lessen each descending strike. 'Please, please!' I begged. 'I'll do anything.'

'Stop, stop it!' I heard Darleen plead. 'Beat me if you must.' She was told to keep her nose out of it by Daniella, who I knew had taken a dislike for me bordering on hatred. I suffered at least another dozen good slaps of the belt before Giotti ceased, lying across his lap only glad that he considered I'd been humiliated enough. The glow in my burning bottom spread through right to my vitals, palpitating both cunt and arsehole.

'Here endeth the first lesson,' cracked Joe Giovanni. 'That was the real thing for once, not set-up like you pay to see in any L.A. or Tijuana cat-house. It was great to see.'

'Great for you maybe,' I complained, too soundly whipped to move off Giotti's lap, rubbing my reddened cheeks. 'You didn't suffer it.'

'Remember,' I heard Daniella say firmly, standing directly before my face so that the most thick and luxuriant thatch of pubic hair I had ever seen was thrust a mere inch from my face. 'Remember her punishment included compensating me for her insolence and attack on my person. She must pay now, it was agreed. I want her on her hands and knees between my thighs – using her tongue . . .'

'I won't, I shan't!' I began to protest, instantly getting one more stinging smack of the belt on my already smarting posterior.

'It was agreed,' Giotti said affably. 'Come, Diana, didn't we all hear you promise just now that you'd do anything?'

'That was while you were thrashing my bottom.'

'And there'll be more for continued disobedience,' he promised threateningly. 'You'd better do as we say.'

I nodded miserably and was pulled off his lap by Daniella none too gently. She held me by the armpits between her strapping thighs as she plonked her ample bottom down at the very edge of the bed. 'Now lick, you haughty bitch,' she commanded, grasping my hair and dragging my face down. A forest of thick black hair covered her plumply curved mound and fat butterfly outer lips guarded her slit. I took a last look around before being hauled closer, seeing a circle of lustful faces eagerly anticipating the show. Then my nose and mouth was being rubbed into Daniella's gaping sex, my tormentor squirming her bottom and grinding her pelvis as she held my head fast.

Her oily lubrication smeared me from nose to chin, her smell the pungent odour of a woman in heat. 'Suck, tongue, lick!' she ordered again sharply and, so help me, her lewdness was gradually making me lewd too. I fought off a growing desire to lap and lick wantonly at her juicy source and nipped her flaring outer lips sharply with my teeth. She yelped, gave me a warning smack on my backside, then pulled me into the fork of her thighs again. My act of defiance made, with a low moan of submission I went into her, tongue extended.

I can't help it, having another woman groaning with helpless sexual pleasure on my face has always thrilled me. Licking, lapping and flicking an engorged clitoris the size of

71

my thumb, I got entirely engrossed in reeming out Daniella's drenched interior, determined to make her climax mightily. In her excitement she let go of my head, falling back across the cabin bed. She reached down to part the lips of her cunt for my deeper access, revealing a glistening pink passage with her clitoris rearing up from its hood like a miniature cock for me to suck greedily upon. She reverted to her native Italian, mumbling and muttering words of obvious delight, raising her large buttocks from the bed and tilting her cunt for me.

I was not unaware of the remarks being used to describe my performance by the delighted male audience. 'What a great cunt-licker!' I heard Joe Giovanni exclaim. 'She has Daniella turning somersaults.'

It was not far off the truth, for the Italian woman was bucking and bouncing as she came off for at least the third time.

'If only her husband could see her now!' I heard Giotti laugh. 'Someone fuck her while her ass is sticking up like that. Who wants her? She'll appreciate a prick the state she's got into.'

It was true. To my undying shame I turned my head and agreed. 'Yes, someone fuck me!' I urged. 'Fuck me while I'm licking out Daniella.' I turned back to continue working on her cunt, moments later giving out a pleasurable groan as I felt a long stiff prick slide up me. I pushed back to get full penetration, feeling the slap of heavy balls between my arse cheeks and a bare plumpish stomach hard against my gyrating bottom. Glancing back I saw the lustful face of Joe Giovanni.

'Oh, baby!' he cried. 'Oh, baby. This is turning out to be one hell of a voyage, and you are one hell of a good fuck.'

'Just make me come,' I ground out through my teeth and, in his final thrusts I came with him strongly, my head falling and my hair trailing on the carpet as he withdrew. On each side of me were Daniella's spreadeagled legs, her toes still tingling as she recovered on the bed with loud gasps and shudders.

In time I got up from my knees, looking defiantly at Giotti and his friends. 'Satisfied?' I asked. 'Now I need to shower, so if it's not obligatory to observe me doing that, please leave. All of you.'

'Diana, you were marvellous,' Giotti said. 'Will we see you on deck later? Please? We'll have champagne and dine and dance under the stars to make it an evening to remember.'

'This afternoon will be quite memorable too,' I said drily, but then could not conceal a smile. 'You were right. I *have* fallen into bad company.'

'You'll be in Bangkok this time next week,' I was promised. 'Even if I have a great desire to keep you here for myself. We look forward to your presence at dinner – and at the little entertainment we shall arrange afterwards?'

'Why not?' I said. 'After the free-for-all that's taken place here in my cabin, what have I got to lose? You've seen it all already.'

I didn't know my Giotti. Or his friends. After landing some days later I really did need a cruise to restore my energy.

Chapter Six
ENGLAND

'Lakeside Abbey,' announced Gerard Manley, turning off the road and into a long tree-lined avenue. 'It's more of a large pond really, dug by the monks in medieval times and stocked with fish to supplement their diet. The naturists here have created a splendid private venue for their nudist activities.'

'I suppose it wouldn't sound so grand called Pondside Abbey,' said I lightheartedly from beside his driving seat, holding baby Peter in my arms. I got an annoyed look for my facetiousness. At a bend in the track the walls of a ruined abbey came into view; we drove through a gate held open by a completely naked man and pulled in among a row of cars. All around were beautifully kept flower beds, trim lawns, wooden chalets, a swimming pool and several dozen absolutely nude people of both sexes and all shapes, sizes and ages. I giggled at the sight and got a rebuke in the shape of an angry shake of his head and another glare.

'Will you behave?' Gerard snapped. 'We're here to work. It's why you get paid the fees you're so eager to get your greedy little hands on.'

'Yes, master,' I teased as his left hand squeezed my right leg threateningly above the knee. 'All right. Sorry, sorry,' I pleaded hastily. 'I'll promise to behave.'

'You had better, I can't suffer your childish high spirits when there is an assignment,' he gave warning in the icily calm tone I had learned at my peril not to ignore.'

'Please,' I begged as he got out to retrieve his photographic equipment from the back seat of his box-like Austin. 'This is like a day out for Peter and me. A change from being in the house and cooking and cleaning.' It was a Saturday morning and my husband was in Coventry all day earning money labouring on pipe-laying.

'We're here to work,' he repeated. 'You really cannot seem to get that into your head.' It didn't seem like work to me, posing nude, and I found I had a natural aptitude as a model. 'I can't believe you were actually an officer in the Wrens,' he added, 'or that you're now a married woman with a child. At times you can be infuriatingly juvenile, Mrs Saxon. Just like a naughty little girl.'

'It's how you like me,' I pouted, 'I know. You enjoy punishing me, smacking my bare bottom when I annoy you.' I knew very well how he relished ordering me to bend over before him with the object of meting out a lesson for some supposed misdemeanour. It was several weeks since my first modelling session at his evening class. On my third appointment I had been ten minutes late at his studio through Harry arriving home late from a college lecture. I couldn't leave the baby, I'd explained. Gerard, who had never before given a hoot about his students, went on angrily about keeping them waiting, something he'd done without qualm the previous week.

'Do you agree you deserve punishment for that?' he suggested severely as I hurriedly undressed. 'Perhaps my docking you a percentage of your fee? We will pursue this issue after class.'

When the students had departed, back in the side room with Gerard counting out his takings, I was about to dress when he looked across at me sternly. He rose, taking off his tan leather belt, purposely slipping it through the loops of his green corduroy slacks that went with the open-necked check shirt and cravat he considered the correct wear for one of his artistic temperament.

'Forgotten something, haven't we, young woman?' he reminded me casually. 'There is the little matter of just retribution for your tardiness in arriving late for my class. Something I won't tolerate.'

The sight of the belt doubled in his hand sent a shiver of apprehension through me. 'What—' I asked nervously, 'what do you intend to do?'

'The time-honoured method of instilling discipline into wayward females,' Gerard said, swishing the belt against his leg. 'A good smacked bottom. The female posterior, and yours particularly, is well suited to receive a good paddling. By hand, strap, or even a suitable crop or cane. I suggest we get on with it, so bend over the table and grip the corner edges to brace yourself.'

He pulled back the chair to allow me access, swept the piled money aside and held out a hand palm upwards to invite me to take up my position. My buttock cheeks clenched as I lowered my breasts to the table top and raised a tremulous rear end. Glancing back, I flinched at the sight of the belt, at his eyes alight with cruel anticipation. He would not spare the rod, I decided, making a last grovelling plea for mercy. That no doubt increased the pleasure of the moment for him.

'Please, please, Mr Manley,' I begged sorrowfully. 'I don't want you to thrash me. I won't ever be late again, I promise. I'm not a naughty schoolgirl to be treated like this. It's shameful.'

'What do you suggest then, Mrs Saxon?' Gerard asked sadistically, the belt raised and his free hand smoothing over my bared bottom cheeks as if lining up his target. 'That we dispense with the well-deserved punishment and I not only deduct your modelling fee but tell you that your services are no longer required? Do you wish that?'

'No,' I whimpered miserably, thinking of the loss of easy money. 'Punish me some other way. Play with my breasts and suck them, titty-fuck them if you wish. I'll suck your cock for you. Fuck me, if you like, front or back, in both places even.'

Behind me I heard Gerard tut-tutting sarcastically. I knew then I was only prolonging my agony, my bottom twitching and tummy churning as I awaited my fate. 'How crude you are,' I was admonished. 'Fuck, suck, cock indeed, from a slip of a girl. I do all of those things you suggested anyway. A good bottom-warming is well overdue in your case. What you are doing behind your husband's back qualifies you for a damned good reminder of your loyalty to him.' He said this unctuously as if he had nothing to do with my infidelity. 'The pity is he hasn't beaten some obedience into you himself.'

'I only do it for the money,' I said with a yelp as the first stroke of the leather slapped down across my raised cheeks. *Thwack, thwack* went his belt until I was pleading for the blows to cease, feeling the heat so generated spreading into my lower abdomen and down to the core of my sex and anus, making the whole region pulse and throb with rising excitement. Gerard simply dropped the belt after a good dozen strokes, lowering his trousers and closing in to penetrate me, unable to contain his urge any longer. Still stifling groans from his beating, thus I was taken, first in my cunt and then in my bottom. So I had been duly punished like his chattel.

Just as with the first modelling session, I left with a throb in my bottom, ten pounds the richer, and the wicked feeling that I had reverted to my true wanton nature. The excitement of other men desiring me was proving irresistible. I told myself it was excusable, the financial gains would make our family life more comfortable. In truth my knickers were soaked and sticky with the urge to indulge in sex as often as possible. I had to satisfy the constant need of my promiscuity.

I told myself too that I was going through a phase, one that would pass. It was a sort of nymphomania forced on me to compensate for the constant strain of keeping a home together. I found it a blessed relief to let myself go and enjoy my secret new life. Even being subservient to the odious Gerard Manley was strangely pleasurable. He took all the responsibility, I had simply to obey his wishes and let him do the planning.

Waiting for me beside his mother's car was an impatient Nigel Lamont. He rushed forward to greet me, agitation mixed with his besotted look of adoration.

'What kept you, Diana darling?' Nigel had blurted anxiously, holding open the car door for me. 'It's late and I'm expected home after class. My mother gets really angry if I get her up to let me in.'

'Well, hard luck for her,' I giggled in my high spirits, my bottom-hole still pulsing and contracting, ten more pounds in my purse adding to my pride in myself. 'You're a big boy, Nigel. Make her give you a key. Tell her you were out with a married woman. That would be a reasonable excuse.'

'You don't know her,' Nigel said mournfully. 'She's so strict. It's awful going home when she's waiting up for me. I haven't got a father. Some fellow got her into trouble and I'm her bastard son. I'm sure she hates men. She brought me up by herself and I've always had to obey her.' He put the car into first gear, eager to be off. 'Tonight I'd better just drop you off near your flat, Diana.'

'That's a pity,' I said wickedly, intent on increasing poor Nigel's misery. It boosted my ego to be coquettish with the love-struck boy, exactly the opposite to my manner with the overbearing Gerard. 'If you had the time I was hoping you would drive me to a dark lane and fuck me.' He looked at me with both hope and anxiety on his face. 'You heard,' I teased him. 'I said if you wanted to you could fuck me, Nigel.'

'Oh, Diana, we've no time,' he said in abject misery. 'You know I want to but mother will be furious. There'll be such an atmosphere at home.'

'Then make it a quickie,' I said, enjoying tempting him. He drove in silence, taking the route to our lovers' lane, despite his fear of his mother. I really wanted him. In the back of the car I kissed him lewdly as we divested ourselves of my knickers and his trousers to get at each other. He brought out his little silver packet with a condom but I told him there was no need, I was wearing a Dutch cap. With my back on the long rear seat Nigel mounted and fucked me with the eagerness and energy of youth, making me come beautifully before he gave his final gasps and inundated me thoroughly.

I borrowed his comb as we sorted ourselves out after the bout. Nigel was calmer now he had relieved himself with me. As I gave back his comb he slipped a crumbled ball of notes into my hand. 'To hell with my mother,' he said grimly. 'That was worth all the silent treatment I'll get when I get in. Three pounds is all I've got on me, Diana, but you must take it to help you at home, with your husband being a student and all.' I thanked him with a long kiss, saying it wasn't necessary, even as I put the money in my purse. Never look a gift horse in the mouth, I say. 'This will probably be our last time,' he added sadly. 'I start full-time at Exeter University soon. I'll be leaving this week for private tuition before the autumn term starts. It's my mother's idea.'

'So you won't be calling to collect your weekly payments,' I smiled. 'I'll miss you marking up my book for services rendered. It was good while it lasted, wasn't it?'

'Worth every penny,' Nigel said seriously, making me blush. We had one long farewell kiss when he dropped me near home, then I bought fish and chips for Harry and went up the steep stairs to our flat. He was sitting at the table engrossed in his studies. 'How's Peter been?' I asked.

'Not a sound out of him,' Harry said, looking up and smiling. 'How was the film, my love? Did you enjoy it?' He unwrapped the fish and chips, eating hungrily. 'This is a treat. I thought we were broke again. I don't know how you do it, Di.'

Just as well you don't, I thought, throwing off my coat. 'It was very romantic,' I said. 'It put me in the mood for a loving session myself. I'm having a bath – want to join me?'

After he had eaten Harry came through to the little kitchen with its bath tub tucked in a corner, and sat on the edge of the bath.

'Aren't my nipples big tonight?' I asked him, thrusting out my breasts. 'That film's made me feel in need of a good fucking. So what are you going to do about it?' Three men in one evening, I reminded myself later as Harry had me in the comfort of our hire-purchased bed. Even in my throes I wondered who would be coming to collect the weekly payments for Lamont's now that Nigel was no longer available.

I still had Gerard Manley and his photographic sessions to boost my income, of course. The trip to Lakeside Abbey nudist resort was one he'd suggested for when I had a whole day free. 'I'll pay the usual three quid an hour,' he'd said, 'so for at least six hours posing there you'll do all right. The pics will be for the nudist publication *Naturism and Fitness*, of which you may have heard. We have to bring along a pretty girl, one with an outstanding figure for these shoots, just to make sure one is available. The real members of nudist clubs come in all shapes and sizes, as you can see.'

I undressed in one of the chalets and, with Peter in my arms, was photographed by the pool, posing as a regular member. There were no end of female volunteers to look after my boy, so later pics had me playing tennis, reclining on the diving board, eating a picnic meal with a group, and engaged in all the healthy outdoor activities one sees portrayed in nudist publications. After lunch I was joined by two beautifully proportioned and well-endowed young men, who were introduced to me by Gerard as professional models like myself. I was photographed with them under a communal shower, relaxing on sun beds and posing with my baby with one of them, as if in a happy family scene.

'Are you here for the extra shoot,' the one called Mike asked me in late afternoon. I thought there could be little else to photograph to portray a day at a nudist camp. He was dark, deeply tanned all over, and his flaccid cock hung at least seven inches over his heavy balls. His partner, Steve, grinned and looked at me, saying he certainly hoped so. He too was splendidly hung, blonde hair covering his lower belly and surrounding a long thick penis. 'Hasn't Manley mentioned it to you?' Mike asked. 'It's twice the rate. Makes it worth while.'

Manley himself then appeared from a chalet. 'Getting to know the boys, Diana?' he asked craftily. 'Have they mentioned an extra service you can do to double your take-home pay? What would you say to some private posing with them? It's a little more risqué than what we've been doing so far. You will like the money.'

'Depends what it is,' I said, intrigued and seeing the two male models exchanging grins. 'Do you mean—?'

'Come into my private chalet and talk business,' Manley offered. 'Peter's in safe hands, it won't take long and you'll be ten pounds better off.'

'Twenty-five pounds is the going rate, you cheapskate, Manley,' said Mike. 'Don't you do it for a penny less, love. He wants to take pics of Steve and me screwing you in various positions. Booklets of sexy scenes, postcards of us on the job for the Soho market. I must say, if you're agreeable, you're the perfect girl for the job.'

'It would be a pleasure,' added Steve, 'but we'll still charge Gerard twenty-five nicker a model as our fee. He'll make plenty out of it. Are you happy about it? Mike and I aren't exactly repulsive. You might enjoy it. Other models haven't complained.'

'Won't the members here wonder what we're up to in your chalet?' I asked, wavering, looking at Mike and Steve and finding them anything but repugnant. 'I don't know. I'm married.'

'When has that ever stopped you?' Gerard said hatefully, taking my arm and leading me off without my say-so. 'No one will wonder where we are. If they do, we're in my chalet for interior shots. Be quick about it and you'll be back in no time, twenty-five pounds richer on top of what you've made already.'

I entered his hut to find it ablaze with bright lights placed so that there was not a shadow in any corner. There was a double bed and an armchair and pictures on the walls to give the impression of a normal bedroom. Gerard adjusted a camera on a tripod.

'You know what to do, boys,' he ordered. 'So make it good. I'm paying you lot through the nose.'

We were all still nude, of course, and I felt Mike brushing into me from behind, his cock stiffening amazingly quickly as he guided it against the cleave of my bum. His arms went around me to cup both my breasts in his hands even as I gasped out my astonishment at the unexpected handling.

'Quit that and look horny,' Gerard rapped out from behind his camera. 'You're getting paid, so give me my money's worth.' My uptilted breasts, held by Mike, were being nuzzled by Steve, who then sucked hard on each nipple, making my insides turn to jelly, his huge prick now nudging my belly while an equally large member was lodged between my buttock cheeks. A girl could only stand so much of that! When Steve lifted his face from my nipples to kiss me I returned it with open mouth and felt his warm wet tongue slip in to twirl around mine. I eased open my bottom, pushing back against Mike.

'She's all for it,' I heard one of them mumble, then I was lifted bodily and spreadeagled on the bed. At one end Steve squatted up over my breasts, feeding his cock into my mouth. At the other end I moaned as Mike pressed his face between my thighs and began tonguing me. I sucked avidly on Steve's thick stem, lifting my bottom and tilting my cunt as Mike lapped and licked at my source. Gerard had taken his camera off the tripod and was moving around us, photographing the action from all angles. I noticed this as my first climax had me jerking helplessly on the bed. Then I was calling out for one or the other of them to fuck me, fuck me, to finish me off with one of those lovely cocks. The boys looked at each other and grunted agreement. Steve pulled me over his body until I was squatting over him, my tits swinging in his face as his mouth stretched up to suck my nipples.

If my husband had walked in at that moment I could not for the life of me have stopped. I groaned as I seized the upstanding stalk under my spread thighs and gratefully guided it to my outer lips, pressing down to impale myself on its girth and length. I squirmed on it, loving the feeling as it distended my cunt walls with its rock-hard size, rotating my bottom wildly as my arousal heightened to fever pitch and coming with coarse cries and shouts.

Then, with Steve's cock still embedded within me, a hand was on my back and I was being pushed forward over him, my bottom tilted high for whatever Mike intended. Twisting my head I saw him wet his fingers with saliva, then rub them on my puckered rear hole, inserting his index finger to the second knuckle. My jerking increased, spasms coursing through me from back to front. 'Yes, yes, there too!' I heard myself cry out.

'Great, great stuff!' I heard Gerard yell. He bent over to catch Mike's stalk entering my rear portal, nosing in through the tight ring and easing up, every slithering inch making me groan. Then both cocks were shunting within me, divided only by the thin membrane separating cunt from arse. My neck stretched, mouth agape, I squealed and gurgled at the intense sensations as their big penises thrust into me. At last, after so many climaxes I lost count, I collapsed across Steve as both young men were shooting their loads inside me. I never saw the photographs but I'm sure they stiffened many a cock and emptied many swollen balls. I settled for the pleasure – and the payment.

Later I showered, dressed, collected Peter from his adoring minders, and was driven home by Gerard in time to make dinner for my husband. In my piggy bank was deposited forty-three pounds for my day's work, enough to keep the wolf well away from the door for many weeks. All the same, as the uncivil Gerard watched me get out of his car, he shook his head. 'I wonder about you,' he said. 'What a sex-mad trollop you are. You go mad at the sight of a prick, I've never met the like. Don't be late for the next meeting of my photographic class or you'll get punished.'

'Yes, master,' I taunted him, sticking out my tongue to show my disrespect. I cuddled my son to me and turned to go.

'I pity your husband,' he said, but he sounded wistful. 'Though I must admit that life with you would never be dull. Get on your way before I want to take you home.'

'That's the nicest thing you've ever said to me,' I laughed. 'Don't be late next meeting or I might punish *you*. I'm sure you'd like it.'

Chapter Seven
ITALY

The cruise of Count Giotti's *Sophia* had been an almost non-stop orgy of fucking, sucking and every other possible permutation of carnal sexual activity. Between times there was dining and wining to excess. I arrived back at my apartment utterly sated and more than a little conscience-stricken that poor Harry had been so rarely in my thoughts during the hectic sea-going salaciousness.

I had sent him postcards from Ischia and Capri of the wish-you-were-here variety. Awaiting my return were several long, loving letters from him which increased my guilt. What I had begun as a one-off lapse with Giotti in return for a favour had mushroomed until I became a star performer on a floating brothel. Adding to my mortification was the undeniable fact that I had enjoyed all of it, for a silly spell even becoming madly infatuated with the beautiful body of the young Riccardo. I'm sure our lovemaking before an eager audience, recorded on cameras, was the *pièce de résistance*, of the many sexual exhibitions that took place.

The freedom of being at sea, the liberal champagne and the company of lecherous men made it little wonder things got out of hand. I had indulged wantonly in lesbian sessions with Darleen. We put on highly erotic displays of female sex for an appreciative audience and the lovely American girl repeatedly vowed her love for me during the voyage. It was high time to straighten myself out, I determined on returning to shore and sanity. In the few days I had left in Rome I swore I would keep to myself. I turned down the offer to stay at Giotti's villa. The remaining time before I flew out to join Harry would be spent as a tourist, taking in the Coliseum and other sights of the Eternal City before I departed.

I awoke late the following morning feeling wonderfully alive. No doubt the sexual cruise had proved beneficial to my health and beauty whether I cared to admit it or not. I enjoyed a hearty breakfast of orange juice, fluffy scrambled egg and crisp bacon and I was about to dress and sally forth in my new guise as a vulture for culture when Darleen rang.

'I had to call to wish you a safe journey and happy reunion with your husband, dear Diana,' she said in her soft American accent. 'I guess you know I'll miss you.'

'And I'll miss you,' I thought it kind to say. 'It was good, our time together.'

'More than good, it was beautiful,' reminisced the girl, sounding wistful. 'I guess it wasn't to be, you and I. I'll never forget you.'

'You will,' I assured her firmly to get her off the subject of her present infatuation. 'I'm married and you have your career in films ahead of you. Think about that, Darleen.'

'Yes,' she answered and said with excitement in her voice. 'That's another reason for calling. I'm at the Cinnacitti studios now and just took a screen test. They want me! I've got a part! It's one of those Spaghetti Westerns, a speaking part too.'

'Good for you, I'm sure you'll make it big in time,' I congratulated her. 'Darleen, I was about to go out. We should say goodbye and not linger over what might have been.'

'What are you wearing, Diana?' she suddenly enquired, her tone sexily sultry. 'Where are you?'

'In my bedroom with just my robe on,' I said somewhat mystified. 'Why do you ask?'

'I'm here in the little dressing room I've been allotted,' she said, her voice still low and husky over the telephone. 'Thinking about you. The excitement of this morning's screen test has got me terribly horny. I want to play with myself. Let's do it together, tell each other what we are doing – as a last goodbye—'

'You randy little thing!' I exclaimed laughing, yet at the same time the very idea of it made my stomach flutter, sending signals to my sex. 'What are you up to now?'

'Lying back on a couch, my hand inside my panties, thinking of you and I making love,' she answered hoarsely. 'I'm so *wet* inside, can you hear my fingers squelching? I'll put the phone there.'

'I can hear,' I said. 'Plainly. Go on, have a lovely climax.'

'I want you to have one as well,' Darleen said in the same aroused tone. 'Together with me. Over this phone. I'm fantasising about your big breasts; kissing, fondling and sucking them. Open your robe and hold them, pluck your nipples, describe them to me and how it feels. Please tell me. Play with your tits and say how it is for you.'

I grew highly aroused at her words, telling myself it was hardly breaking my vow to not fuck again with anyone before rejoining my husband. I was beyond the point of no return anyway and jammed the telephone receiver between my chin and neck to free my hands, my thighs beginning to grind together as I sat at the edge of my bed. I drew my robe wide apart, my hands cupping both heavy spheres of my breasts,

feeling the swell of tumescence as they seemed to grow in my
grasp, flicking the tautening nipples, savouring the pleasure
with low moans in my ecstasy.

'I can hear you sighing,' Darleen announced exultantly.
'What are you doing—?'

'I've bared my breasts. I'm holding and squeezing them.
My nipples have got so big and stiff,' I told her, my voice
now almost as impassioned as hers. 'I wish you were here to
suck them, and lick out my cunt like you do so beautifully,
Darleen. God, I shall come soon just with grinding my thighs
together! Oh, oh, I *am* coming! Yes, yes, you've made me
come, you horny little bitch! Are you satisfied now – now
ugh, oh, I can't help myself! Lord, Lord, that was *good*, as
good as any.'

'I'm coming too!' I heard Darleen croak, then all was
silent for long moments and I imagined the telephone had
fallen from her hands in her throes. When she retrieved it her
breathing was as laboured as mine. 'There's someone
knocking my door, I'm due for costume fittings,' she said.
'Wasn't that a lovely way to say goodbye?'

It was, and now Darleen was out of my life. Yet even as I
lay back recovering my senses the apartment intercom buzzed.
I answered it to hear Riccardo asking to be let in.

'I don't think I dare,' I said lightly. 'You were more than
a passing fancy. Let's call it quits. It was nice knowing you,
young man.'

'I have your air tickets from the U.N. office,' Riccardo
answered. 'There's other stuff for you as well, Lady Saxon,'
he added, trying to be formal. So I had to let him into my
apartment.

He entered bearing a matching set of expensive luggage.
'A present from Count Giotti,' he informed me, his eyes
taking in my figure with intent. Along with my air ticket on

Air Italia to Bangkok in three days' time was a letter saying I must vacate the apartment the next day for Harry's replacement in Rome. 'Don't worry about that,' he smiled. 'There's a place for you at the Villa Appia.'

'That would be going into the lion's den,' I laughed, refusing the offer. 'I'll find an hotel, thank you. I don't trust you or your boss, and you've both had more than your share of me. Let's shake hands and say goodbye.'

It was a mistake, his hand lingering in mine, then drawing me to him in his forceful way. 'No,' I said as firmly as I could. 'No, please, Ricky. I don't really want to. I'll soon be joining my husband.'

He made no reply, his eyes steady on mine while he unzipped the fly of his jeans and drew out his massive penis, already startlingly thick and tautly upright. My hand was wrapped around its girth. It felt hot and throbbing under my fingers. I wanted to stroke it, to have it between my thighs penetrating deeply. 'No, no,' I repeated weakly. 'I promised myself to be faithful for the rest of my time in Rome. Put it away, please. Don't tempt me.'

'Not even one last fuck?' Riccardo said disbelievingly. 'Look at my cock, see how it's straining for relief. Would you be so cruel?' He took my hand again to circle its thickness. 'Go through to your bedroom. I can't leave without being satisfied.'

It was a beautiful thing, I had to concede, rearing in its huge magnificence. Weakening still further, I found the determination to resist a fuck. 'I could suck it,' I offered as a way out of the dilemma, my mouth watering at the thought. That, after all, would not exactly be reneging on my vow. 'I'll suck it off for you, that's all,' I insisted, his prick still in my hand as I went on my knees before him.

He grunted, placing his feet apart, his hands holding my

face as I covered his circumcised bulb with my lips, giving the first tentative sucks. Its warmth and pulsating throbs made me draw in more of the shaft, sucking with increasing greediness as my arousal grew in intensity. I was absorbed in the pleasure of suctioning his beautiful cock, bobbing my head while he moaned and moved his hips against my face. Then, with almost an animal growl, he tightened his hold on my face and thrust even faster, fucking my mouth until I felt a succession of strong spurts striking my throat.

As I saw him to the door a little later, he turned and took the thick gold chain with its ruby pendant from around his neck, handing it to me.

I showered and dressed, deciding I must find a suitable hotel to move to until my flight, when the intercom buzzed again. It's like Piccadilly Circus here this morning, I told myself as I answered the call. It was Daniella Siracusa, the voluptuous Italian who had been on the cruise with her plump daughter Gina. Before the trip was over we had become friends, despite a bad start.

'We've come to wish you well in your new country,' she said, so I let the pair of them into the apartment, thinking I must be more popular than I'd thought. I served coffee as requested and we sat around chatting.

'Your daughter looks beautiful,' I said, and indeed she did in her youthful way.

This brought an amused laugh from them both. 'Gina is no daughter of mine,' said Daniella smiling. 'She came up from Naples to work in my establishment and some of my clients thought I was her mother. They liked to think they were fucking the madam's daughter so we let them carry on as it improved their pleasure. I run a house of pleasure after all, so why not? They pay extra for the privilege.'

'So Gina was not exactly your virgin daughter on the

cruise?' I laughed with them. 'Good for you. Those men were so keen to think so – drooling at the mouth over a young fresh piece.'

'I'm the eternal virgin,' Gina said slyly. 'My young looks and puppy fat fool them.'

'Men are such fools anyway,' Daniella said. 'When you run a brothel you see every side of human nature. With you, Diana, at first I resented you because you were an amateur along for the fun, while with us it's strictly business. Then I got to know you and like you.'

'I am an amateur,' I confessed. 'An enthusiastic one, you must have noticed. Sexual urges prove too strong for me to resist, I admit. Everything I did on the cruise I wanted to.'

'Except perhaps taking a shine to Riccardo?' said the shrewd Daniella, fingering the ruby pendant at my throat. 'It happens. My clients fall for my girls and my girls fall for my clients, some even marry them. I wish you were one of my girls. You would be kept busy, I assure you. Never be ashamed of your sexuality, Diana. Let pleasure be your best guide, the pleasure of being a desirable woman. Two things are limitless: to be wanted and to take advantage of that fact. I'm sure I don't have to tell you that.'

'I have to find a hotel for three days,' I said, thinking that Daniella would know of a suitable one.

'Why not come and stay at my house?' she offered immediately. 'You would not be expected to entertain my clients, of course, although I am sure they would all ask for you.'

'Don't tempt me,' I giggled. 'You know my nature.'

'Your nature is what you are born with. You have no choice about it,' Daniella said. 'You are highly sexed, and that is given to you like your eyes, shape or even your colour of hair. There are private rooms in my house, comfortable bedrooms with private bath which you can choose. I run a much respected establishment, visited only by the members of the best families of Rome, male and female. Come back with us and see how better it is than an hotel.'

I took up her offer and was soon being shown over a large house set back from the road among woods. The huge lounge contained large sofas and deep armchairs, thickly carpeted and sumptuously decorated. Beautiful young girls in flimsy underwear and gossamer-thin negligees were chatting to afternoon clients while maids circulated with trays of *hors d'oeuvres* and wine. There was nothing cheap or sleazy about the set-up. Passing through, on our way upstairs for me to choose a room, a well-dressed middle-aged man with the stamp of wealth about him stopped Daniella on the first landing. He was outside a bedroom door with a well-built young girl wearing only a bra and brief knickers, obviously about to enter with her. That did not stop him eyeing me up with avid interest, marking me as a future prospect for his pleasure. Daniella noticed it too, wagging a finger at him as if he were a greedy boy.

'Not for sale, Guido,' she told him with a smile. 'Diana is a guest, a visiting friend who is passing through Rome. Diana, meet Senor Guido Salero, one of my best customers and rumoured to be the most wealthy man in town.'

'I need to be with the prices you charge,' Guido remarked, his handshake turning into a fondle until I disengaged my palm. 'Such a pity that this charming creature is not on the menu here. She is exactly what I've always advised you to have in this house: a mature, ripe, firm-bodied woman with superb breasts and buttocks to match. Unfortunately I have to leave Rome for business in Switzerland tonight. Will the lady be here when I return next week? I'm sure we could come to an arrangement profitable to all parties.'

'I leave Rome in three days,' I answered for Daniella. 'So hard luck, Guido. You seem to be doing all right with what you have.'

'You make the girls here look like boys, my dear,' he smiled, turning the door handle of the bedroom. 'I should have loved to have had you. I'd have paid your price, whatever it was.'

I was shown several excellently furnished bedrooms, but was advised to wait until I saw the special one Daniella thought was best. The size of the house impressed me and I was told of the restaurant and swimming pool on the ground floor and invited to use them as I wished. In the bedroom Daniella wanted me to have, I could only express my delight at such comfort.

'It's a room reserved for clients who come here for rather special pleasures,' she told me. 'Voyeurism. I have several who pay extremely well to watch others having sex.' She crossed to a wall, lifting down a framed picture to reveal a two-way mirror that allowed a full view of the next bedroom.

'Mmmm, kinky,' I said. 'Does the viewing lady have a man with her to satisfy her while the show goes on next door?'

'None of them,' Daniella said. 'However, if the watching is arousing enough to make them want to have something special, come and see what there is in the room next to your bathroom.' She looked at me with eyes wickedly alight, throwing open a door and standing back.

I saw what seemed to be a rocking-horse: a full-sized horse's body, minus the legs, mounted on a stand with four piston-like cylinders about a foot long holding up the animal. I walked around it, felt the lifelike feel of a live horse and noted there were reins but no saddle.

'What do they do with this?' I couldn't help laughing as I asked.

'You have a rhyme in your country, I believe, called Ride a cock-horse to Banbury Cross,' Daniella said enjoying my wonderment. 'Well, this is indeed a cock-horse. Fancy a ride?' She touched a switch set in a small indented panel in the horse's side and it began to jog, slowly at first, and increasing its pace to a canter as she pressed a second switch. 'There,' she said proudly.

'I've heard that riding a horse, with all that powerful flesh between your legs, can get you aroused,' I conceded, still highly amused. 'Don't tell me that's how your lady voyeurs get their orgasms, riding bareback on a stuffed nag. I've never known the like.'

'Watch,' said Daniella, pressing a third switch. From the back of the horse, exactly where its rider would be sitting, sprang a marvellously realistic human penis – a thick dildo of a good eight inches with a plum-shaped crest that shunted up and down.

I swallowed my amazement, impressed by the ingenuity of the thing. 'That should do the trick,' I had to admit.

'Guaranteed climaxes, as many as a woman could wish,' agreed Daniella, switching off. The dummy dick retracted as the body of the horse slowed to a halt.

Her driver took me back to the apartment to pack my things and on my return I dined with my hostess. As the evening grew late I went to my room. In bed I thought back on all that had happened during the past week, looking forward to my trip out to join Harry, wishing he were beside me in the huge comfortable canopied bed. Trying to sleep, I was aware of muffled noises from the adjoining room. Intrigued, I arose and went to the framed picture covering the trick mirror. I lifted it down more out of curiosity than a desire to spy on people.

Yet I was immediately made captive, hopelessly aroused, by the scene taking place through the looking glass. I saw a man and two lovely young girls attending to his needs. They kissed him in turn with open mouths, offering him their breasts, sharing his prick with their lips and tongues. He lay on his back with a firm cockstand while one girl mounted his thighs and impaled herself to the hilt on his prick, and the other girl sat on his face and rubbed her cunt over his mouth.

Thus engaged, all three naked bodies moving in unison, the girls leaned towards each other to kiss and fondle each other's breasts. The way they lewdly pleasured each other was surely no act. It made me rub a hand across my own tits, the other hand going down between my thighs.

How I wished Harry or Riccardo were present to give me what I craved, a cock instead of a finger probing my pulsating cunt. Then it occurred to me to try out Daniella's cock-horse.

I approached it apprehensively and mounted up. I felt the rough hair rubbing my cunt lips quite pleasantly as I straddled the broad back. Reins in hand, I nervously pushed the first switch to start the slow jogging movement. Rub, rub went Dobbin's back against my quim, making it pout for something more, making *me* respond by wanting something more. I touched the switch to turn the dildo on, looking down to see it rear, before my crotch, its crest pumping up and down, begging to be inserted up my cunt. I eased myself up over it, one palm on the back of the horse to steady myself, the other grasping and guiding the dummy prick to my opening. Then it was fucking me so realistically that I lowered myself to get its full length. I held tight to the reins, gripped the sides of the horse with my legs and prepared myself for the most unusual ride of my life.

Relentlessly the jogging continued, the deep insertion of the dildo increased by its pumping action. I gave a low groan and came off within moments, going on to multiple orgasmic spasms – one continuing come that in time had me draped forward across the neck of the horse, for once fucked to a frazzle. I desperately sought the switch to turn the thing off and found the wrong one in my haste, setting the thing going faster and being jogged about and penetrated more furiously than ever. When I finally got it to stop I fell off and stumbled to the bedroom to climb gingerly into bed. My innards were pounding from the assault and the aftermath of at least a dozen sapping climaxes.

I did not make use of the horse again during my stay. All the same, when put to use by one familiar with its mechanics, I could well imagine how popular it was with Daniella's regular clients.

I spent the next two days sightseeing in Rome. On the last evening before my flight I returned to Daniella's house of ill repute to find her waiting for me. She took me into her private office.

'We have had an offer that will be hard to refuse, I think,' she began. She held up a letter written in Italian with a bold hand. Attached to it was a cheque made out in lira to an amount ending in a long row of noughts.

'This is worth over two thousand of your British pounds,' I was informed with her eyes watching my reaction. 'I want no commission on it, only to grant the wish of the letter writer who has stated you are the one chosen to fulfil what he has in mind. It is from Senor Guido Salero, whom you have met. Agree to his request, Diana, and you will leave for Bangkok tomorrow over two thousand pounds the richer.' She looked at me hopefully. 'I wouldn't ask this of you if it were not that Guido has been a special friend of mine, advancing the money to buy this house and start my business for me. There is also, of course,' she added shrewdly, 'a great deal of profit in it for you—'

'It's a lot of money to pay to fuck me,' I had to agree, finding the offer extremely tempting. 'Has he returned from Switzerland just for that? What does the letter say—?'

'He is still on business in Switzerland,' Daniella said. 'This refers to his making a birthday present of *you*. No doubt he was greatly impressed when he saw how desirable you are to men – and women,' she added knowingly, her eyes regarding me with a wicked twinkle, no doubt recalling Darleen's passion for me.

'Guido wants me to sleep with someone as a birthday present?' I asked. 'That beats giving a set of cuff-links, I suppose. Who—?'

'He is the most generous man,' agreed Daniella. 'One of his firm beliefs is that youths on the verge of manhood should be initiated properly into sex with an experienced woman. One who would tutor the boy in all the sexual arts and variations, which would stand him in good stead throughout later life. He brought his eldest son here on his sixteenth birthday to lose his virginity. Actually he spent the night with me.'

'What a lovely man,' I giggled, finding it rather unusual while admitting it made good sense. 'Don't tell me, Daniella, he has another son aged sixteen today whom he wants initiated?'

She held up two fingers, smiling. 'Twins,' she announced to my shock and horror. 'Both are nice boys, at good schools, big for their age. I will show them to you, they are in the dining room having their celebration dinner.'

'I don't think so,' I said. '*Two* horny and eager youths at me all night! You know what boys are like at that age, inexperienced or not, they'll never be randier.' The cheque was waved before my eyes as an incentive. 'You can put that away,' I said ruefully. 'What would their mother think of all this anyway?'

'Senora Salero?' Daniella shrugged. 'She has many lovers, as is agreed between her husband and herself. The room you are in is often used by her to view others fucking, then she rides the cock-horse with Guido and other men present. She brought her boys here and will return in the morning for them.'

'This house of yours is hardly the Y.M.C.A.,' I said. 'What you've told me makes me think my past life has been *almost* exemplary.' I had to laugh. 'Two boys indeed!'

'Think of how many women would beg for the opportunity,' Daniella said lowering her voice, sounding deliberately salacious and sexy. 'A fresh young body on either side of you throughout the night, fumbling excitedly at your womanly charms, so eager to have you, so grateful for everything you allow them to do, obeying your every demand, worshipping your lovely breasts, rigidly erect as only youth can be and always eager, always ready.' She poured me a stiff brandy which I lifted with a trembling hand and drank off too quickly. She replenished the glass while I still held it. 'Think of all that, Diana.'

'Shut up,' I told her shakily. 'You are trying to get me pissed and randy.' I swallowed the second brandy, hoping it would strengthen my resolve but it seemed to have the opposite effect. 'I suppose it wouldn't do any harm to take a look at the birthday boys,' I heard myself saying. 'Just a look, mind.'

'Of course,' Daniella agreed cunningly. 'And don't forget your reward. I can arrange for the money to be available in traveller's cheques for you to take with you tomorrow.'

I am well aware I am a weak woman and a greedy one at times too. It must be a hangover from the poverty-stricken days of my childhood and the poor but happy times of my early marriage years. I was a lady by title if nothing else, hardly in need of a cash incentive any more, although I might use it to buy Harry an extra special present to salve my conscience.

Later I stood smiling nervously at a pair of identical adolescent youths who were ushered into my bedroom by Daniella. I kissed each in turn to welcome them and break the ice and received a tongue in my mouth from each of them – so they were not exactly novices! There followed one of the most sexually athletic and hectic nights I have ever spent. I was undressed and made to walk around the room while they discussed what they saw. As they spoke in Italian I can only guess that they approved of my breasts, pubic bulge and bottom. Next I was laid out before them on the bed while they inspected and felt every inch of me. This quickly turned me on. Their slim young bodies were so beautiful, and their smooth rigid pricks so suckable. I gobbled their cocks eagerly when told to do so in schoolboy English. My excitement was evident in the way I welcomed the first one between my thighs. His name was Paulo and he fucked me to a strong climax before his brother, Dino, took over and gave me a good second one with me on my hands and knees. Throughout the night they were insatiable.

They left me in the morning sprawled across the bed, my neck, breasts and inner thighs purple with juvenile love-bites. In my fucked-out state I wondered just how I would explain them to Harry, who would of course want to make love to me nude on my arrival. I slept soundly only to be awakened by Daniella, who guided me to the shower, packed the expensive pigskin cases Giotti had given me, showed me the wad of traveller's cheques I had earned for the night's debauch and then drove me to Rome airport.

I was never madly keen on flying and in my sexually-exhausted state I could not keep my eyes open. I dropped into a sound sleep as the jet circled over Rome and set course for Thailand and whatever awaited me in the mystic East. With my past track record, it could be anything.

Chapter Eight
ENGLAND

Manley had moved on to pastures new, so I was back to typing addresses for a mail-order firm for slave wages to make the extra income we needed while Harry completed his studies. Gerard had gone to the South of France, a much more fertile field for his photographic forays in the world of nudist resorts. He had been offered a lucrative post by an international magazine on the strength of the pictures of me taken on our day's visit to Lakeside Abbey. Apparently they had been admired and published in dozens of naturist magazines from the United States to Germany.

'You were too good and put yourself out of work as a model while getting me this marvellous chance,' he admitted when saying goodbye. 'Of course I would like to take you with me, and the magazines all want more of your marvellous naked figure, but since you refuse to leave your husband I have to accept your decision. You are missing a wonderful life, you know, in the South of France. Inflated fees for modelling, mixing with the rich and famous.'

But I was content to stay Harry's wife, the mother of Peter, used to making do and counting the pennies. Nigel's position as the collector of my weekly hire-purchase instalments was taken over by another Lamont, a grim-faced uncle who took the money wordlessly and left promptly to visit his next client. My freebie was over.

Expecting his arrival one day, I opened my front door to be faced by a handsome middle-aged woman, a blonde with a full figure under a soaked raincoat. She introduced herself as Ellen Lamont, to whom I would be making my weekly payments while her brother Hector was ill. 'The stupid man has got pneumonia,' she said grudgingly, and I guessed I was faced with Nigel's mother, the woman who ruled his life. 'No wonder, perhaps, out in all weathers doing this job.'

'I've a good fire on, you're welcome to dry off,' I offered, inviting her in. She entered, looking around the sparse attic flat, handing me her raincoat, her cardigan bulging with full rounded breasts. Her tweed skirt too was packed tight with plump strong thighs and the seat stretched across her firm swelling buttock cheeks.

'Is this the best your husband can do for you?' she asked bluntly. 'And you such a pretty young thing too. Still, that's men for you.' She nosily pulled aside the draped curtain that separated our bed and cot from the living area. 'And a baby,' she said, seeing Peter at his afternoon nap. 'Men will give you one of those every chance. Ten shillings a week you pay, I see from my book. You're almost clear. We've a nice range of female clothing just in. Pop into Lamont's shop and cheer yourself up with a nice new dress.'

'I don't need cheering up and I can't afford a new dress,' I said, laughing at her overbearing manner. 'I take it you have no high opinion of men. Are you married?'

'Certainly not,' she stated, 'though when I was young and attractive like you, my dear, I made the fatal error of trusting a man. I'm not ashamed to tell you he gave me a child. He's like his father, a weak creature. Will we wake your baby by talking?'

'No chance,' I assured her. 'Peter sleeps every afternoon. I take him to the park, play with him and he is so strenuous he tires himself out.' I smiled inwardly at her remark about Nigel. 'I'm sure your son is a nice young man but you won't admit it. Would you like a cup of tea?'

'I'd rather have something stronger,' she said, sitting down in one of our comfortable old armchairs and reaching out finely tapered hands to warm at the fire. 'Tea will do if you've nothing else. Have you got any sherry?'

'I like a sherry, the sweet kind,' I said, 'but we never have it. We will one day, however. My husband is going to be a civil engineer. He's at the university after serving in the army. It won't always be like this. I'm happy to wait for better times.'

Ellen Lamont chuckled. 'Romantic little fool,' she said. 'Make sure there are no further babies while you're so hard-up.' I assured her not, although I wanted one more at least in time. She sipped the tea I gave her. 'You really are a good-looking girl,' she said eyeing me over the rim of her cup. 'Most attractive.' As she left, collecting ten shillings and marking it off in my payment book, she paused and suddenly stroked my cheek gently with her long fingers. 'You're too nice to be stuck in this hole,' she said of the little home I had made so comfortable and took pride in. 'Don't let that husband of yours play you up. They're not worth it.'

I had a smile to myself about Ellen after she had departed, wondering about her hatred of men. She had never got over being left pregnant by one, I decided. I thought little more of her although I liked her brusque manner and frank way of speaking her mind. The following week, she walked in without invitation. 'Get out two glasses, girl,' she said, producing a bottle of sherry from her large shoulder bag. 'We'll cheer ourselves with a drink. Maybe two. Sit on your bottom instead of fussing around. Your flat is spotless and your baby asleep, for goodness sake, relax a little.'

After the second sherry I felt tipsy. Not being used to drink I almost wished I could take myself off for a lie-down on the bed. Ellen came to sit on the arm of my chair, balancing her ample bottom there, leaning over me with her fingers idly stroking the nape of my neck. Pleasant as it was, and I had experienced sexual advances from women before and allowed it to go further, the unexpected was a shock. I edged slightly away from her, for once embarrassed for us both. 'Please,' I said weakly.

'Please what?' Ellen said. 'Please stop? Has my touching your neck like this made you uncomfortable? I find it hard to resist stroking your soft young skin.' She did not appear put out by my protest and continued to brush her fingers lightly over my neck, chin and cheek. 'I'm sure that feels nice to you, doesn't it? What harm is it doing?'

'I don't know,' I said, my voice beginning to tremble. 'I mean, should you? It is nice but should you be doing that? Why?'

'Because I want to,' Ellen said assertively. 'I want to know if you would like it too. Relax, my dear, I feel you're so tense. Let yourself float, enjoy the feeling.' Suddenly she leaned across and kissed my mouth lightly, then with more ardent pressure, lingering until I turned my face away after returning her kiss for one brief moment. 'Don't be so silly,' she said sharply. 'You were just beginning to enjoy that.'

'I wasn't,' I said, trying to deny it and also to deny the feeling of excitement stirring in my body. 'You're trying to seduce me. You deliberately brought that drink. You, another woman.'

'And what's so wrong about that?' she said, continuing to stroke my face and lips tenderly. 'It is the sweetest kind of love, the most erotic, as you would discover, my dear. Women know each other's bodies so much more intimately than rough males. They know what pleases most, what they enjoy best and where. Exactly where! Do let me kiss you again.'

Ellen turned my face and lowered her opened mouth over mine, pushing a warm wet tongue tasting of Bristol Cream sherry between my teeth. For a long passionate moment the kiss continued, my resistance weakening as our mouths clung together. In the welter of thoughts that swirled through my excited mind as her lips and tongue devoured me, I recalled that both mother and son had desired me in this room. I felt her hand undo the top buttons of my dress and slide down inside my bra to cup one breast. She circled her palm over the rounded flesh, plucking at the nipple. I held her wrist as our mouths parted, our breath coming in laboured gasps. I was trembling and Ellen regarded me lovingly.

'Enough,' I managed to get out. 'Really, what makes you think I need that. I've got a husband.' I fumbled to button up my dress. 'Do you set out on purpose to seduce young married women?'

'Of course I don't,' Ellen snapped. 'You especially appeal to me. There's something about you that makes me certain you've made love with another woman before. I'm right, aren't I? It takes one to know one. Why all this fuss?'

'I've other things to do,' I said lamely. 'I've got the baby to see to when he wakes up and my husband's dinner to prepare. I hardly know you, anyway. I didn't expect anything like this—' I expected her to start kissing and fondling me again and I wanted her to. In truth, my resistance was token. Instead, I thought I had blown it, as Ellen sat back up on the arm of my chair with a shrug of compliance.

'As you wish, you silly girl,' she said easily. 'I thought that you and I might find a lovely way to pass an hour or so on a dull afternoon. What a waste if we don't take the chance. Perhaps I rushed things and surprised you. I respect that.' Her hands clasped one of mine, stroking it.

'Let me tell you a story if you feel ashamed because you became aroused. When I started as a young girl in the Lamont family business, my first job was what I'm doing now, collecting payments. One of the customers I called on weekly was a widow in her early fifties, still a handsome woman and very lonely because she always kept me talking. It was her that gave me a fondness for sherry, always pouring me out a glass or two. She'd say how nice I was, such a pretty girl. She always seemed to brush herself against my breasts, which were big even then, and squeeze my waist at times.'

She paused to squeeze my hand and smile at me. 'It got so that I made her house the last call on my round as the sherry made me quite tipsy. I'd sit in an armchair, just like you, with herself perched on the arm, like I am. One day she kissed my cheek, just like this—' Ellen leaned forward to press a kiss half on my mouth. 'Then one of her hands caressed my breast through my dress, just like this—' She held my left breast, applying increasing pressure.

'What did you do?' I asked intrigued, enjoying her hand fondling my tit.

'I was shocked, of course, but didn't like to hurt the woman. Then she began kissing me, just like a man does, rolling her lips over mine so eagerly, putting her tongue in my mouth as well.' Ellen suddenly swooped, kissing me lingeringly several times before drawing away. 'Like that, exactly like that,' she said. 'I was trembling, not knowing how I felt, then her hand was pulling up my dress.'

My dress was pulled up just as she described it, revealing my thighs and cotton knickers. Her hand cupped my mound, making me part my legs as she compressed it in her palm. 'I heard her mumble that I must do it, I must,' Ellen continued, drawing down my knickers, and slipping to her knees in the fork of my thighs. 'The woman was doing this, pulling down my panties. Then, then, she wanted to kiss me *there*, right on my vagina, and lick it and push her tongue inside me.'

Here she paused, her mouth a bare inch from my tilted cunt which I expected her to assault any moment. Peering down I saw the flat expanse of my belly, my knees spread with her head between and the raised mound with its tuft of rich auburn. 'Go on, go on,' I told her hoarsely, expecting and desiring to be tongued. 'You let her!' I urged. 'You let her lick you out?'

'I pushed her head away,' Ellen said disappointingly. 'Saying no, no, it wasn't nice, not right, two females. I pulled up my knickers, grabbed my bag and fled the house. Then I was in the street, all of a dither I could tell you.' I resisted pulling her face in to my crotch, awaiting the outcome, desperate now that she would use her tongue to pleasure me.

'So there I was, in broad daylight and surrounded by people,' Ellen laughed softly. 'And all I could think of was her long wet tongue making me writhe and gurgle like a horny slut, which I *never* considered I was. You fool, I told myself, you were enjoying that, loving it, in fact.' She smiled up at me and gave the first peck of a kiss to my throbbing cunt. 'So I turned about, went back to her door and knocked. All the rest of that afternoon I was naked with her, discovering what delights there are in sucking tits, licking cunts and rubbing cunts together. So I developed a life-long taste for this,' she added slyly, pressing her face onto my pussy as I parted the outer lips for her expert tonguing.

Several massive climaxes later I was slumped in the chair with legs outstretched, my softened cunt folds palpitating as she took her leave.

One of her last acts was to tear up my payment book, announcing that the amount outstanding had been settled. 'Pop into the shop and I'll make sure I serve you,' she added. 'Pick yourself a nice dress and fancy undies. I'm sure we're going to be close from now on.'

On my next supposed night at the cinema I found her waiting as arranged with her car parked in a nearby street. When I got in she drew me into her arms for a long passionate kiss. She drove me to her house which was like a palace compared to mine, as befitted the home of a director of a haberdasher and furnishing business. I paused before a picture of Nigel set on the mantlepiece, sneakily enquiring if that was her son.

'He wouldn't know what to do with a girl like you,' she scoffed, little knowing that her boy had been fucking me regularly. 'Let me show you my bedroom, Diana. I've a little surprise for you there. Perhaps not so little though,' she smiled wickedly.

We stood apart beside her double bed to undress. It was my first view of Ellen naked and an impressive sight she was. I guessed she was in her middle forties and she was most shapely, with heavy hung breasts that dwarfed even mine but were of the same firm flesh as the rest of her, including broad round buttocks. I admired her huge nipples, dark brown and thick as my thumb, and the inrolling lips of a plump cunt mound which was clean shaved to entice kissing and licking. We flew into each other's arms as eagerly as any pair of lovers, breasts squashing breasts, cunt rubbing cunt, our mouths locked together. I was laid back across the bed and her great breasts descended on my face as my greedy lips sought to catch her nipples. Then she was covering me, my legs curled around her waist, hands grasping at her solid buttocks, humping up into her as our cunts met and ground together.

'How I wish you had a prick, a big prick to fuck me with,' I moaned as our thrusting grew in pace. 'Rub harder, make me come, Ellen! Fuck me like a man!'

'Just what I hoped to hear you say, you randy young baggage,' the older woman said triumphantly. She rolled off me and crossed to a dressing table. She opened a drawer with her back turned to me. 'Close your eyes, Diana,' she ordered. 'Don't open them until I tell you.'

I did as I was told, annoyed that she had left me while I was so aroused, my hand fingering away at my quim. I heard a soft laugh from beside the bed.

'You dirty girl,' Ellen chided me. 'Fancy playing with yourself! Open your eyes and see what Ellen has for you.'

I turned my head sideways and gave out a squeal of surprise and delight. Ellen stood beside the bed, tits thrusting, hands on hips, and from her shaven crotch curled up the most monstrous dildo. It projected from her cunt where no doubt an equal length of it was inserted, held in place with straps around her loins. It was utterly lifelike, even to the veins along its thick stalk and the plum-shaped helmet. I could not resist reaching out to clasp it.

'My God, can I take all of *that*?' I gasped, holding out my arms and spreading my legs to tell Ellen I wanted to try. She eased the monster in until I was grunting out loud. Its mass filled me to my deepest recess. Then Ellen fucked me, thrusting and withdrawing, making me arch my back, heave up my bum from the bed and cry out that it was killing me, *killing* me! But I revelled in every thick inch and came time and time again gloriously.

The dildo became a trusted appliance over the next few months. I knelt to take it, rode over it, and returned home on my evenings spent with Ellen still dizzy from its effect. Between my husband and his real prick pleasuring me nightly, and the dummy one on my visits to my lesbian lover, I was a fully satisfied young wife.

My trysts with Ellen continued until Harry's graduation. By then he had found work as a civil engineer which entailed a move to London. With the baby and our bits and pieces packed into a furniture van owned by Lamont's, courtesy of Ellen, we said goodbye to Oxford and set off for life in the big city and – I couldn't prevent myself from hoping – more lusty adventures.

Chapter Nine
THAILAND

Bangkok airport bustled excitingly: it was crowded, noisy, hot and smelly, a scene throbbing with Thai life that immediately endeared me to the country. As I left the aircraft and entered the arrivals terminal I was vividly reminded of happy years spent in East Africa. I searched the sea of faces for Harry. The waiting crowd at the barrier thinned out but I saw no loving husband rushing forward to take me in his arms. A tall thirtyish honey-blonde woman in a tailored white linen suit and matching broad-brimmed hat advanced on me. Her startling blue eyes behind round designer spectacles were fixed in my direction.

'Lady Saxon?' she said in the distinctive voice of the American-south. Her top teeth protruded slightly, parting her heavily glossed lips in a fetching manner. 'You are Lady Saxon?' she repeated. 'Of course you must be. Who else looks like a lady here?'

'Your estimate could be a little generous,' I said smiling. 'Who are you? Why isn't my husband here?'

She held out a white-gloved hand just long enough for me to make contact with it. 'I'm Magnolia Bouverie Wentzel. My husband, Howard, is the United Nations High Commissioner for Refugees in South-East Asia. He's with *your* husband in the north, on the border with Burma and Laos, and they've been delayed. It's most annoying. Senior officials don't usually have to go to such dangerous areas.'

'That's my Harry from the sound of it,' I said, trying to disguise the pride in my voice. It would also give time, I thought with some relief, for the multitude of love-bites that the Italian teenagers had inflicted on me to fade before his return. 'My husband likes being in the thick of things.'

'Yes,' said Magnolia Bouverie Wentzel drily. 'I blame him for their absence. Howard has plenty to do in his office here in Bangkok, and your husband too, without chasing off into the jungle to dig wells and start farming projects. Frankly the peasants are quite content to grow opium. Anyway, Sir Harry got a message through to say he'll get back as soon as he's able, and that I should meet you. Oh, and that he loves you.'

'I'm glad to hear that at least,' I laughed, making light of the fact that Harry was not at the airport.

'You don't mind his not being here?' Magnolia said uppishly. 'I would be furious with Howard. He wouldn't dare.'

I could imagine that. 'We make up for it when we do get together,' I said mischievously. 'Absence makes the heart fonder and the sex stronger, as I'm sure you know.'

'I don't,' Magnolia said scathingly. 'I consider that a very over-rated obligation. Now that Howard and I have had a family, I feel I've done all that is expected of me. I'm practically celibate, thank God.'

Poor Howard, I thought. And what a waste of the lovely woman he had for a wife. 'So what do I do now?' I asked. 'Where do I go?'

'Your apartment is across the hallway from ours in the Sunyat Court building,' she announced, raising a gloved finger. A ragged Thai boy appeared beside us and picked up my luggage. 'The taxi rank is just outside. It's about a fifteen minute drive, Lady Saxon.'

'Never call me that,' I said. 'My name is Diana. What shall I call you – Magnolia or Maggie?'

'Certainly not Maggie,' she answered abruptly. Conscience got the better of me as the elegant Magnolia walked ahead and I relieved the little Thai ragamuffin of my heaviest suitcase. The taxi was a yellow-painted cab like those in New York. My luggage was piled in the boot by the driver and Magnolia waited for him to hold open the rear door for her. As she made to enter he produced a handful of printed business cards and pressed them into our hands.

'The very best night spots, cabarets, massage for ladies in whole of Bangkok,' he said cheerily in an attempted American accent. 'Live sex show, you name it, madams.'

'Keep your trashy filth,' Magnolia snapped furiously, leaving the taxi-driver in no doubt he had misjudged his client. I was left with a handful of cards and, while the driver was recoiling from Magnolia's outrage, I slipped them into my shoulder bag. As we drove on we passed through streets crowded with humanity and ablaze with neon lights advertising bars and other places of entertainment. 'Bangkok is a disgustingly depraved city,' I was told disapprovingly. 'It's getting worse if that's possible. Tourists flock here for sexual deviations and drugs. Both are readily obtainable. We rarely go out.'

'I've heard there are beautiful places to visit,' I said. 'The beaches are meant to be wonderful and the old Siamese temples should be worth seeing. What do you do?'

'We take in movies at the United States Embassy and go to various receptions,' she said. 'There's a very good private pool at our apartment building for residents if you like

swimming. No doubt you will find like me that remaining
within *our* community, U.N. people and others of the
diplomatic service, is the only way to survive. As you've just
arrived I've had my cook make dinner for you in my apartment.
No doubt you would like to shower after your journey. As
there'll be no hot water in your bathroom until you settle in,
you may use ours.'

The apartment, and I presumed mine would be similar, was
spacious, air-conditioned and luxuriously furnished. On
entering with Magnolia we were welcomed by a pretty teenaged
girl beginning to fill out into curves, her smile spoiled by
silver braces on her teeth. I was then introduced to Nicola –
never Nicky I was warned – the sixteen-year-old daughter of
the Wentzels. Two Thai women in their local pyjama-style
dress were laying a table with a fine lace cloth, flowers and
candles. Magnolia showed me through to the bathroom and
gave precise instructions on how to operate the spray.

The bathroom itself was magnificent, with tiled glass
mirrors, pink sinks, a round bath and a frosted glass cubicle
for showering. I let the cold spray refresh my hot skin,
striking my breasts like needle points and erecting my nipples.
I turned off the water when I'd finished lathering and sluicing
away the suds. I resisted the temptation to hold the shower
head in my hand and play it directly onto my sex, parting the
outer lips with my free hand so that the spray struck my
clitoris and guaranteeing an orgasm. It was only because
Magnolia and her daughter Nicola would be waiting for me
to join them for dinner that I desisted – I would have welcomed
the relief of a good come after the long flight. As I stepped
from the shower cubicle, Magnolia entered the bathroom
bearing a huge fluffy towel. I saw her eyes linger on my
figure for a long moment. She blushed as she held out the
towel for me.

'You have such *breasts*, my God,' she gasped, unable to refrain from remarking on their size and shape. 'They are beautifully firm and proportioned, I admit, but don't you find them *tiresome*? I mean, just the weight of them? I know men like breasts like yours, but I'm glad mine are smaller. I can see my daughter's bosom growing alarmingly, I'm afraid. The silly girl is quite proud of them, I am sure. You could have been a model with that figure.' Thankfully she did not remark on my love-bites.

'I have done some modelling,' I said, accepting the towel. 'I think your Nicola is growing into a lovely girl. You have a son too, haven't you? Where is he?'

'At the Carolina Military Academy,' she said. 'We felt the discipline would be good for him. I didn't want Nicola to go to a girls' boarding school in the States, there are so many temptations for young girls over there. She goes to the American School in our embassy so that I can keep an eye on her.'

With Magnolia's outlook, that figured. I dined with them on delicious Thai food and found Nicola a friendly, lively girl. She chatted away until a severe glance from her mother told her she was being unladylike in talking so much about her life in Bangkok. Later she was sent off to bed reluctantly. She kissed both her mother and myself as she went, offering to show me the sights of Bangkok until silenced by another look. Then I shared the contents of a cocktail shaker with Magnolia before she gave me the keys to my apartment and I crossed the ornate carpeted hallway to my new home, alone and feeling that the night was but young.

I still thought so after I had unpacked and hung my clothes in the built-in wardrobe in the master bedroom. I looked at the huge double bed and wondered if Harry had had some female in there with him during his stay without me. I would not have blamed him if he had, Bangkok with all its temptations being a bit much for any man on his own to resist. From what I had seen of the Thai people, especially the young girls, they were a good looking race, pretty-featured and enticing. Sex, I considered, is one of the nicest gifts bestowed upon us, and did not see why one shouldn't enjoy the pleasure as often as possible.

I had slept all day on the flight and now I felt excited and restless in a new city. It was then I remembered the cards pressed on me by the taxi driver and I dug them out of my shoulder bag to see what they offered.

Cards such as these, I was to discover, were offered to foreigners in every shop, taxi, cinema, restaurant throughout the city. One that caught my eye advertised Madame Tan's massage emporium for educated ladies. Intrigued, I took the lift to the ground floor, wondering what Magnolia would think of me if she knew I was heading out into Sin City. At the door a smiling commissionaire hailed me a taxi. I showed the driver the address on the card and, with a sly grin to himself, he drove off.

Madame Tan's establishment was, I noted with relief, no backstreet clip joint. It was brightly lit, on a well-populated thoroughfare, and looked like a shop. As I hesitated in front of the door, for one never knows what might lie beyond, the taxi driver leaned out to offer me yet another card. 'You like ladies, madam?' he asked. 'Licky-lick, sucky-suck? Big dildo you like? Pretty girl fuck you? Maybe you fuck girl —?' I accepted his card, blushing at his frankness. 'This card tell you of best horny place in town for lady's pleasure. I take you now—'

'Thank you but no thanks,' I said firmly, on my dignity. 'I want a proper massage to relax me, nothing more.' With that I hurried through the door, finding a smiling Thai woman of middle-age at a reception desk, who welcomed me in sing-song English. 'I want a massage, just a good massage,' I said to make sure I was understood. 'You can do that, can you?'

'Of course, madam,' she smiled again. 'Very good massage and a special treatment if you wish. Very relaxing, very relieving for up-tight ladies.' She named a price in the local currency, adding that the special treatment was extra if required, and that discount would be made for dollars, Australian dollars, yen and pounds or francs.

I paid for the basic massage, thinking I would enjoy that enough, and was led down a corridor to a room furnished with armchairs and potted plants. Thai music piped softly into an atmosphere already heavy with the scent of burning joss sticks. Several women of around my age sat in the chairs, avoiding my eyes as I entered. None looked butch or submissive, all being well-dressed and obviously wealthy with rings and jewellery. Two were European or American and the other pair I took for Japanese.

They were led away in turn by pretty Thai girls in short white nylon overalls, the two Jap women leaving together, until I alone remained. I was joined by a new arrival, a large woman who addressed me in German. When I shrugged to show I didn't understand, she spoke in gutteral English. 'First time for you?' I was asked. 'I have not seen you here before. If you want the special, ask for Miss Chong. She is the best, very wicked girl. Worth the money.'

'I just want the massage,' I said. 'I've been on a long flight all day and feel a little tense.'

'Ach, *liebchen*,' the buxom woman laughed. 'Let Chong make you come and come until you forget tense, only that you are *kaput*, so satisfied that you cannot move a muscle. So relaxing.' She arose and went back to the reception desk, returning with a Thai woman of about thirty with another Thai in tow, a very young girl with slanted eyes. She was as pretty as a picture with her eyes rouged and a wide red mouth. 'Chong is training one of the new assistant masseuses so you will get two for the price of one tonight,' the German woman said as if it was all decided. 'Put yourself in their hands, my dear. Forget you are British and discover what pleasure they can give you. I promise you will thank me afterwards.'

I was led away, Miss Chong holding my elbow and her trainee going ahead to open one of the white-painted doors for us. The building was deceptive, for the room I was ushered into was surprisingly spacious, containing a padded massage table, a shower cubicle that was open-fronted and several chairs set against the wall.

'Who is the German woman?' I asked. Miss Chong stood back while her assistant began to take off my clothes gently and carefully, hanging each article in the wardrobe until she was behind me unclipping my bra and I was down to my panties.

'That is Frau Gretel Mannlicher,' Miss Chong said solemnly. 'We work for her, this is her place. She recognised you as a new customer and wants you to return.' She stood back and studied me as the girl trainee drew down my briefs and I was left naked.

'What are these, madam?' she enquired politely, indicating the purplish love-bites on my body. 'Did a lover give them to you?'

She indicated that I should lie on the massage table and I had half-lifted myself over it, bum raised prior to rolling over to stretch out, when I felt a soft hand lightly fondle both cheeks. I turned my head to see the trainee girl standing behind me, eyeing my nakedness with an undisguised look of

approval and desire. The minx was turned on, I plainly saw.
Young as she was, she wanted me. The lewd thought made
my sex throb and sent a thrill of sudden arousal rushing to
my belly and breasts.

'Chi-Chi likes you too much, I think,' Miss Chong smiled
enigmatically, watching my reaction as I laid myself out.

I thought of Harry, away in the bush, and of my already-
broken vow to save my sexual energy for a memorable
get-together session on his return. 'Just the massage, thank
you,' I said firmly. 'That will do nicely. Tell Chi-Chi to
behave herself. I could be her mother—'

I noticed Chi-Chi was busy filling a plastic bucket with
warm water and adding a thick liquid that turned into a
glutinous ooze not unlike wallpaper paste. She stirred it
vigorously with a long-handled brush of soft yellow hairs.
The handle was a good nine inches long and carved in the
shape of a male penis complete with bulbous knob and the
ridge of a drawn-back foreskin.

'Chi-Chi is new here, she does not understand English
yet,' Miss Chong said soothingly. 'You must relax, madam,
leave it to our hands. These?' she smiled, referring to my
love-bites again as her fingertips played sensuously over my
breasts and stomach. 'Are they from your lover? It must have
been very hot affair.' Her fingers stroked down until they
reached the curling strands of my pubic bush. 'A lady lover?'

'No, damn you, two young men,' I said defiantly, not
seeing why I should make excuses while she was attempting
to arouse me so cunningly. She was doing a good job of it
too, I had to admit. Her narrow eyes widened in delight and
she gave a short laugh, now drawing a single fingertip along
the parting of my outer lips, making my quim pout and part
and for me to moan softly and arch my back. Had Magnolia
remarked on the love-bites I was ready to tell her some

concocted story about returning from the toilet during the flight when sudden turbulence had thrown me about, knocking me into the corners of seats.

'*Two* young men,' I repeated, fighting the desire to thrust up my thighs to her. 'This is *seduction*,' I ground out in complaint, my will weakening by the second. 'No, no,' I gasped. 'You mustn't—'

'But you *want* us to,' Miss Chong insisted slyly. 'You are very sexy lady, need relief. See, your big breasts, how they thrust out, and make your nipples so long and hard. This cunt likes me to play with it, I think. It is *so* wet for me. Tell me of the two young men. They fuck you good, eh? Fuck you together, both holes? Very nice.'

'Oh, you bitch!' I moaned, her finger now probing me slowly and expertly, touching and circling over my clit, making its hood peel back and project erect and stiff. I thrust against her hand as if to urge her to go faster, but she withdrew as my throes increased, leaving me in an agony of suspense.

As if by arrangement, Chi-Chi advanced on me, still stirring the bucket of gooey slop, the motion making her pert pear-shaped tits wobble under the thin white nylon overall, her sharp nipples impressed through the material. The next moment she was slathering me with the contents of the bucket, sploshing it over my breasts, belly and between my thighs. It felt wonderfully sensuous, the soft hairs of the brush slap-slapping up and down from my breasts to my cunt, covering me thickly with the scented gunk down to my toes.

They rolled me over on the massage table and the treatment was continued from my neck to my buttocks. I felt Miss Chong part my cheeks widely as Chi-Chi flip-flopped the teasing brush hairs up and down over my rear-hanging bulge and puckered arsehole. While sighing and muttering my pleasure at the treatment I was penetrated by the phallic brush handle I assumed. It slid easily to its final inch up my cunt, the slippery paste covering me.

My grunts, groans, oohs and aaahs of abandoned licentiousness were for real as the brush handle was worked in and out, fucking me. I turned my face to see Chi-Chi smiling behind my prone form, nodding her head as if to say, you like? She withdrew momentarily and deftly slid the brush-dildo up the inch or so necessary to press the knob to my anus, manipulating it forward to enter and stretch my back passage. I cried out in surprise and approval, revelling in the wanton sensation created by its size and shape. I writhed, pleaded, bucked and gyrated to the lovely intruder, driven madly lustful by its shunting inside me. 'Ah, yes, yes,' I heard myself urging Chi-Chi. 'Go on, on! Make me come, come—'

But it was withdrawn even as I was on the very verge of a climax. Miss Chong bent over as I turned my face in frustration, smiling her enigmatic smile. 'You like *real* prick now, madam?' she enquired salaciously. 'Real hard flesh prick to please you? See, look at Chi-Chi, what she has got for you. Very good proper prick.'

I turned on one elbow with some difficulty in the slippery goo. I was annoyed at being so cruelly interrupted on the verge of a come. Pretty little Chi-Chi was beaming at me, opening up her white overall button by button and revealing her firm pear-shaped tits with long taut nipples dark purple against the light brown skin. As she threw the garment aside I gasped with surprise to see a rampantly erect prick rearing over small tight balls at her crotch. The cock looked so genuine, straining upright; very lengthy but also very thin, at least to my eyes, for all the world the size and shape of a big

Havana cigar. 'It can't be,' I said in my amazement, looking at her lovely face, the perfect shapely breasts and then down again to the standing dick. 'What – what is she?'

'One of Bangkok's many boy-girls,' said Miss Chong. 'Chi-Chi is on hormones, awaiting the operation to make her a real female.' She was one for smiling secretively. 'Looking at her I wonder if she should have it. She still likes to fuck very much. She wanted to fuck you, madam, as soon as she saw you. She has satisfied many ladies like you.'

'I can't believe it,' was all I could find to say, the experience unique even to me. Chi-Chi advanced, taking my hand and curling it about her prick. Sure enough it felt exactly as it should: warm and alive, stiff as a poker and the outer skin slid over the interior stalk as she moved my wrist up and down to stroke it. Her free hand cupped my neck, bent me forward and kissed me, her lips clinging and a sharp pointed tongue pushing into my mouth.

'No! I don't know about this,' I protested as she made to get on the massage table with me, turning me over on my back. Her lips went back to mine in another long kiss, then lowered to suck upon both of my nipples in turn. Aided by the slippery fluid covering my body she seemed to glide over me. Then she was positioned between my thighs with her lithe girlish body covering mine, her nipples pressed to my tits.

'Oh, you little she-devil,' I groaned as Chi-Chi's crotch went hard to mine and I felt the long thin stalk pierce my cunt and thrust deeply as her flanks began a steady shunting. 'Yes, yes, yes!' I was imploring moments later as she fucked me clinically and masterfully. Chi-Chi withdrew to the knob, making me heave to get what I craved inside me, then met me by shoving forward. The angle of penetration was altered, making me crow with ecstatic pleasure as the knob rubbed on my clitoris and nudged back to my cervix. I forgot what was fucking me, I only knew the delight was out of the world. My legs curled around the slim waist and my hands cupped the delightful girlish cheeks of a taunt round bottom to haul my fucker closer. Then I was heaving and humping, at times only the back of my head on the massage table, as I came and came in the most shattering climaxes. Chi-Chi cried out loudly and jerked on top of me. Then I was flooded.

I could only slump on the table in a stupor not caring that the Thai pair were giggling at my complete submission. My cunt throbbed and palpitated, my head spun from such a fucking. Then I felt warm water being sprayed over me and Miss Chong was directing a thin hosepipe to wash off the goo from my heated body. It was absolutely delicious, being sluiced down back and front. When I arose from the table I was handed a large fluffy towel and I allowed Chi-Chi to dry me off luxuriously. When I was dressed, the girl-boy accompanied me to the front door and found me a taxi. As I made to leave Chi-Chi suddenly embraced me. Her lips pressed to mine voluptuously.

'Come back and see me, nice lady,' Chi-Chi cooed, 'I like to fuck you very much.' Evidently her English was knowledgeable enough to say that. 'Next time I lick you out good, suck your big titties, fuck ass too. You ask me come to your house, yes?'

'No,' I said, smiling at her opportunism. 'I think Miss Chong was right, you'd better think hard about dispensing with your lower equipment, even with those breasts of yours. Goodnight, Chi-Chi, I can only say it was an experience I'll never forget.'

'Make you come very much,' the little creature reminded me as I got into the taxi. 'You will be back.'

At least, I consoled myself as I tiptoed into my apartment

at two in the morning, I had not been unfaithful to Harry with another man. Not exactly anyway! For my first foray into Bangkok I could only conclude Magnolia was right, the whole city was a delightful den of iniquity.

Chapter Ten
ENGLAND

Houses were as rare as hen's teeth in the post-war London of the early 1950 years. This was the result of wholesale destruction in the Blitz and a complete halt in the construction of new homes during the war. To buy a house or flat was well out of our budget and renting the tiniest room meant paying an extortionate weekly amount and making a substantial deposit. I thanked Gerard Manley in my prayers for the vital nest-egg I'd accumulated to get us a roof over our head. Harry always concluded that it was thanks to my Scottish thrift that we had a little spare cash. His first job as a civil engineer being based in London, we settled for an attic in Bloomsbury which was even smaller than the one we had left behind in Oxford.

However, both he and I were supreme optimists, happy together whatever the circumstances and convinced better times lay ahead. Harry had his new job and regular pay and I saved every penny I could. I only bought essentials and was determined to achieve the deposit for a mortgage on a nice new house in the suburbs. I spent hours in a nearby park with baby Peter, guiding his first steps, feeding the ducks, giving him the fresh air and exercise not available in our attic abode. Once a week Harry insisted I have my outing to a cinema. A film show was the only luxury I allowed myself, unless you can count nightly sex.

Every Wednesday I left Harry pouring over his work and, with little Peter tucked in bed, I spent a few hours at a local picture palace. On my way home I always passed a brightly lit café with steamy windows. One night I went in and was enveloped in the warm smell of sausages and chips. I stood at the wooden counter with its glass-domed plates of sandwiches and meat pies wondering whether I would invest a shilling in some Cornish pasties for Harry and I. We were always hungry in those days.

The man who served me was as broad as he was tall and powerfully built. The curly fuzz of black hair at the open neck of his spotless white shirt covered his thick arms. He was about forty with thick jet-black hair combed back from a ruggedly handsome face. His smile was friendly and his dark eyes shot me an instant admiring look. 'Two of the sixpenny Cornish pasties, please' I said, realising at once that this man was greatly taken by my face and full figure. 'Will you wrap them up for me to take away.' I held out my shilling but he held my hand.

'That all, love?' he enquired pleasantly. 'Can't I tempt you with a hot supper? Anything you like on the menu—?'

'Just the pasties,' I said firmly, disengaging my hand. He smiled again, considering the shilling in his palm.

'Didn't mean to offend, young lady. I was just struck by how nice you look.' He said it in a most disarming way, with no evident ulterior motive such as all attractive young girls suspect. 'Two Cornish pasties,' he added, using tongs to place them in a bag.

'This is a treat,' Harry declared when I got home and heated them up. We sat at our table eating and drinking tea. Indeed it was a treat, as tasty as any of the gourmet meals we were to have in restaurants and embassies around the world in later years. 'Are these from Georgiou's?' Harry enquired, munching. 'That Greek chap is renowned for his food. All made on his premises. If we're working around here my squad always uses his café for pie and mash.'

So on my way home from the cinema in future I called in for sausage rolls or meat pies. Georgiou always seemed available to serve me, even leaving other customers. He chatted in the manner of one keen to please, even though my patronage of his café would never make him rich. One night I had to tender half-a-crown for my purchase. As he handed me my change he winked. Looking down to count the change I totalled coins worth ten shillings. I held it out to show he had given me too much, only to get a shake of his head and a stubby finger held up before his lips to silence me.

'Pop in tomorrow lunchtime and have a meal on me, love,' he said kindly. 'I don't want to know your business, but I guess money is tight with you. You're always smart and nice though. Come in around one and I'll have something special for you. Chicken, the works.'

'And what would you expect in return?' I asked cheekily, the coins in my hand held firmly.

He looked hurt, shrugging his broad shoulders. I did not take up his offer, but thought seriously about it. I had granted sexual favours often enough before not to be shocked at his offer – or the extra change. Besides, I was set on saving every penny I could for a mortgage down-payment. Georgiou was clean and attractive in his way and was no doubt virile enough to be a satisfying lover. In my situation it would be the easiest way of earning money. I subscribed to the old adage about women, that they were sitting on a gold mine if they cared to sell it.

My first rebuff to him did not turn him against me. I

invariably got extra change when I went to his café, was presented with a box of chocolates from his confectionary shelf and offered packets of cigarettes which I refused because Harry and I never smoked. At last I agreed to have lunch on him, adding that I would have to bring my son along too as there was nobody else to look after the toddler.

That did not put him out in any way. He set up a special corner table with a new cloth and a high chair. I dined on roast chicken, roast potatoes and a selection of vegetables topped with a gravy as good as the kind my mother used to make. Peter too had a feast of the same, mashed up for his convenience. When Georgiou came to clear the plates after an ice-cream dessert, I plucked the corner of his apron to delay him.

'Just what would you like from me, Georgi?' I asked. 'You've been very generous to me for months. What can I do to repay you? Don't be afraid to say.' I considered that as far as I dare go, at least without blatantly offering myself. He pulled up a chair and sat beside me, choosing his words carefully.

'You're a nice girl, a beautiful girl, a good mother as I can see by this lad here. What I ask is not for myself, if I dare ask—'

'Try me,' I said in a flat voice. 'You might be surprised.'

'I can't talk now,' he said, looking around his café packed with customers. 'All I can say is that I'll make it well worth your while.' He held up a hand. 'Don't be insulted, Diana, but I'm talking more money than you'd earn cleaning offices. I know you've done that, going out at dawn before your husband leaves for work.' He certainly could not insult me talking of money. 'Pop in next Wednesday night before you go to the cinema and I'll try to explain.'

I was intrigued. The following Wednesday, without Harry

noticing, I wore my best dress and put on extra make-up. At the café Georgiou guided me upstairs to his living quarters. In a cosy overfurnished lounge he indicated an armchair for me to sit upon, going to a cabinet and bringing me a tiny glass of ouzo, his national drink. I drank it and was given a refill, feeling its warmth penetrating to my stomach, and making me bold.

'I'm here,' I said. 'What must I do?' I looked him directly in the face. 'I think you want to—'

'Very much,' Georgiou admitted awkwardly. 'I always have since you came into my cafe. But I have a brother, much younger.'

'You want me for your brother?' I gasped. 'Can't he get a girl? Do you arrange everything for him?'

'I have to,' Georgiou said seriously. 'The boy was badly injured in a motorcycle accident. It was I who bought him the powerful bike, curse the day. He is completely paralysed, he cannot move.'

'How awful for him,' I said sincerely. 'Is he in a hospital? I don't see what I can do for him. I'll visit gladly, if that would help. I wouldn't want to be paid for that.'

'He's here, in his bedroom,' Georgiou said. 'I look after him, dress him, change him and feed him. He's my brother. I have a nurse come in as well to help when I'm busy in the café. She bathes him. You know what? His neck was broken and he cannot speak except in sounds, he cannot use his limbs. Yet when the woman comes to bathe him, he has an erection. A good stiff one.'

'Poor young man,' I had to say. 'He has feelings there evidently. How frustrating it must be for him, confined to bed and not able to get about and, well, meet girls. Has he ever?'

'Sure,' said Georgiou. 'He was married when he was

eighteen but his wife left him after the accident. He has few pleasures now. I got him one of the first televisions. That's a poor substitute for making love. At least his eyes have expression, they light up if he likes something. His brain is okay, it's just his body.'

'Except his penis,' I said, delicately using the proper term instead of a cruder version. 'That works obviously.'

'Too damn well,' Georgiou said sadly. 'It breaks my heart to see it standing up so stiff. I've stood there wishing the nurse would rub it or suck it for him. Anything to relieve it. Do I disgust you saying that?'

'No. I would wish she'd do that myself. I take it that is what you want me to do,' I said levelly. 'Did you never think of getting a prostitute to give him relief?'

'Just once,' I was told sadly. 'She looked the part. She breezed in and straight away called him a cripple. I paid her off and threw her out there and then. When I got back to the bedroom Ari was crying, real tears down his cheeks, trying to shake his head as if to say, never again. That's why I decided it would have to be a nice girl, a good wholesome girl like you.'

'Ari' I said reflectively. 'My husband is a Harry.'

'It's short for Aristotle,' Georgiou said. 'It's a common Greek name. What about your husband? Would he know if – if you were kind enough to help in this situation?'

'I would hope *not*,' I said. 'It would be strictly between you and me and Ari. Shall we go through and see him?'

'Let me suggest something first,' Georgiou said, looking at me appealingly. 'To make him think you are not just here to relieve him for money, would you mind dressing as a doctor?' While I sat wondering at his subterfuge he went to a sideboard drawer and brought out a folded white starched medical coat and a stethoscope, offering them to me. 'He is used to doctors calling. I have paid many in the hope of some miracle. Put on the coat, please, and stick the stethoscope in a pocket so that he can see. That way he'll be reassured.'

'If you insist,' I said. 'What do I do then—?'

'Make a show of examining him,' Georgiou insisted. 'You'll do as much for him as any of the other docs I've paid big dough to look him over. Pull the blankets back, I'll help you strip him. Poor Ari. A lovely girl like you roaming her hands over his body is certain to get him erect. Then maybe you can be nice to him.'

'I'll do my best,' I agreed. 'I won't push it, only if and when he gets a good erection will I take interest in it. Maybe I can examine it. Then I can pretend it is having an effect on me. If he responds by growing harder or his eyes show me he is pleased, I'll take it from there.'

Georgiou looked delighted as I put on the doctor's white coat, the stethoscope poking from my hip pocket quite professionally. 'Fifty pounds if this goes to plan,' he promised, 'or even if it doesn't, you are worth that for trying.' Suddenly he kissed my cheek, his eyes filling. 'Such a lovely girl. What more could he want?'

We went through to the bedroom where I saw a handsome young man with a dark shock of hair lying on a bed. He was perfectly still except for enquiring eyes that took in my arrival with a frown. I was introduced as Doctor Saxon, whom Georgiou had brought to inspect his brother. I nodded sweetly at Ari, glad that the white coat was tight in the bust, the buttons straining to hold the bulge of my breasts. We drew back the bedcovers and drew off Ari's pyjamas. Everything was spotless, including his still athletic-looking body which showed no sign of twisted limbs. I made a pretence of feeling his muscles, tapping his back as we sat him up, lowering him again for me to place my hands on his stomach and upper thighs as if seeking some sign of life.

The response I got was for the long flaccid prick which had lain at rest over heavy black-haired balls to rear up in a most proud cockstand, positively thick with arousal and stretching to its full eight or so throbbing inches. I looked at him, smiling, and saw his eyes register embarrassment and shame. He was unable to turn his face away and no doubt was suffering mental agony.

'Why the apologetic look, Ari?' I said to him mischievously. 'I'm flattered. Is it so big on account of me? I'd like to think so. What a beauty! It looks so big and hard I hope it's not painful.' Again I looked very purposefully at his eyes, nodding and smiling to reassure him of my sincerity. I saw an expression of gratitude in the pupils. 'I think it time your brother left the room,'

I turned to Georgiou and I said in my most officious voice. 'This is a private medical examination and any information regarding the patient's infirmity will be made to you in my report.'

Georgiou left the room, trying to disguise his glee. I suspected that he was hovering outside the partly opened bedroom door. I turned back to my patient. 'In my medical opinion,' I told Ari, 'a young adult male like yourself in that condition should naturally seek satisfaction. Obviously you can't help yourself. Would you be shocked if I recommend your erection be relieved? I advise it strongly, both for your comfort and peace of mind. Would you be agreeable for me to ease your condition with my hand?

It was a lot of clap-trap, I knew, but I did not want to appear anything other than a concerned doctor with my patient's welfare at heart. I saw Ari look at me like a starving man who had been promised a feast. I gently clasped his upright stalk, feeling its warm pulse. 'You can blink, Ari,' I said. 'Blink once if you wish me to desist. Twice if you want me to continue.'

Two definite blinks of his eyelids gave me the go-ahead to begin a slow sensuous stroking of his rigid stalk and I felt tremendously aroused at the smoothness and heat in my grasp. My mounting excitement was evident in my face and I judged that Ari, lying back as I manipulated his prick, was increasingly aware of my mounting stimulation.

'Yes, yes,' I said to him, my voice strained. 'I didn't mean to, but I like it too. It's such a lovely prick to rub, lovely to hold—' At that moment, no doubt worked up by my admission that I found it highly arousing to massage his beautiful cock, Ari grunted and jerked almost imperceptibly as he came, strong spurts of his stored emission jetting out in a series of arcs. His spunk was hot and thick, covering my hand and wrist and splattering his stomach. No doubt it was a blessed relief for him to unload it all.

I washed my hands at the sink in a corner of the room, returning to him with a damp hand towel to gently dab his prick and stomach clean. He lay back regarding me with some wonder.

'Don't be so surprised,' I teased him. 'What woman wouldn't lose control and get fruity with that lovely cock in her hand? Wicked Ari, you had me turned on, didn't you? Good Lord,' I giggled as the prick in my hand stirred again as I washed it thoroughly. 'Don't tell me it wants more of the same. As a doctor I shouldn't, you know. As a woman I very much want to.'

I gave the growing shaft a few tentative strokes, feeling it thicken under my fingers. 'Would you like to *see* me, Ari?' I said. 'This is awful of me, but I can't help myself. Blink twice if you want to see me, *all* of me.'

His two blinks were forthcoming even as I spoke. I arose,

taking off the white coat, unbuttoning my blouse and dropping my skirt. His eyes never left me as I cast aside my bra, looking at him almost as if I were shy but unable to resist showing off my large breasts. My knickers and stockings followed and I posed for him with uplifted tits and out-thrust pubic bush. I'm sure if he could have moved he would have raised his arms to receive me, perhaps he tried valiantly.

I moved back to the bed, nursing my breasts to his face, and feeling his lips suckle. Then I looked down to see his fine prick rearing in its full glory again. Unable to resist, I cuddled it into my cleavage, rubbed my breast flesh up and down on the stalk as both orbs encompassed it. Then what I wanted was to suck it, bobbing my head over its length while Ari sighed and gave pleasurable moans. His cock felt so big and hard, I wanted it badly, not out of kindness for him but an ache in my cunt demanding to be filled. I mounted the boy and directed his stiffness into my cunt, squirming down upon it until I was plugged to the hilt. With my breasts swinging like bells I rode him and came strongly. Then I went on for a second climax, matching his final spurts that drenched me even as I shook in helpless spasms over his prick.

If I felt overpaid as a delighted Georgiou slipped me his promised fee as I left, he assured me it was nothing to what he had paid members of the medical profession who hadn't done half as much for Ari as I'd done that night. From then on, on my supposed cinema-going night (and I lost count of the films I never saw) I called to give Ari his therapy and enjoyed his magnificent prick. This continued until Georgiou decided to sell his café and take Ari back to the family home on the island of Kos, where he could lie out on a sunlit verandah with the blue sea and sunshine all around instead of the cell-like bedroom he was forced to occupy above the café.

'I haven't lived there myself since I was ten,' Georgiou told me while announcing his plan to leave London. 'Ari will have people all around, the fishing boats at sea, everything but you, Doctor Saxon,' he added with a smile. 'You must come out to visit us. You have been wonderful for Ari and made his life worthwhile.' He pressed a wad of banknotes into my hand. 'That is for all your kindness.'

'Then I'll do one more kind act,' I told him. We were in his overfurnished lounge and I began to take off my clothes before him. 'I know you've always wanted to fuck me,' I laughed. 'Fuck is the correct term, isn't it? So strip off and let me see what you've got.' What he'd got was a hirsute muscular body with a good thick prick which he used to shaft me strenuously before we parted.

My bank account had increased dramatically and I truly felt I had made a stricken young man's life a lot more tolerable by my visits. I hoped that when Georgiou was settled in Kos that he'd find another such as me for Ari. After all, there are other things in life to want to look upon than the fishing fleet putting to sea. I refer to the naked female form, which men seem never to tire of gazing upon in magazines, films – or in the flesh.

Chapter Eleven
THAILAND

Having done her duty in meeting me at Bangkok airport, Magnolia left me to it. If we chanced to pass in the hallway between our luxurious apartments, she was polite but her usual snobbish self. She always had a reason for hurrying off, such as arranging flowers at the U S Embassy, attending a reception, or hosting a musical evening of Mozart. I did not mind as I was quite happy with my own company until Harry's return. That was another thing, she blamed Harry for dragging her husband Howard into the wild hinterland. Therefore took her irritation out on me, a wasted emotion if ever there was one. Magnolia was lovely and desirable but as cold as a fish. Her teenage daughter Nicola had more life in her. She greeted me cheerily when we met, usually on her return from school which she referred to as 'a drag', 'the pits', and other Americanisms of the with-it young.

Nicola had a carefree air about her that made one feel that there was a wild spirit in her waiting to be released. She was an animated girl who, if allowed the chance, would burst out. She was made all the more so probably because of the strict regime her mother imposed, determined her daughter would be a mirror image of herself as a woman. I met Nicola by chance on one of my daily forays to enjoy the sights of

Bangkok, taking in the splendour of the Temple of the Emerald Buddha and the Grand Palace. Nicola was there with a school party of girls in their straw hats and uniform dresses. She spotted me and attached herself to me as the school party moved on.

'I've seen all the temples and golden buddhas I can stomach,' she said when I expressed concern for her deserting the party. 'You wouldn't like to take me to the Sky Lounge on Rajaparop Road, would you, Lady Saxon? They serve afternoon drinks.'

'Do they?' I said, thinking that the girl reminded me of myself as an over-developed and boisterous teenager. 'Well, tough luck, young lady, I'm not buying you a drink stronger than a Coke. And while we are at it, your mother would kill me if she knew you were with me.'

'She's a complete no-no to anything I want to do,' Nicola pouted. 'I wish she were more like you. You're a real titled lady, just what she'd love to be. I think she's jealous of you.'

I'd wondered if she was even attracted to me, remembering how she had been so nervous and flushed on seeing my nude body in the bathroom of her apartment. 'You must never be disloyal to your mother, Nicola,' I said. 'I'm sure she wants what's best for you. Mothers are like that.'

'Not all of them and I'll bet you aren't,' the girl smiled. 'My mother can be a witch. "Don't talk to boys". "Don't go to the disco". You don't know her or you wouldn't be so kind. She even talks about you. I've heard her with friends who asked how our new neighbour was.'

'I'm always interested to know what others who hardly know me say about me,' I laughed. 'Nothing nice from the sound of it.'

'She said you were one of the most beautiful woman she'd ever seen with your burnished chestnut hair and full figure.

She thought you must have been an actress or model in your day, and probably married your husband to get the title.'

'That's not too bad,' I laughingly agreed, thinking back to the attic rooms of my past with Harry a hard-up student. 'Quite flattering, in fact.'

'She said you've probably had lots of lovers and love affairs,' Nicola went on meaningfully, with a questioning look in her wide blue eyes. 'Mother said you were the type that men go silly over and make advances. Have you had lots of lovers?'

'That would be telling,' I teased her. 'Of course not.'

'Well, I hope men go silly over me and make advances,' Nicola sighed wistfully. 'And that I have lots of lovers and love affairs too. Look at me in this awful school drag! I'm growing into a woman and I've got woman's feelings. I'm as horny as hell at times but I can't talk to my mother about it, she'd collapse with a nervous breakdown. I say, I hope you're not shocked or offended with me saying these things? It's just that I've got to tell someone.'

'These are natural urges at your age, my dear,' I said, trying to conceal my amusement at her honesty and appear the older, wiser head. 'I felt exactly as you do when I was your age in Scotland. I couldn't wait to spread my wings, if that's the right term,' I said, well aware that spreading my legs would be more accurate. 'Your time will come, you're already a very pretty girl with a lovely figure.'

'There, see,' Nicola pointed out. 'My dear mother would never say anything like that to me. What about masturbation? Do you agree girls should relieve themselves? Especially when they are not allowed to meet boys. And what about girls, well, doing things to each other, I mean kissing and fondling and such? Girls do at my school and I like it. Does that mean I'll turn lesbo? I still like boys though.'

141

'We're getting into deep water here,' I said, smiling kindly to assure her I was not disturbed at her questions. 'Really, you should talk to your parents about those important things.' To change the subject I indicated a nearby open-air café. 'I'll buy you that Coke I promised and a coconut ice-cream. Let's take a seat at one of those tables. In this heat I need an ice myself.'

As soon as we were served, a handsome Frenchman in a bow-tie and a linen suit, obviously a resident, chanced his luck by bowing his head in a slight incline and pulling back an empty chair as if wishing to join us.

'What a delightful picture,' he began. 'Such a charming mother and daughter, both of you so beautiful. May I join you? I live here and would be privileged to show you the sights of this splendid city.' I admit the creep was using other than his native language, but his obvious intent and choice of words had both Nicola and I giggling. He stood before us a little disconcerted. 'Believe me, ladies, I intend only French chivalry.'

'Are you serious?' I said, choking over my ice-cream. What I could have said was that the lecherous chancer fancied fucking me or Nicola and most likely both. 'Thank you but we like being on our own,' I added. 'Better luck next time, monsieur.'

'I do not understand,' he muttered, frowning. Beside me, Nicola spoke rapidly in fluent French, making the man turn abruptly and stalk off, glancing back angrily.

'You see,' my young companion said as we laughed at the incident. 'My mother was right, men are attracted by you so much that they make an approach without an introduction. He was quite handsome too.'

'And quite obvious,' I said. 'Whatever did you say to send him off with a flea in his ear, as we say in Scotland?'

'I told him to fuck off,' Nicola said mischievously, looking to see how I reacted to the F word. I shook my head, returning her grin.

'You're obviously benefitting by your French lessons,' I had to admit. 'You're very fluent.'

'What about the other kind of French lessons?' Nicola asked of me insistently. 'What we girls at school talk about as Frenching? Of course it's really called fellatio or oral sex. It means putting a man's penis in your mouth and sucking it.'

'I know what it means,' I said. 'Again, your parents are the ones to advise you, or if you can't ask them then your teacher. Or you should study a good manual on what it's about.'

'But I want to ask someone like you, a woman of the world,' Nicola pleaded. 'You didn't answer any of the things I asked you – about masturbation and girls arousing each other. And the Frenching thing. Is it too disgusting or perfectly natural, the same as for a man wanting to lick a vagina? Oh, that's the sort of word my mother would use! It's *cunt*, isn't it? We've got cunts.'

'I could talk to you of these things,' I told her seriously, 'and I respect your wanting to be fully aware about sexual matters as a young person on the verge of womanhood. But if I did, and your mother found out, she might accuse me of putting salacious ideas into your pretty head. If you talked of what we discuss to a schoolfriend, might it get to a teacher who would inform your parents? That would be a situation I could do without. Just how old are you, anyway, young lady?'

'Sixteen but going on seventeen,' Nicola answered. 'Girls my age back in the States have lost their virginities by now. And I wouldn't breathe a word of whatever you tell me.

Anyway, if I said anything it wouldn't be that I learned it from you.' She crossed her heart with a finger. 'On my honour, Lady Saxon. Won't you?' she pleaded, weakening my resistance. 'What about masturbation? Is it dreadfully wrong and how often should one do it?'

'It's not wrong, it's perfectly natural in fact, as all the experts agree nowadays,' I said. 'All the more so for young people like yourself who feel the need for sexual release when no other way is available. The harm is to feel guilt about it. That is unnecessary. As to how many times, well, as many times as you feel like it.'

'Did you masturbate?' she asked daringly.

'Of course, everyone does, I suppose. Many times.'

I saw her face light with impish delight. 'Do you still, with your husband away?'

'We're getting personal now,' I warned, 'but as we are being honest with each other – yes, at times when I feel the need. What about you?'

'Almost every night,' she admitted. 'With my fingers or my pillows bunched up between my thighs. That gives me great climaxes and the feeling is lovely. Have you ever used a dildo or a vibrator? They sell them in the sex shops here, I know.'

'Yes, I've used a dildo and vibrator,' I said. 'By the time you are of my age, I'm sure you'll have tried them too. I shouldn't be telling you all this, but I must admit it seems perfectly natural to instruct you.'

It was also perfectly natural to feel a certain arousal in discussing one's private sexual habits. Looking at Nicola, I saw it was having its effect on her too. She was squirming her round little bottom in the cane chair and blushing. Enough was enough, I decided, it was becoming erotic sex talk instead of an enlightening tutorial for an inquisitive girl who, I was beginning to suspect, knew more than she let on. She was revelling in the revelations, her own as well as mine.

'Just fancy,' she said in hushed wonder. 'A beautiful adult lady like you still masturbates! Do you think my mother does? No, never, surely. Has a man ever used a vibrator on you, or a woman even? I know it happens from stories. Some of the porno they sell here is bought by boys to pass on to girls at school, knowing it will get them horny. Has a man used a dildo on you, or a woman you were lovers with?'

'Both, if you insist on knowing,' I conceded. 'As I said, by my age no doubt you'll have experienced such things yourself. Yes, and I've performed fellatio as you call it and had cunnilingus—'

'Sucked a man's prick and been licked out too,' Nicola said delightedly. 'I can't wait for it all to happen to me. And I won't feel guilt about any of it, like you said, or be ashamed of my natural sexuality. That's my mother's problem, I'm sure! What a good sport you are, Lady Saxon. What else have you done that I should know about?'

'Things you will find out for yourself as you get older,' I advised her. 'I think we've gone far enough into the subject to start off with. You'd better call me Diana now we've let our hair down.'

'Diana,' repeated the girl, pleased I had said so. 'But I won't call you that in front of mother. What's your husband like, Diana? Is he a good lover? Do you make love often? Do you have passionate sex?'

'Get on with you,' I told her humorously. 'You want to know everything. For your information he's a terrific lover. That's all I'm going to say.'

'Would you let him make love to me?' she asked wickedly. 'As part of my education? Would he want to?'

'You horny little baggage,' I said, laughing at her boldness. 'I suppose he would want to. Practically all men would want a juicy morsel like you, so young and fresh and obviously willing with your tits and bottom rounding out so seductively. But you won't get the chance with my man if I can help it, and here endeth the sex lesson. You know more than enough to get on with, I'm sure. More importantly, can I get you a taxi to take you back to school?'

'Take me home,' Nicola said positively. 'I'll tell my mother I got separated in the crowds at the Temple of the Emerald Buddha so you met me and saw me safely back. That should make her grateful to you as she's always nuts about my safety in Bangkok. She says it's the devil's playground, if ever you heard such a corny description. That's her guilt complex showing up again. I'm sure she never lets father fuck her. They have separate rooms, you know.'

'Don't be so uncouth, it does not become you, child,' I said. 'What they do or don't do is their own affair. People have as much right to be celibate as those who—'

'Screw each other like rabbits,' Nicola finished for me cheekily. 'As I bet you and your husband do. My poor husband won't be able to keep up with me, whoever he'll be.'

'Just get in the taxi,' I ordered wearily as a yellow cab drew in to the kerb. 'I'm beginning to sympathise with Magnolia and know why she keeps tabs on you, my girl.'

'She thinks I'm her sweet virginal little darling with never an impure thought,' grumbled Nicola. 'It's all her fault for not letting the real me do things girls my age do.'

At the apartment we went up in the lift together and as I sought my key she cuddled up to me fondly. 'It's been great to have someone adult to talk to about sex,' she enthused. 'And my mother is right about one thing – you are an absolutely beautiful lady. I hope I look like you in time, with a figure and breasts like yours, and attract handsome strangers. I think he was hoping to lure us off to his flat and slip dope into our drinks and fuck the both of us. They do such things in Bangkok.'

She was still holding me but the cuddle was now more of an embrace, her body hard against mine, her young firm breasts pressing into me, our thighs engaged, standing belly to belly. As I tried to prise her off her soft young mouth sought mine, clamping to my lips with passion, her tongue seeking to force an entrance. For a brief moment I was tempted to let her continue, feeling my stomach turn over and my sex respond by starting an insistent throb. But I summoned the will to push her away, angry with myself for being so easily led on by such a little schoolgirl seducer.

'Oh, that was *nice*, why did you stop me?' Nicola sulked before I had recovered my composure enough to give her a sharp reminder never ever to attempt such intimacy again. The little witch smiled at me seductively, not in the least put out.

'Go!' I ordered. 'Go to your mother, for evidently she doesn't know what a wanton little bitch she's got on her hands.'

I went into my apartment trembling, acknowledging that her kiss and the pressure of her pliant young body to mine had made me weak at the knees. While I showered to refresh myself after the heat of Bangkok I calmed down somewhat, even smiling at the thought of myself at Nicola's age, already engaged in sexual liaisons with two older men and experienced in female love with a woman more than twice my age. Nicola, no doubt, was by nature highly sexed and the urge to express her desires uninhibitedly made her act as she had with me. Not on my doorstep though, I decided firmly. I had miraculously escaped unscathed from so many near scandals and sexual entanglements in my time that I recognised the danger signs. I knew enough to walk away when the flesh is weak and temptation strong, as in Nicola's case.

Still drying myself from the shower, casting the towel aside as I entered my bedroom to dress for the evening, I was drawn up short at the sight before me on my bed. Nicola was stretched out naked, smiling seductively, leaning up on her elbows with her pert already woman-sized breasts thrusting up, the nipples taut and rosy pink. Her thighs were parted, presenting to my startled eyes the unrestricted aspect of a sweet fig-like cunt with the inrolling lips on the plump little mound festooned with a light wispy covering of the honey-blonde hair inherited from her mother. To make matters worse, her school uniform lay on the floor.

In comparison to her lithe girlish figure I saw myself directly in the long wardrobe mirror opposite: the large heavy rounded tits of maturity, the strong firm curves of my limbs and buttocks, the thick triangle of hair curling about the bulging prominence at the fork of my thighs.

'Your body is so beautiful, Diana,' I was told in a hushed whisper by the forward girl. 'Come to bed with me—'

'Get dressed,' I said, trying to steady the catch in my voice. 'Go home. I don't want you here.'

'Yes, you do,' she said defiantly. 'I know you do. I could feel you start to respond when I kissed you.' She smiled at me again. 'Don't worry, my mother is out. I found a note saying she's having tea with friends in the Royal Orchid Sheraton and then staying for a display by some Siamese dance troupe. One of our servants is giving me my dinner later.'

'So that makes it all right,' I said crossly. 'She would freak out to know you are here like this. I've a good mind—'

'A good mind to what?' she giggled teasingly.

'To tan that wicked little arse of yours. To beat some sense into you.'

'I might like that,' Nicola said sweetly. She sat up with her tits bobbing, holding out her arms to me invitingly. 'I'm *sure* you want to. Are you afraid you'll be introducing me to wicked ways? I've slept with girls at school when I've boarded.'

'That's hardly the same,' I said acidly. 'Damn you, I'm old enough to be your mother.'

'And with one of my teachers,' she added proudly. 'The French tutor. She's your age too, so you needn't worry about leading me astray. Please, please, I *want* you.'

'You've been having me on, playing the little innocent,' I accused, shaking my head. I approached the bed, meaning to haul her off it, but in a flash she was up on her knees with her arms encircling my neck. I swung my right arm, giving her two or three good hard smacks to her firmly fleshed bottom, making her squeal momentarily before seeking my mouth with hers, overbalancing me and drawing me down across her over the bed. I felt her warm body lift to merge with me and she clung on, pushing her breasts and nipples into mine, squirming her crotch to my crotch as I haplessly straddled her. Our kiss was long and passionate, then I rolled aside, trying to push her away. 'No, no,' I said desperately. 'Not with *you*, Nicola. We musn't, musn't!'

I was now on my back, breathing heavily, hoping against hope that she would go. I closed my eyes, only to endure light sweet kisses pressed to my lids, my nose, mouth and chin before her lips were brushing my nipples, sucking gently on each in turn while she held my breasts. 'This shouldn't be happening,' I protested weakly. My low moans came unheeding. 'You're so young.'

149

'But it's so *nice*,' my expert little seductress cooed. 'And I'm as much a woman as I'll ever be. Isn't this lovely?' I could only groan in submission as I felt her slide down between my spread thighs, raising my knees and planting the soles of my feet on the bedcover as her wicked tongue flicked at my sex. Her fingers parted the outer lips, going in to lap, probe, lick, swirling around my responsive clit until I was raising my bottom for her, groaning in helpless pleasure, my hands gripping and twisting the bedcover.

'I'll come,' I gasped. 'You'll make me *come*. Oh, oh, I'll come—'

'Then you must do the same for me,' I heard in my throes, mumbled eagerly against my cunt in its acute spasms. 'Aren't you glad you let me?'

She wriggled her way up into my arms and we kissed lingeringly, for my part almost in gratitude for the delightful pleasure she had given me. I found I was fondling her tight breasts, lost in the ecstasy of two bodies caressing each other beyond the point of return. I kissed and licked my way down between her thighs and gave her what she had given me until her body stiffened and she cried out, grasping my hair as her climax sent her into convulsions. How long we lay in each other's arms I know not, only that the room darkened and eventually I told her she must leave.

Watching the little minx dress, I warned her that my lapse had strictly been a one-off, that with my husband away she had caught me at a weak moment. 'I'll believe that, dearest Diana,' she laughed, bending to kiss my lips sweetly, 'when my mother dances naked on a table at the Hilton International during one of her charity dinners. You and I are two of a kind.'

I couldn't imagine the aloof Magnolia dancing naked anywhere, and her daughter was quite right about the two of us being highly sexed. All the same, I had lapsed again and I wished that Harry would return quickly. As ever, temptation overtook me wherever it lurked, and it never lurked so lurkingly as it did in old Bangkok, of that I was sure.

Chapter Twelve
ENGLAND

A year of striving to increase the Saxon bank balance passed. I was determined to own a real house instead of rented rooms, with a garden for Peter to play in and where we would give him a little brother or sister. Since I'd bid farewell to poor paralysed Ari, I had truly been with no one else but my husband, who kept me well supplied sexually. To add to the family savings I got up at five every morning to work in a nearby newsagent's shop. I prepared the papers for the delivery boy to take on his rounds, served the early customers, and was back home by seven-thirty to see Harry off to work and make breakfast for our son. The money was nowhere near as good as paid to me by Georgiou but I settled for it.

The delivery boy was a handsome and athletic youth of Jamaican extraction aged seventeen, earning money to add to his grant to fund his training to be a dancer. Wayne was a forward young man and big for his age. He took an obvious fancy to me. Coming into the shop each morning he'd pass where I stood behind the counter, pressing close in the narrow space, his strong thighs sliding across my bum. This did not go unnoticed by Sybil Paterson, the buxom widow in her forties who owned the shop. Once when the boy had left with the newspapers, she remonstrated with me.

'I sincerely hope you are not encouraging young Wayne, Mrs Saxon,' she said. 'He's just a boy, although he's big.'

'I'm sure he is,' I retorted. 'I don't need to encourage him. He doesn't need to pass behind the counter. You're the boss, you tell him.'

She stalked off displeased to the back room behind the shop full of papers and magazines. Empty confectionary and cigarette cartons filled the spaces between an old couch and the table that doubled as her desk. I was left with a regular early morning customer, a shrewd-eyed skinny little woman in her fifties who regularly drove a van to the Cotswolds to seek out antiques for her market stall. She was always friendly, well dressed and lively as a cricket.

'That bitch is jealous of you, my love,' she said, laughing. 'Afraid you'll pinch her supply. Before you started here, there was just her and that black lad in the mornings. I've often come in and caught her slobbering over him. Found them kissing and cuddling, I did.'

'What?' I laughed. 'Mrs Paterson and Wayne!'

'Why not?' said the woman. 'No doubt she's paying him more than a paperboy's wages. He'll need it, going to that dance school. Students are always hard-up. She's upset that he prefers you.'

'Well, I'd never pay for it,' I said, with a giggle. 'Not for Wayne or anyone else. My husband sees me well supplied. It's just as well. By the time I've paid the rent, there's little enough left to pay for that!'

'They'd pay you, pretty thing that you are,' she said. 'Just what is the rent of that attic, if I may ask?'

When I told her she raised her eyes and whistled. She listened as I explained, eyeing me closely.

'I've a top flat empty,' she said at last. 'On the second floor above the one my hubby and I occupy. Our last tenants went off to Australia. They were a nice couple with two kids. Since then we've been cagey about letting it again, so many don't keep the flat clean or come in drunk. I'm asking only half the rent you're paying now. Are you interested, my love?'

Was I? Before she left I was given her address and a note to introduce the bearer to her hubby, as she referred to him, a retired copper name of Richard. I went straight there on finishing work and rang the doorbell of an imposing house. The door was opened by a giant of a man in a singlet, trousers and slippers, with a slice of toast in his hand. He was about fifty, with sandy hair and a gleam in his eye as he regarded me approvingly. He read the note and moved aside to invite me in. The hall and stairway was well-carpeted and spotless, very different from the entrance to where we lived.

'So the old lady sent you,' he boomed. 'Then she must like you. Diana, is it? You'd better come up and see the flat. It could be yours if you want it, girl. After you on the stairs.'

I went up ahead of him, sensing that his eyes bored into my behind, and as he was several steps behind me he was getting an eyeful. As I climbed the stairs the motion made my buttock cheeks grind and jiggle from side to side.

I was not mistaken about him enjoying the view. I'd already realised from the appraisal he'd given my tits at the door that here was a fully-paid-up lecherous type. 'You've got a fine arse on you, young woman,' he said appreciatively as we reached the landing. 'The rest of you goes with it nicely too. All this is the upstairs flat. Wander about by yourself and look it over, see what you think.'

I did so, finding it an absolute palace compared to the hovel where we presently lived. There were two bedrooms, which meant Peter could have his own; a spacious living room; an adjoining kitchen with a gas cooker and a large sink in front of a window that overlooked a lawn bordered with flowers; plus a separate bathroom and toilet. It seemed too good to be true and I was already imagining telling Harry of my wonderful find. There were good carpets throughout, plus odd pieces of furniture to add to our own bits and bobs, which meant I wouldn't have to buy any more things to fill the rooms adequately. The one fly in the ointment, I already hazarded, was going to be the leering landlord. But my husband would be there, and his scrawny little wife, so he couldn't be too obvious about his intent, could he? That was what I thought.

When I went back out to the landing he was leaning against the newel post, size fourteen slippers planted firmly apart, eyeing me expectantly. I tried not to appear too excited, but the thrill of seeing such a splendid flat and the hope that I would be granted the tenancy, was imprinted on my face. 'Like what you see, do you?' I was asked smugly. 'It is a superior place for the rent asked. I'm not a greedy man, not in all things, that is. It's impossible to get a decent flat in London now without some consideration—'

'You mean key money?' I said, willing to use some of my savings if necessary. 'I could find a reasonable amount.'

'Lord, no, I consider that a racket. There's other ways.' His voice was now hard and flat, suggestive. 'You want the flat? I said right away it could be yours.'

'Your wife implied that too,' I said to remind him. 'She told me you were careful about renting it to anybody.'

'She's nothing to do with it, the house is mine, bought and paid for. Clara is never here anyway, she's always dashing about looking for junk and running her stall. I do all the cleaning and cooking. We've lived our separate lives for years now, before I retired from the force. Let's go below and see what agreement we can come to.'

This time he led the way, showing me into a little room furnished with a roll-top desk, two armchairs and a coffee table, with one of the television sets which had just appeared on the market. 'My domain,' he announced, sitting his huge frame in a swivel chair and unlocking a drawer of the desk, bringing out a little red cardboard-covered book and tapping it on his knee. I knew what it was, of course, and I desired it as much as he desired my body. It was a rent book.

'There's a queue of folk a mile long would do anything to get this,' he said confidently as he waved the book in the air. 'Don't you think so, lass?'

I was growing to dislike him more every moment, wanting very much to tell him where he could shove his rent book. There are many such men in this world and this is a fact of life and there are also women like myself who fall prey to them. I wanted the flat very much and had met his kind before. I was certain I could handle him.

'Come out with it and say what I must do, Mr Long,' I said as calmly as I could. 'Whatever it is, do you guarantee I get the tenancy of the flat? You don't intend to interview other women I hope.'

'I doubt I'd find any as good-looking as you.' His smile was almost kindly. 'I'm a self-confessed randy man with an eye for a pretty girl. You get the picture? Do me one or two little favours and I'll do right by you and your family. The last tenant here was a young wife like you. She went with her husband and kids to Aussie and she had no complaints. Saved a bundle staying here so they could emigrate and her man didn't have a clue. I'm careful about that. So what do you think?'

'What do you want me to do?' I asked, my voice throaty at the thought of allowing him his way with me, a strange excitement creeping up from my loins. His face was set, matching mine as the atmosphere in the little room became charged with sexual electricity. I remembered Harry and how he would be made late for work for once, no doubt giving Peter his breakfast in my absence, wondering where I'd got to. It would all be worthwhile if I came home in triumph with the rent book.

'So what do you want me to do?' I repeated still in the same hoarse voice. 'I can't let you make me pregnant. Anything but that.'

'Those marvellous tits,' said Mr Long, sitting up erect on his chair. 'I'd love to see them for a start. Bring 'em out, love. You don't mind that, do you? Give me an eyeful.'

I stood before him pulling my blouse out of my skirt, not at all surprised by his request. My breasts had always been an object of admiration, heavy and full as they were, perfectly shaped and of a matching spherical size that make them nestle together tightly, the nipples thick and long when aroused. I could feel them growing as I undid my bra and bared myself under his watching eyes. I stood with shoulders drawn back to give him the full effect and heard him gasp.

'What beauties! By God you are well hung there, girl. Perfect, they are. How old are you, about twenty?' he said admiringly. 'I've never seen such a good pair of tits. Come here. Let me feel 'em.'

I stepped forward a pace or two to stand directly before him and his hands went up to cup and fondle my breasts while I tried to remain perfectly still. He had surprisingly soft hands and gentle fingers, squeezing and then hefting both tits together as if testing their weightiness, his thumbs flicking over the projecting nipples. In truth it was a most pleasurable feeling that brought a suppressed low moan from my lips. With my sensitive boobs, and the feeling of arousal I invariably got when they were fondled and my nipples touched as he was doing, what could a girl do?

'Suck them if you want to, Mr Long,' I heard myself offer. 'Would you like to do that? I don't mind.'

His lips began to suck first one and then the other, the bristles of his moustache digging into my breast flesh and exciting me. I nursed his head, finding that in his ardent sucking I was experiencing the warm flush in my sex that preceded a mounting orgasm of strength. I wanted him to continue but he pulled his head away, pleased with himself for making me so responsive. 'So you do love those big tits played with and your nipples sucked,' he stated flatly. 'Anytime, darling, anytime! Now let's see all of you. Drop your skirt and knickers for me. You can keep your stockings on if you like. I don't mind that.'

I felt annoyance at being denied the good come I'd been brought so near to experiencing. 'I can't be too long about this,' I grumbled. 'I've a husband and baby waiting for me at home.'

'This won't take a jiffy,' he said. 'There's something I like to do and you'll like it too. You're just about there, I reckon, from the moans and shifting about your arse was doing when I was sucking your tits. Strip off like I said and I'll show you.'

I stepped out of my skirt and knickers, standing before him nude but for my stockings held up by elastic garters. 'Oh yes,' he intoned lewdly, eyeing me up and down, walking around behind me and inspecting my rear. 'What a lovely little minge and a fine arse you've got, a matching set with those tits. I bet you like a bit of crude talk. So do I. I call a spade a spade. Now lie back across that table, love.'

'I said I couldn't risk getting pregnant,' I warned him, lying across the coffee table with my legs over the edge. 'You'll be careful, won't you?'

'This won't harm you, you'll love it,' he said, getting down on his knees between my legs, parting my thighs with his huge hands, his face mere inches away from my quim. 'Does your husband lick you out, girl? I'll bet you'll beg him to do it for you after this. Lift up your knees, park 'em over my shoulders if that's more comfy. Ooh, I'm going to enjoy this, going downstairs for lunch as we used to say at the nick. Lovely grub.'

I felt his tongue rasp along my outer lips, his thick moustache scratching my mound, then he went at it voraciously, tonguing and reeming every nook and cranny of my crevice. His was a rough, thick tongue, stiffened and poking at my inside almost like a prick as he worked away. His head bobbed as he heard my groans increase. My thighs writhed and my pelvis lifted to the treatment. 'More, deeper, yes, Y-E-E-S-S-S!' I cried out as I came. He sat up on his knees, grinning.

I arrived home and excitedly explained to Harry about the flat, showing him the rent book I had earned. Once he had seen the place he was delighted and we moved in the following day. Our luck had taken a definite turn for the better, I decided, even if it meant submitting to the occasional demands of the burly Mr Long. Surveying our comfortable roomy flat, who cared if he had a surreptitious grope at my tits when we passed on the stairs or felt my bottom in the hallway? I didn't. Just a week or two after moving, Harry's firm of contractors sent him to work on a large reservoir development site in the remote Highlands of Scotland, the Loch Tummell project, so that he came home only every few weeks. No matter that it was wonderful experience in his career and an increased salary, it was our first time apart.

Another piece of ill-luck was directly occasioned by this. Now I had young Peter to look after on my own I had to give up my job at the newsagents. It was no big deal perhaps, but to a thrifty Scot like myself who counted the pennies and whose favourite reading was her bank book, I gave in my notice with regret. My employer, the sexually active widow Mrs Paterson, was glad to accept it, feeling she had got rid of a threat to her love life. Regarding Wayne, the strapping Jamaican stud himself, before I left the shop for good he gave me a ticket for his ballet school's annual show. Harry had been away six weeks and the only reason I had been able to work on so long was that our landlord's wife baby-sat for me each morning before antique-hunting.

She always had a cup of tea awaiting me on my return, with Peter playing happily with his toys on the carpet. I was not in the best of moods with no husband around, my job finished, and in our general conversation I showed her the ticket.

'Go, my dear,' Mrs Long insisted at once. 'Lord knows you're stuck in your flat enough, a young girl like you. I'll baby-sit gladly. Have a night out, the ballet is lovely. Here,' she added with a gleam in her eye, 'I'll bet young Wayne never gave a ticket to old fatso who employs him. Go and have a good evening.'

I went, thinking it would break the monotony and went into the foyer to find Wayne in the milling crowd looking out for me. 'Great, I wondered if you'd come,' the handsome black boy said. 'We've never really had the chance to talk, what with the boss keeping an eye on us. And there'll be a party after the show to which I'm inviting you. Say you'll come.'

I sat through the show spellbound by the music – Tchaikovsky, Prokofiev and Gershwin among others – and the brilliance of the dancers, not least Wayne who filled his tights with a very prominent bulge at the crotch. After the finale he guided me backstage where the performance's success was toasted in lavish style in champagne donated by a wealthy patron.

It was my first night out for so long and I got quite light-headed on the drink.

'Who's your pretty friend, Wayne?' enquired one of the ballerinas. 'You've kept quiet about her, you sly boy. You must bring her to the party.' This quite made my evening and I found myself later trooping along the pavement with the dance group to a nearby house.

I might have guessed what would happen. I danced with Wayne and in the crowded room, with the lights low, found myself clinging closer, pressing my breasts to his broad chest. I felt his undeniable response in the hard bar of flesh that rose to nudge against my stomach. The champagne had made me giggly and rather wicked.

'I'll bet Mrs Paterson would go berserk if she could see us now,' I teased. 'Not that I'd blame her. I saw you in your tights tonight. It's even bigger now, isn't it? Have I done that?'

This is what is known as asking for it. He danced me out of the door, along a passageway, turning the handle of a door and guiding me into a little room with a single bed, a small wardrobe and nothing else apart from ballet posters on the walls. He put on the light as he firmly closed the door behind us. At once he took me in his powerful arms, kissing me deeply, his tongue probing my mouth.

'Undress,' he said urgently. 'I've wanted to see you without your clothes since you started in the shop. Don't say no, please.

I didn't. I stripped off my things while he stood before me doing the same. In the light his ebony frame gleamed. There was no doubt, I thought, that his dancer's body was beautiful, but most remarkable of all was the huge penis thrusting up from his groin. It reared thick and menacing, an awesome ten inches over tight balls, surrounded by crisp wiry hair, my first sight of a black man's prick.

As he came forward to kiss me, his hands on my breasts, I stumbled backwards, sitting up on the edge of the bed, at eye level with his massive erection. I reached for it spontaneously, spellbound by its size and nursed it lovingly to my breasts, kissing the bulbous head, covering it with my lips almost in a state of reverence.

It filled my mouth with its girth, taking up all the space between my tongue and palate as I sucked in inches of the great stem. Wayne stood holding my cheeks, moving his hips to fuck my mouth until he withdrew, making me cry out with the disappointment of being denied the beautiful thing in my greedy mouth.

'Lie back, Diana,' he said, 'part your thighs for me.' To hear was to obey such was my desire to get more of his splendid weapon. I fell back and opened myself shamelessly for him, knees raised and cunt presented for penetration. First he licked me wetly as if to prepare me, then hoisted my legs high so that the back of my knees rested on his broad shoulders. It was my hand that grasped the rigid stalk and directed it to my cunt. As it entered inch by inch I gasped at the fullness within me, until at last I had taken every lovely inch of it, our pubic hairs meeting and grinding together. We started fucking slowly at first, as if to savour the delightful sensation of cock in cunt. Then I matched his quickening thrusts with my back arching and my bottom lifting on his forward heaves.

'Heaven, heaven, heaven,' I repeated each time he jolted me. 'You're the first black one I've had, Wayne, and it's heaven. Keep fucking me, don't you dare come! Don't you dare come at all! Just keep fucking me, fucking me.'

'You're my first married woman,' Wayne grunted into my face, 'and my best fuck yet.' I presumed he wasn't counting a widow, thinking how Sybil Paterson must enjoy what I was getting. 'Such a lovely cunt to fuck, it's what I always wanted.'

'And such a lovely prick to fuck my cunt with,' I cried out, bucking madly in the throes of a magnificent ongoing climax, seeing for the first time that several men and women had entered the room and were standing in a circle around the bed with glasses in their hands watching the show. By then, jerking and crying out as I came in a succession of orgasms as Wayne's prick rogered me in ever-increasing thrusts, I couldn't have cared if we were performing before an audience on the stage of the ballet school. Such was my delirium I was screaming out loudly to be fucked, fucked harder, and cradling him hard to me with my thighs, legs, arms and hands, uncaring if he shot his hot load into me in my desperation for his cock.

At last he tore himself apart from me to sit up on his knees between my thighs, his magnificent prick pulling clear and rearing up as jet after jet of thick gruelly spunk flew in a high arc over my body. It fell on my chin, breasts, filled my belly button, splattered my still heaving stomach. I let out a last low groan, sated after weeks of not being brought to a climax other than by my own hand.

I was brought back to reality by the sound of applause as our strenuous exhibition was cheered and clapped. Short of breath, I could not find the effort to sit up and covered my face with my arm as if to hide. Then a warm flannel was being used to clean the spunk from my body. I looked up to see the ballerina who had praised me earlier. 'That was quite a show,' the girl smiled pleasantly. 'I know what Wayne can do to a female with that beautiful weapon of his, believe me.'

'I think I'd better go home,' was all I could think to say, knowing I had had a lucky escape with Wayne having the will to withdraw at such a hectic stage in our wild coupling. I'm sure there would have been a black child on the way for certain if he hadn't. Still dazed and tremulous from the terrific fucking I'd received, I ordered a taxi, feeling the expense worth it, as I was still weak at the knees. I arrived back at the flat, letting myself in and trying to compose my shakiness and flushed features. Mr and Mrs Long appeared in the hallway as I entered, disturbed and anxious. I felt as if I were a teenager, coming home late with my mother waiting grimly to hear my excuse. 'Am I late?' I said apologetically. 'The show went on and on. I hope I haven't kept you out of bed or that Peter was a bother.'

'Nothing like that, my dear,' Clara Long said kindly at once. 'It's your husband, he's been injured at his work.'

'His firm's London office just phoned ten minutes ago,' her husband explained. 'Evidently there was a fall or cave-in in the tunnel where he was working. He's alive, don't worry,. They got him and the others out, and your Harry is in a hospital at Inverness. There's been arrangements made by the firm for you to travel up to be with him. They're sending a car within the hour.'

I felt my knees give and Mr Long's hand steadied me. 'Help her into the lounge and give her a brandy, Dick,' I heard Clara say in my confused brain. 'Don't worry about a thing, Diana. Your Harry is a big strapping lad, he'll be up and about in no time when he sees his pretty wife at his bedside. And don't worry about Peter, either. He knows us well enough now and I'll enjoy looking after him while you are away.'

I was guided to an armchair, choking over the brandy I

was given. All I could think of was that Harry needed me and hopeful that his injuries were not too severe, remembering the Greek boy and his infirmity. Then there was a ringing of the doorbell and the car had arrived for me. I arose steadily to pack a case for the journey, determined now to face the worst.

Chapter Thirteen
THAILAND

Harry returned from his travels up-country and for two weeks we shared blissful togetherness again. The first day saw us leaving our bed only to satisfy another kind of hunger, sitting naked in the apartment kitchen while we ate to sustain our strength. We arose early the following day to watch the sunrise from the ornate Memorial Bridge, coming up like a great ball of fire as it does in the East. We crossed to Phak Klon Talad and the fresh produce market, enjoying the bustle and Thai coffee and delicious Chinese pastries for an *alfresco* breakfast. We explored the ancient Royal City, Chinatown, took boat trips on the canals, ate seafood lunches of steamed ray and roasted crabmeat with noodles. At night we dressed in evening wear and danced in the many smart clubs and fine restaurants on both sides of the Chao Phraya River and even on a cleverly converted rice barge.

We explored the temples, tried selections of Thai, Chinese and Japanese dishes, rode over the whole of Bangkok in the tuk-tuks, those bright blue and yellow three-wheeled taxis whose name comes from the sound of their two-stroke engines. We swam and had saunas and massages to combat the heat. Nights out on the town often carried on until dawn and time to enjoy the sunrise again before arriving home to fall into bed and each other's arms in a second honeymoon.

But the good times had to end and Harry left for an important U.N. conference in Singapore. I packed his case as he showered and later drove him to the airport.

'I shouldn't be away more than a week,' he said as we parked before the departures entrance. 'I've too much underway in North Thailand to spare time for this junket. There'll be the usual cocktail parties and dinners. However, delegates from all over South-East Asia will have to submit budget estimates for next year's projects. I'm going to hit them for every penny that I can squeeze out of them. There's so much I can do with it in the northern region. It's not like Bangkok up there.'

'Is Howard Wentzel going to this conference?' I asked, smiling at the thought. 'His precious Magnolia will have kittens if he leaves her so soon again. She blames you for his being away on the last trip.'

'She'll probably blame me for this too,' Harry said as a boy came to take his suitcase. 'Actually, poor Howard peed his pants when he knew he'd have to tell his missis he was leaving her again for a few days. He told me himself that life wouldn't be worth living at home. But it's his job, and he's got to go.' He curled an arm around my waist and kissed my cheek. 'I'm bloody glad you aren't like Magnolia, Di. What an awful woman. I'm sure Howard never gets the leg over *her* and he'd be too afraid to risk it with any female while she's at home.'

'Would you, Harry?' I asked sweetly.

'Why should I? You're too much for me as it is,' he joked. I squeezed his hand as if gratified. I refrained from mentioning that the maid had come to me with a single earring of the type worn by Thai women which she'd found under our bed while cleaning. She thought it was one of mine. But I understand men. I don't think having a one-night stand is grounds for a divorce.

As we entered the arrivals lounge we saw Magnolia with Howard, both of them standing sullen and silent. Nicola was there too, spotting me and giving me a sly smile. 'Good morning, Lady Saxon,' she said as a polite and properly brought-up girl should, the scheming little bitch. 'Mother and I are flying out too, we're going home to the States to visit my brother while daddy is in Singapore.' She gave Harry a beatific smile. 'Lady Saxon and I became *such* close friends while you were away. Did she tell you?'

'Nicola, it's time we went to board our flight,' her mother said sharply. 'Say goodbye to your father. Howard,' she said, tilting a cold cheek for him to kiss, 'we're off. We shall be back in two weeks. I'll give your regards to Junior when we visit the military academy and we shall stay with my mother in Atlanta if you need to contact us. Make sure the servants turn up for work when you get back from Singapore and that the apartment is spotless for my return.'

She stalked off with Nicola grinning back at us, or me in particular, I believed, to remind me of my lapse with her. Harry kissed me fondly and went through the departures barrier with Howard, leaving me on my own again. When I went outside to our car the rain was lashing the roadway, a typical tropical downpour that drenched my dress in moments. I drove off, wondering how I would spend the day alone, already missing Harry.

A policeman under a huge umbrella was on a railed dais a few streets on my way back, directing traffic to a detour around a flooded road. Moments later I was hopelessly lost and pulled up to the kerb to get my bearings from a street map. Through the sweep of my windscreen wipers I saw Madam Tan's Massage Emporium, directly across from me.

I was soaking wet and I thought, why not? Locking the car, I dodged taxis and rickshaws, entering the innocent-looking establishments with my rich rust-coloured hair plastered to my cheeks and my wet dress clinging to my figure. Talking to the receptionist at her desk was the buxom German woman, Gretel Mannlicher, whom I'd met briefly on my last visit. She recognised me immediately, her eyes lighting up. 'I've looked for you returning to us, *liebling*,' she gushed. 'Little Chi-Chi especially hoped you'd be back, the wicked creature. You did enjoy the treatment my Madam Chong and Chi-Chi gave to you, I know. They told me *all* about it.'

'I'm sure they did,' I replied coolly, 'but I'm not here for any of that today. I'm soaked, bedraggled, and would like a hot bath and *ordinary* massage, if that's possible in this place.'

'Of course, but it's such a pity,' Gretel tut-tutted. 'One of my ladies will see you to a cubicle and your clothes will be dried, pressed and ready for you when you've finished.' She rang a little brass handbell sitting on the reception desk and a handsome Chinese woman in her late twenties appeared to escort me to a cubicle. I refused her offer to join me in the shower, enjoying the tepid water streaming over my body while she sat in a chair watching, no doubt considering loss of a tip if I didn't require the special treatment available.

When I emerged dripping she arose to help me dry myself, her hands seeking my vulnerable places such as my breasts and inner thighs, murmuring in her few words of broken English how big and beautiful my tits were, and how unusual the colour of hair on my mound. Only an hour or two before I had been very satisfactorily fucked by Harry and, getting up on the massage table, decided that with him hardly in the air

I could resist temptation for that day at least. It seemed only fair.

So I gritted my teeth and tensed my body as the masseuse stroked, rubbed and worked expert fingers over my prone form, and that in itself was a pleasant experience. I willed myself not to give in to the feelings of arousal her hands generated as she massaged my breasts. It was pure pain/pleasure as I fought not to emit low moans, to urge her to do as she wished with me, even shaking my head when she undid the overall to bring out firm pear-shaped breasts presenting her inch-long sharply pointed nipples to my lips. I turned over for her and she gave my bottom a series of hard smacks as if to make me more compliant and finally, when I was on my back again, the massage completed, she darted her head between my parted thighs and fastened her mouth to my cunt. I pushed her away as firmly yet gently as I could, thanking her but refusing her attentions. My clothes were returned dried and beautifully ironed, and I gave a tip to both the masseuse and the laundry woman as I left, feeling pleased with myself for resisting but also feeling amazingly randy.

In the passageway I met Gretel Mannlicher, who was with an unusually tall and powerfully built Thai in grey military shirt festooned with badges and rows of medal ribbons. He doffed his peaked cap to me and was introduced as Colonel San-joi, head of the Bangkok vice squad, which I refrained from saying must be about the most unnecessary job in the world. His clasp of my hand remained long enough to tell me, along with the look in his almond-shaped eyes, that he considered me a most desirable fuck.

I resisted Gretel's offer to take tea and sweet noodle cakes in her private lounge, not knowing what that would lead to. She walked me to the front door, her ample arm encircling my waist. It had stopped raining and I said I had other engagements just to get away from her.

'Don't make it so long before you come back, *liebchen*,' Gretel said, taking my hand. 'You know I came here as a tourist after I was widowed and I fell in love with Bangkok. It is *the* wickedest most delightful city on earth. A beautiful woman like you could do very well for herself here. For instance Colonel San-joi took an instant fancy to you and he's a powerful man, he could open many important doors while you are here. Since I bought this place he has been a good friend of mine. With me guiding you, I could arrange many opportunities to our mutual advantage.'

'You mean you'd be my pimp,' I said with a laugh. 'Good try, but I'm not taking you up on it. I don't think my husband would agree.'

'A great pity,' she laughed with me. 'Husbands can be funny about such things. We shall remain friends. Would you give me your name?'

'Magnolia,' I said in a sudden flash of inspiration. 'Maggie for short. That's all I'm telling you.' I went back to my car, passing by chance The Cup restaurant in Peninsula Plaza. I'd dined there with Harry and found it very elegant, with the finest Continental quisine, and I decided to treat myself to lunch. Then I spent the afternoon sight-seeing at The Marble Wat, with its community of saffron-robed monks and visited Vimarn Mek, the world's largest golden teak palace. Yet despite these distractions my mind wandered back to the Chinese masseuse and her determined attempt at pleasuring me. It had left me maddeningly aroused, so much so that I considered retracing my steps to let her finish the job. What stopped me was that I did not care to get too involved with Gretel Mannlicher. She had plans for me, I felt, which might even include kidnapping and being kept as a sex-slave. Well, this *was* Bangkok.

Later I swam in the apartment building's private pool, having it all to myself as the tropical storm resumed and heavy rain lashed down to dapple the pool's surface. I did not want to go back to my empty apartment, not after the happy time I had spent there with Harry. When I did force myself to go up in the lift it was dusk. I showered and wrapped myself in a towelling dressing gown as the night was chill. I decided I would have a nightcap and settle for my lonely bed, certain I'd relieve my loneliness and the lingering arousal I felt with a spot of self-relief. For old times sake I would bunch the pillows between my thighs and grind my crotch into them, a sure-fire method of obtaining a good come when allied to a favourite fantasy.

Often this was one that had stood me in good stead since I was a girl, of being out for a walk in the Scottish countryside and passing a group of workmen digging a ditch. After making coarse remarks about my breasts and bottom, they'd lead me behind the hedge and undress me, then all of them would have me in turn. An added touch to this scenario was that, after fucking me singly and together, I was left naked when they drove off with my clothes. Rescued by a passing motorist, he too would insist upon screwing me.

When I went to the front door before retiring to make sure all was secure, I thought I heard a noise in the hallway, a sound not unlike a person sobbing in distress. The safety-chain was in place so I opened the door as far as it allowed, peering out to see a figure huddled in the doorway of the Wentzels' apartment. It was a youth in a soaked sweatshirt and jeans, his hair cut to stubble, a picture of misery in his cold damp state as his shoulders heaved. He looked up with scared eyes as I opened my door and approached.

There was something very familiar about his face as he sprang to his feet. 'Who are you and what are you doing here, son?' I asked kindly. 'The Wentzel family are away and their apartment locked up. By the look of you I'd say you are their boy, Howard. Your mother left just this morning to visit you. Aren't you supposed to be at some military school in Carolina?'

'I couldn't stand it any more,' he blubbered. 'It was awful, ma'am, drills, bullying, shouting at us new guys all the time. The senior cadets are the biggest sadists of all. I had to get away. I didn't know my mother was coming to visit. She'll kill me for this, I know.'

He was wringing his hands in his utter dejection, shivering like a whipped pup. It brought out the mothering instinct in me. All the same I could imagine his terror at his mother's wrath when she found out he'd bolted from school and hopped a plane to Bangkok. It was Harry's dressing gown I was wearing and I found a large handkerchief in one of the deep pockets and handed it to him.

'Dry your eyes now,' I said, 'your mother will certainly not kill you and it's not the end of the world. You're a big boy, so cheer up and act like one. First we'd better get you out of those wet things, then you can use my shower. And I expect you'll feel better with something hot to eat. You'd better come in, you certainly can't sit in this hall all night.'

He followed me dutifully, stopping his sniffles and accepting that help was at hand. I gave him a large towel, showed him the bathroom, then left him to it and went to the kitchen to make him scrambled eggs, bacon and coffee. It occurred to me that he couldn't get back into a wet sweatshirt and jeans, which was all he wore apart from socks and shoes. I changed Harry's dressing gown for one of my own, deciding that the male garment would be more suitable for him. I knocked on the bathroom door and enquired if I could enter. On hearing a sort of muffled reply I went in and handed over the dressing gown and collected his wet clothes. He stood naked, towelling himself, his clean white body athletically formed and youthful.

'Put on this gown,' I told him. 'I've made you something to eat in the kitchen. After that you can sleep in the spare bedroom. I'm sure things won't seem so bad in the morning.'

He ate ravenously while I questioned him. There were people I felt should be contacted about his whereabouts. With the telephone numbers he'd given me, promising he wouldn't have to talk to his mother as I'd tell her he was asleep, I showed him in the spare bedroom and wished him goodnight. I called Atlanta, where Magnolia was staying with her mother and got no reply. Then I got through to the military academy, telling a female receptionist why I was calling and being put through to a Major Calvin Gruber, United States Army Retired, principal of the Carolina Military Academy for Boys, as he announced crisply. When I explained why I was calling, his tone changed.

'You can tell that little bastard there's no place in this fine establishment for his kind,' I was informed sternly. 'He has goofed off from the day he got here, been sloppy in his uniform dress and a bad influence all round. Madam, if I never see nor hear of that corrupt little wimp again it would be too soon. You get the message, we don't want *him* back.'

'He had some choice things to say about your place too, Major,' I said, enjoying the chance to get in on the act. 'He said it was a prison run by sadistic morons and it sounds to me as if he was right. What did he do there – refuse to salute you?'

'You really want to know?' I heard Major Gruber spit out. 'He besmirched the good name of the academy having *sexual relations* with my best staff instructor's wife! I don't need to tell you that *she* has been banished. Wentzel got the hell out just in time before he was tarred and feathered. I think this conversation should end here before I really say what I think of him!'

I replaced the receiver and reassessed my opinion of Howard junior, now hopefully sleeping, his worries over until morning. How the haughty and forbidding Magnolia would take to learning of her son's sexual liaison with a married woman made me smile, giggle, and finally burst into laughter. I poured myself a large vodka, thinking back on a day replete with surprising events. Before bed, I cleared the dishes and washed up, washed Howard's clothes and hung them out ready to iron in the morning. Then I sat thinking again about the day's events with much amusement while having two more vodkas. After that I went through to go to bed. I'd figure out what I'd do about my unexpected guest tomorrow.

In the passageway outside his bedroom door I paused and heard the sound of heartfelt sobbing, interspersed with anguished moans as if all the worries and troubles of the world had descended on his young shoulders. I knocked softly, putting my head around the door to enquire whether he would like a hot drink to help him sleep? He sat up, switching on the bedside lamp, his young chest smooth and hairless.

'Sit with me for a while, please,' he begged, holding out a hand for me to take. 'I'm in the most terrible trouble, and you've been so kind to me. I – I – just don't want to be alone right now—'

According to the incensed Major Gruber, Howard's terrible trouble had been of his own making, but boys will be boys. He looked so forlorn and dejected, with his eyes and nose pink from blubbering, that I accepted his hand, sitting up on the bed beside him. Harry's handkerchief lay on the bedcover, so I dried his tears like a sympathetic mother. 'Now, now,' I clucked. 'Such a handsome young face to spoil with all that crying. One day you'll look back on this episode and laugh about it, as I do about some of the awful scrapes I got into as a girl.'

'You?' he said, trying to stifle his sobs and heaving shoulders. 'You must be Lady Saxon, the neighbour my sister Nicola wrote to me about.'

'I'm sure she did,' I said, wondering just what the scheming little minx had written about me. 'Lady Saxon is a bit of a mouthful, you can call me Diana. What is it that worries you most? That you ran away from school or what your mother will do?'

Mention of the malevolent Magnolia brought an immediate cry of terror and a resumption of his miserable sobs. It seemed so genuine that as he leaned towards me I took him in my arms, holding him to me, patting his back to comfort him. With a sense of shock I felt his face burrow into the divide of my dressing gown, parting it to the waist with his nose and mouth buried between my breasts, his breath warm in the snug depth of my ample bosom.

'I don't think you should, Howard,' I began hesitantly. '*No*, you must not! Oh, oh, what are you doing *now*, you wicked boy?' His lips had fastened to my left nipple, sucking at it greedily while he made little sounds of comfort at my breast.

'*Please*, please let me,' he moaned pitifully, my treacherous nipple growing tight and stretching, a thin string of his saliva bridging from its tip to his lips as he paused in his avid suckling to beg me: 'It feels so *nice*, Lady Saxon. Just for a while, please! It does make me feel better.'

I'll just bet it did, I thought grimly, and his going on to suck my other nipple, without my say-so but not with much resistance on my part, I confess, was beginning to feel more than nice to *me* on the receiving end. Strong arousal surged through my loins, my breasts swelled as he drew in each bub in turn with his suction. Giving up the contest, I nursed him, muttering little comforting noises as I held his head, cupped each breast in turn and fed my nipples to his eager lips. Almost on the point of no return, my thighs grinding together, I discerned he was trying to draw me into the bed with him.

'Oh, no you don't!' I said sternly, finding the will to untangle myself from his embrace. 'This has gone too far. Settle down and sleep, boy!'

I hurriedly fled to my own bedroom, throwing off my dressing gown and getting into bed trembling. That I had wanted to continue the seduction was more than apparent from my greatly aroused state, and the feel of the cool silk sheet moulded to my hot body only increased my agitation. But not with that boy, I told myself sternly, putting out my bedlamp and rolling over, knowing sleep was impossible with my mind racing, thinking of his mouth on my tits. Then he was beside my bed, Harry's dressing gown hanging from his frame several sizes too large. Without turning my head I demanded to know what he wanted now, my voice hoarse.

'Do let me come to your bed,' he said, almost a plaintive whine. 'My pillows and sheet are wet from crying.'

Ten out of ten for trying, I had to admit. 'I'll get you fresh ones,' I said. 'Go to your room and wait for me.'

'I'm sure I could sleep now,' he pleaded. 'With company. I won't disturb you, Lady Saxon. I'll lie on my own side, honest.'

Lie was what I was sure the persistent boy was doing, yet I weakened. He had undoubtedly been through a deal of stress, fleeing his school and finding his parents away. 'Get in then,' I said tersely. 'Let's get some rest. On your own side of the bed, mind you. I'd be in as much trouble with your mother as you are if she knew about this.'

'She never will,' Howard said and I thought I heard a note of triumph in his young voice. It struck me forcibly, too, that I was sleeping nude. I moved away to the far edge of the bed with my back turned to him as I felt his weight on the mattress. The storm had continued and I heard heavy rain drumming down, a soothing sound, and in time, hearing his regular breathing in the darkened room, I fell asleep and dreamed my husband was beside me. It seemed so real, his breath on my neck as he leaned over me, soft kisses on my neck, then a gently exploring hand smoothing over my buttock cheeks, trailing up my back. In the position in which I slept, on my side facing away, the hand sneaked under my outstretched arm to gently fumble at my breast and squeeze it lightly, as if gauging its shape and mass, touching the responsive nipple.

In half-sleep by then, I must have sighed and murmured something, turning on my back and wanting the tender foreplay to continue. The roving hand went down over my stomach, barely touching until stroking fingertips played among the growth of hair on my *mons*, the prominent split mound of my sex, already throbbing in anticipation of a finger pleasuring it, lubricating for ease of penetration.

With heightening arousal came some awareness. In a muddled mind, fresh from deep sleep and now wantonly active in the sexual area of my brain, I recalled with shock that Harry was away. One finger, then two, was slipped inside me, titillating the excitable nerve ends of my cunt folds and clitty. I moaned pleasure, stretching my legs and widening them, taking the wrist of the hand that so gently worked at me as if afraid of disturbing my sleep and making it move faster. I wondered if I could still feign sleep, deciding that was impossible with my pelvis writhing and bottom lifting, hearing the boy beside me quicken his breath, feeling the rigid stalk of his erection pressed to my hip.

'Oh, Lord, yes,' I moaned, a gone goose as he had his way with me in the wee small hours. 'It's you, isn't it, Howard? Oh, you shouldn't but – do you like that? It's wrong, but it's *so* g-o-o-o-d-d—'

'Yes, oh yes, Lady Saxon,' Howard agreed in a voice as tremulous as my own. His probing fingers had my back arching, cunt tilting, having me on the very edge of a climax. I fought to hold back, not wishing the intense pleasure to stop. 'I'm so stiff doing this, it's bursting. Please let me, I want you so much! I want to fuck you—'

My lips crushed to his, our tongues meeting, my hand grasping a stiff bar of flesh at his crotch. Even as he made to get between my legs I was pulling him across me for the same purpose. 'Then fuck me!' I cried deliriously. 'I want it too. Take your time and fuck me properly. Make it last, sweetheart. Make me come for you. Oh yes, I want it so badly. I want your nice hard prick deep up my cunt to make me come.' Such crudities came naturally as I eagerly directed his young prick to me, groaning with relief as it entered.

If I considered myself the older, more experienced head, it soon became evident that, once in the saddle, Howard was no novice at pleasuring the opposite sex, whether girls of his own age or older females like myself or the instructor's wife. No doubt she had capitulated to his wiles as I had. He almost leered down upon me, thrusting in and then withdrawing, making me cry out for more, going fast then easing up to have me implore him to keep it up, fuck me harder. I had several strong orgasms of the kind that drives sanity from one's mind, humping to his heaving flanks, using my arms and legs to keep him belly to belly with me. I kept muttering how good it was, heaven, what a lovely fucker he was, as yet another climax wracked me in spasms, saying that he could fuck me any time he wished. These vocal admissions pleased him no end.

'I love to make women come,' he said lewdly in a hard voice very different from his earlier whines, which made me think that his tears and abject misery had been mainly to soften me up. 'The woman at the academy,' he told me with boastful delight, 'never had a climax with her husband. I certainly made her come – plenty! Just like you!' I cringed even as I thrust back at the little sod, realising that Major Gruber's assessment of his runaway pupil was generous. But who cared right now as his dick made me wild for more, throwing myself up to match his inward shunting, wanting it to continue until I heard him gasp and jerk violently, emptying his load into me.

'That was as good as any I've had,' the cheeky devil declared. 'How was it for you? I'll bet your husband doesn't screw you so good.'

It was then for me to tell him, as I'm certain older women who have misbehaved with adolescents have done since the dawn of time, that no one, but *no one*, must ever know what had happened between us that night. He agreed too nonchalantly for my liking, saying, 'Sure, sure, of course I won't let it get out,' while trying to fondle my breasts again. I hoped that Harry or Magnolia didn't get to hear of it, certain that when he was in his next school he would regale the other boys with a full account of the older woman he had fucked so successfully in Thailand. I ordered him away to his own side of the bed but, with dawn lightening the curtain, I felt his hand sidle between the cleft of my bum as I lay turned away from him. He had been there, as they say, so I let him continue, thinking what had I to lose? He climbed over me after playing with my cunt, and hard as ever, took me from the rear with my face in the pillows until I was made to come.

It was while I was giving him his breakfast later that the phone rang. 'Magnolia Bouverie Wentzel here, Lady Saxon,' came the annoyed voice, making me fear the worst for her son. 'Howard junior is with you, I've discovered, by a roundabout way incidentally, through my visit to his previous school. You might have told me.'

'Just a minute,' I said, deciding to take no nonsense. 'I took your boy in, got your telephone number in Atlanta and received no reply. Then I called his school and spoke to a Major Gruber. Meanwhile your son has been given a bed, fed and looked after.' I did not care to say just how well. 'He's here now having breakfast and I was about to call you again.'

'I want him back here with me,' his mother said, not deigning to thank me. 'There's a flight from Bangkok today and I've arranged his ticket. Eleven o'clock this morning, Thai time. You will see that he is put safely on the aircraft. I want him here with me.'

'Don't be too hard on the boy, Magnolia,' I said. 'It seems that school of his is an awful place.'

'I'm glad he's left there and I attach no blame to his running away,' she said surprisingly. 'I think Howard junior did the right thing and acted bravely. You tell him that to put his mind at rest. I've now met that moron Major Gruber who is head of the so-called academy. Poor Howard, you'll never guess what that uncouth man accused him of.'

'Do you care to tell me?' I asked, tongue in cheek.

'That my son, *my* son, had been having some sort of sexual affair with a married woman, the wife of a member of the school staff. It is quite unthinkable, don't you agree? Howard junior is not like that.'

'Of course he's not,' I agreed, looking across to the kitchen table and receiving a suggestive wink from the boy in question. After all, what else could I say?

Chapter Fourteen
SCOTLAND

My concern about Harry's accident, the shock and the energy
I'd expended having such hectic sex with Wayne had drained
me and I could not stay awake on the drive north. I sat beside
the driver, who had introduced himself as Charles Groves,
the managing director of my husband's firm, trying hard to
keep my eyes open. The Humber limousine was warm,
comfortable and quiet. As it ate up the miles through the
night I nodded off frequently, forcing myself awake each
time he addressed me.

'The latest report is that things might have been much
worse,' Charles Groves said in a kind cultured voice. 'It
seems Harry has been banged up a bit but he's made of stern
stuff. He's one of our best site managers, by the way. We've
great expectations of him. Gained useful experience as a
major in the Royal Engineers during the war, I've been told.'

At last he got the message, pulling over into a lay-by. I
came slowly to awareness, blinking heavy-laden eyes and
sitting up straight as he patted my knee with his soft well-
manicured hand.

'Into the back seat with you and stretch out,' he ordered
firmly yet courteously as he reached across to open the door
beside me. 'There's a travelling rug to cover yourself with,

my dear. I have a thermos and packed food; perhaps you'd like a coffee or a sandwich? There's brandy too, if you feel like something stronger.' He produced a silver flask and poured a measure into the cup. I drank it gratefully and lay on the long rear seat, something I'd done in a Humber before when about to get screwed.

Charles Groves was obviously a gentleman. He made sure I was tucked up in the thick tartan rug and told me not to worry but to sleep soundly. It was grey daylight when I awoke, sitting up as the roadside verge flashed by and the big car sped on.

'Good morning, young lady,' he said affably, turning his head and smiling. 'We're well into bonnie Scotland now. You've slept well too, the best thing for you. I'm stopping at the first reasonable hotel we pass, to get a good breakfast in you and let you freshen up your pretty face.'

But Harry lying injured in hospital was the only thing on my mind as sleep left me. 'I'd prefer that we went on to Inverness,' I said.

'As you wish,' he responded. 'But I've booked rooms at the Highland Glen Hotel and I shall take you there first. Your husband will be heavily sedated, he won't be sitting up awaiting your arrival, you know. We'll have lunch to give you the strength to visit him – you can't go on an empty stomach. Then you can bathe and change and look your best for him. I didn't know Harry had such a lovely young wife. He's a lucky fellow.'

He turned his handsome head again and I decided he was a man like all others, not averse to trying it on. I smiled back, thinking I was probably wrong in my assessment and he was merely being nice to me. He was a well-fed, elegant male in his middle-forties, at ease with the world and confident in his executive position in life. I asked why he was driving me? 'I mean, one of your firm's drivers would be more usual, wouldn't it?' I said. 'Though I do appreciate it.'

'I was due to go up to look over the scheme,' he admitted, 'and when this emergency occurred I was happy to do my bit. Leave everything to me, you'll see Harry soon.'

The hotel was luxurious beyond my experience for those days. In my en-suite room with its huge bed, thick tartan carpets and matching curtains, overlooking a breathtaking view, I wished I could have been there in happier circumstances. I used the telephone to call the Long household, hearing Clara tell me that young Peter was enjoying the change, that he was then in the park with her husband and that the following day they were taking him to the seaside at Clacton. After lunch I changed into my best dress and was then driven to the nearby Cottage Hospital. I saw Harry swathed in head bandages, getting a bright smile from him as I squeezed his hand. Then he was trolleyed off to the operating theatre for treatment to a broken leg, ankle, crushed ribs and various cuts and bruises.

I awaited his return until evening but he was still unconscious from the operation and I was told he'd be that way until morning. 'So you can come back then, lassie,' I was told by the gruff Scottish surgeon. 'No use you getting in the way. Your man will be fine, good as new in time, so dinna worry. Go and get a good nicht's sleep and come back and hold his hand in the morning. Tell him I told you he'll be making a full recovery. The sicht of you will be his best medicine.'

I was cheered considerably, knowing Harry would get better and that Peter was being well looked after. So I was happy to agree when Charles Groves telephoned to ask if I would join him at dinner. I found him in the dining room wearing a beautifully cut lounge suit with a whisky glass in his hand. He rose from the table to greet me. 'Do you feel better now?' he asked. 'I spoke to your husband's surgeon myself. He's a strange old coot, but obviously the best in his profession. He swore he'd attended lots worse cases successfully, so now you can relax and enjoy this evening. I've ordered champagne to toast Harry's health.'

'You've been very kind,' I began sincerely.

'Nonsense, I'm the privileged one, sitting here with the most lovely girl in this hotel,' he said. I raised my glass to him, not sure I should appear so friendly, but I was never one who considered that moping and being miserable made things better. If I was to enjoy a nice dinner with wine and a suave and handsome companion, would that be so treacherous to Harry in his unconscious state? Definitely not, in my opinion. There had been enough Monday mornings, wet-washing days, and scrimping and saving over the past few years. Besides, Harry would be the first one to say, enjoy yourself to the full. So I let Charles Groves refill my glass and tucked into a splendid dinner in the relaxing atmosphere of the fine old hotel. In the background a pianist played the romantic tunes of that era, waiters circulated unobtrusively, and it was all very luxurious. Replete with smoked salmon, pheasant, chocolate gateaux and too much wine, I couldn't prevent giving a loud hiccup which turned heads.

I excused myself, feeling dreadfully embarrassed and fled to the ladies' room to splash water on my face, seeing my image rather blearily in the mirror over the basin. I forced myself to straighten up and walk sedately back to the dining room. I was about to negotiate the tall screen set directly behind our table when I heard voices and paused.

'I've been sitting across from you during dinner thinking about your lady companion's tits, Charles,' a man said in a refined voice.

'A noble thought, Jeremy,' I heard him reply, 'but I saw her first. She's a real beauty, isn't she?'

'Positively the essence,' the man he'd called Jeremy agreed. 'I couldn't keep my eyes off her – or *them*! What a gorgeous pair of ripe bouncers. Who is she? Model, actress? I suppose you intend to make free with those magnificent mammaries later on, you lucky dog.'

'She's the wife of one of my employees,' Charles replied.

'Since when has that stopped you from rogering them?' I heard laughed. 'Personal assistants, secretaries, wives, but I must say she is the best yet. I envy you. I love the hint of tight cleavage revealed by her dress. It let's one imagine the treasures within. I say, you wouldn't like to introduce me, would you?'

'No,' Charles said flatly. 'So toodle off before she returns. I have no intention of trying to seduce the girl.'

In my tipsy state I didn't know whether to find that complimentary or not, waiting behind the screen for the man to leave. 'I don't believe you,' Jeremy said. 'Since your divorce everything has been fair game. You don't seem heartbroken that dear Vanessa walked out on you.'

'Why should I? She got herself fucked by half the Chelsea set and by you too I suspect,' Charles said calmly. 'I didn't mind that so much. What got to me was her bitching, accusing *me* of playing around. I wasn't then, so I've made up for it. I paid her plenty to leave.'

'Always the generous Charlie,' agreed the man. 'You were too kind to her. I admire you for that. Well, I'm off. Good hunting.'

I waited a few moments, as much to compose myself as allow the man to leave. 'I think I should go to my room,' I said. 'This has all been a bit much.'

Charles nodded, leaving his coffee to escort me from the

dining room, which by then was circling slowly around my head. In my room he led me to my bed, standing back as I collapsed across it, and tried to focus my eyes on the chandelier above as it appeared to go around with the room. I giggled, feeling wanton and silly. 'Do *you* think my breasts are gorgeous ripe bouncers?' I teased him.

'You heard that idiot Jeremy,' Charles said, looking down upon my prone form. 'Take no notice of him.'

'But do you think so?' I insisted mischievously.

'If you press me, yes. Your breasts are spectacular, as is your figure. I wouldn't be a normal man if I hadn't noticed. Now, are you all right? I think you'd better sleep it off.'

'Then you'll have to undress me, I feel as weak as a kitten,' I slurred. 'Is it awful to ask that, Charlie? I really don't think I could struggle out of my clothes.'

'If you are trying to seduce me, young lady,' he said, 'you would regret it in the morning, I think. Is all this because you are not used to being tiddly and in a hotel room with a man? Or because you wish to take your mind off your husband's injuries? A psychiatrist might say that.' He gave a short laugh. 'He could be right. The way they think it might be the appropriate therapy in such a case. Do you really want me to undress you?'

'I don't think I could manage it by myself,' I said feebly.

'Let's have you then,' he stated boldly, sitting me up and feeling for the zip at the back of my dress. He drew it off over my coiled auburn hair, making the tresses fall to my shoulders, pausing to stare momentarily at my overfilled brassiere. I struggled to unclip it myself, throwing the bra carelessly aside, shaking my liberated tits, enjoying the release from confinement.

'God!' I heard Charles exclaim softly. 'How they wobble so beautifully when you do that.' I fell back on the bed again while he rolled down my stockings and draped them over a chair with my dress. I looked down between my uplifted tits, seeing him on his knees between my parted legs as they hung over the edge of the bed. All that remained on me were my brief panties.

'These too,' I told him dreamily, aroused now in that semi-inebriated state that makes one so lazily uncaring and uninhibited.

'My pleasure,' I heard quietly as if from a distance. I craned my neck to watch, straining to lift my bottom as he eased them down my thighs and lifted them free of my feet. His head was steady and his eyes level an inch or so away from my cunt mound with its bush of chestnut hair.

'You are indeed the most delightful creature I've ever seen,' he muttered as he began to kiss my split bulge over and over. I sighed loudly, my head heavy as it fell back on the bed, half-asleep but loving what he was doing to me, awaiting the entry of his tongue.

'Go on, go on,' I urged him in a trance-like murmur. 'Do you like it? *I* like it. It's very naughty of me, but *so* nice. Oh, oh, I don't want you to stop – what would my poor husband think if he knew what we were doing? Poor Harry!'

'You make sure you never tell him,' Charles said sternly. 'I'm beyond stopping now even if he walked into this room which, thank God, he can't.' His long tongue slid up me, lapping my juices. It was warm and slippery, its tip seeking my clitoris and then flicking rapidly against its stiffening nub, making me squirm with the pleasure. In my fuddled state I just lay back letting him do as he will, knowing I was in the hands of an expert.

Almost at the point of climax, I held off the urge, and bathed in a warm glow throughout my cunt and lower belly. I wanted it to continue longer. Then I gave a soft moan of complaint as his tongue left me. I tensed, waiting to feel his slow lascivious licking at my greedy source again. I heard a plaintive plea escape my lips, but his tongue travelled up, wetting my mound, kissing my belly and probing my navel. 'Mmm,' I muttered as first one nipple and then the other was washed by his busy tongue. My breasts were cupped tight in strong hands as his mouth descended.

My excitement was so intense that I felt my tits swell and my nipples stiffen. 'Yes, do, suck my tits and suck them hard,' I begged him. 'Suck them deep into your mouth, as hard as you like.'

He teased me, ceasing to suck and roaming his tongue over the rounded globes of tight flesh, lapping into my cleavage, at times on the point of going back to my aching nipples, tormenting me by moving on until at last I shamelessly grasped his head.

'Suck, suck,' I pleaded. '*Please*.' I needed the return of his mouth to continue the pulsating messages his sucking sent down to my throbbing cunt. 'Oh, please do it to me.'

'How you love those lovely big tits played with,' I heard Charles say, but he did as I begged, suctioning both nipples in turn eagerly, sucking hard and greedily the way I like it. Hot ripples surged through my stomach, into the very depths of my womb, taking me to the verge of an exploding orgasm. My cunt felt so juicy and soaking, it tingled, and my outer lips pouted, yearning to be strenuously fucked and filled. Then the bulbous head of a thickly stiff prick nudged an entrance past the swollen labia, the ultra-satisfying girth sliding in to fill me right up. I curled my arms and legs around his body, feeling the roughness of his suit against my skin, pulling him as close as I could, my hands hauling at his buttocks.

My cunt felt marvellously stretched and he drove into me

harder and faster, making slurping, squelching sounds as he thrust. I felt my first climax reach its peak, screaming out that he was making me *come, come, come*, the spasms welling into several other orgasms that shook and shuddered through me.

'Keep fucking, keep fucking!' I implored him, speared to the hilt and throwing up my bottom from the bed to get even more inside me. Then he too was groaning, his flanks heaving faster, jerking out of all control as he flooded me.

The full impact of what we had done hit me even as I recovered. I realised that I had not only encouraged sex with Harry's employer but, the biggest lapse of all, I had allowed him to go all the way – shooting his sperm up me and risking impregnation. I did not speak, but lay with my arm across my face, and heard Charles leave the room.

I went down to breakfast after a disturbed night. But what had happened had happened and, as ever, I accepted the sequence of events. The sex itself I felt no guilt about, we were simply two randy individuals who had been unable to resist each other. I've always considered that excusable. But it was another matter if I became pregnant. I'd bathed and washed thoroughly after Charles had left my bedroom. Now I found the breakfast table laid for one and the waiter told me Mr Groves had left early. He's getting out fast, I thought, but later at the reception desk I was informed a taxi had been laid on for me to visit the hospital and I was handed a fat envelope by the receptionist.

I ordered coffee in the conservatory and, with no one near, opened the envelope. 'Dear Diana,' I read the flowing writing. 'It's best that we do not see each other again for I should surely want to continue our relationship more meaningfully. I truly mean this, you are a sweet girl and I'm already too fond of you. Don't be offended by the money I enclose, it's for your expenses while you are here with your husband. Also, your hotel expenses during that period, no matter how long, and taxi fares incurred, have been taken care of by an arrangement of mine with the hotel accountant. I'm sure Harry will make a full recovery with you here. My very best wishes for your future. Sincerely, Charles.'

I counted ten crisp notes in my hand, amounting to a hundred pounds, and slipped them into my handbag like a thief, in case others were watching me. I tore the letter up into small pieces and considered the episode over as far as Charles Groves was concerned. If I had his baby he would never know of it.

At the hospital I found Harry looking considerably the worse for wear with his bandaged head, bruised chest, and one leg almost fully encased in plaster to his thigh. A nurse in the corridor had told me he was remarkably cheerful and had eaten a full breakfast of porridge and bacon and eggs. When I bent to kiss him he grabbed me for a long open-mouthed passionate one, even if the contact made him grimace in pain.

'There's not much wrong with you,' I laughed, disentangling myself from his clutches. 'Private room, breakfast in bed, pretty nurses to chat up. I was so worried about you, my love—'

'No need,' Harry declared. 'This Cottage Hospital is a regular four-star hotel, I'll be sorry to leave it. That is as long as you are here, Di.' His nearside hand went to my breasts as I sat on the chair at his bedside. 'As good as ever,' he said seriously. 'The best boobs anywhere. I've been dying for a feel at them.'

'You're supposed to rest quietly,' I teased him. 'Don't tell me you feel like that.'

'I'm as randy as hell, thinking about you, love,' he

chuckled. 'Lift the sheet, see what I've got. No pyjama trousers with a plastered leg, just me. Take a gander.'

I lifted the white cotton sheet and saw that Harry had a superb erection. I giggled and covered it quickly. 'There's nothing wrong with that,' I had to say. 'It's beautiful.'

'Then do something about it, Di,' he said seriously. 'I woke up with a massive hard-on this morning and it won't go away. Lock the door if you're worried, love. Don't you want to as much as me?' He watched happily as I went to lock the door, pulling back the sheet again to reveal his upstanding prick. 'Oh, darling, I've missed you these few weeks.'

'It hasn't been easy for me either,' I said, and what kind of a fool would I have been to say otherwise? 'I think it's time we did something about *that*,' I said officiously. 'The patient's prick has been out of use for six week, so he says but I don't believe it, and obviously it can't remain in its rigid state.' I took the swollen stalk lightly between my finger and thumb as if testing its pulse. 'It has a temperature, I'd say. Does the head ache, is the whole length painfully hard?'

'Oh, yes, nurse,' Harry grinned. 'What treatment do you suggest? Put it somewhere cool, like between your tits or in your mouth.'

'Why not both?' I laughed, 'and I'll do the prescribing here, thank you. But if that's what you want—' I said, starting to unbutton my blouse, 'What if someone knocks at the door?'

'I'll shout go away, I'm fucking my wife,' he said merrily. 'It comes under patient therapy.'

'Could you manage that?' I said thoughtfully, my blouse and bra discarded and my breasts swinging over his mouth. I was remembering Charles filling me with his sperm. 'I mean *fuck* me, Harry? Really fuck me in your condition?'

'My condition is a dirty great hard-on bursting for relief,' he joked. 'Of course I could fuck you, Di. You'd have to squat over it and do all the work, but I'd be fucking you, wouldn't I? Now that we've mentioned it, I think it's worth a try. You must be quite eager for a shag, my love, after six weeks' separation.' He nuzzled my breasts with his face, tried to catch the nipples in his lips. 'Let's do it, shall we? I've never needed a good fuck more.'

'I thought you'd never ask me,' I teased him. 'Of course I'm ready for a going over, I need a real good come from a real good prick.' I stepped out of my skirt and panties, even peeling off my gartered stockings, and offered myself naked to him. 'If anyone wants in now they have had it,' I declared. 'This is husband and wife stuff, nobody else's business.' I nursed his upright tool between my cleavage, giving it a little fond hug, then lowered my mouth over it and sucked gently for a few moments. Harry gave a moan of pleasure, then of pain as I leaned on his chest.

'Never mind me,' he ordered. 'Just keep sucking! This must beat the hell out of grapes or orange juice. Get up on the bed, Di, squat over my belly and guide it in. Jesus, I'm about ready to burst. Let me feel my dick up you.'

I got over him carefully, excited, my knees pressed into the mattress either side of his waist. His prick was hot and hard in my grasp as I directed it to my crotch, entering the plum head and easing down on several thick inches of it. After a few jiggles, making sure I was not hurting him, taking his stifled groans for pleasure, I pushed down with my pelvis feeling every inch filling me wall to wall and back to the farthest recess. 'How does that grab you, my love?' I said in a croak, loving every inch of his cock inside me. 'Isn't it just heaven?'

'Bloody marvellous,' he agreed, reaching up to clasp my swinging breasts. His groans were a mix of pleasure and pain as I ground down on his weapon, gyrating my hips and arse, getting the surge of an impending climax in the acute pulsing and throbbing in my cunt. 'Go on, go on!' Harry said gallantly, suffering I was sure but too lost in the wild lustful fucking to want me to ease the pace.

'God, it's great to be up your lovely cunt again, Di,' I heard him say as my neck and head tilted back and strange garbled sounds issued from my throat in my excitement. Impaled to his balls, my greedy cunt gripped at his stalk like a vice as I made it shunt within me. Then his hands were at my outer thighs as if about to lift me. 'I'm going to COME, Diana!' he shouted in a strangled cry. 'I can't hold back.'

'Then put a baby in me, Harry!' I yelled in the midst of a body-shaking climax. 'I don't care, I won't stop! Fuck me, fuck a baby up me – oh, aaagh, I'm coming too! Let it all go, Harry darling.'

'Yes, yes!' said Harry excitedly, valiantly trying to thrust his hips up to meet my final thrusts, his prick jerking within me as his spurting began, jet after jet of sperm shooting deep inside my receptive cunt.

I climbed off him with great care, seeing how he had slumped back, eyes closed and breathing heavily. Despite the wonderful warming glow still pulsating through my sexual parts I wondered if I had not overdone things.

'Are you okay, darling?' I asked anxiously. 'I didn't hurt you, did I?'

'You just made my day, that's all,' Harry said to my relief, opening his eyes. 'Too good to stop, wasn't it, love?' he grinned. 'You realise, of course, that the bout we just enjoyed courtesy of this Cottage Hospital, went the whole way? I mean there's a good chance I've got you well and truly preggy.'

'I'm well aware of what we did,' I nodded, sorting out my clothes by the chair, preparing to dress again. I had my back to him and felt his hand rove across my bum cheeks. 'You could be right. I'd like another baby anyway. Do you mind?'

'I'd love one,' he said seriously. 'I always thought it was about time, but you've been so set on buying our own house first. Now that we're in a decent flat with Dick and Clara Long, why wait?'

I bent to kiss him. 'That's how I feel,' I said. 'Now we must wait and see if you've done the necessary.'

'If not,' Harry said wickedly, 'there'll be other visits you'll be making here, won't you? If at first you don't succeed, try, try again. I'm already looking forward to seeing you this evening.'

'Then I'd better give up wearing any underwear when I call,' I said, clipping on my bra. 'Are you sure you'll be up to it?'

'Up to it is exactly how I'll be,' he vowed. 'Up and rearing. Do you fancy having a little girl this time, Di? A sister for Peter. I've heard the woman on top position is best for making baby daughters.'

'You'll have to settle for that anyway, my lad,' I told him, giving his plastered leg a tap with my knuckles. 'It's just as well for you that woman superior is one of my favourite positions.'

'Along with all the other ones,' Harry said good naturedly. 'Dear Di, I wouldn't want you to be any other way.'

Chapter Fifteen
THAILAND

Harry returned from his conference only to leave within a week to continue his work in the north of the country. 'Howard Wentzel will be coming with me too,' he said with some malice. 'Magnolia will have a fit when she returns next week to find him gone, but he *is* with the High Commission for Refugees and up on the borders with Laos and Burma is where all the refugees are. Where else should he be? They're pouring in from as far away as Cambodia and Vietnam as well as Burma. We'll need camps for them, a good water supply, and ground cleared so they can farm. I'll have to see to all that.'

'And you enjoy doing it,' I pointed out, packing his case yet again. 'I just wish it didn't keep us apart so much.'

'I'm working on that, love,' he said. 'Once I've got a base set up I'm hoping you'll join me. All mod cons in the jungle. It will be like our time in Africa again. As for Howard, I very much doubt if Magnolia would care to rough it in the wild. Thank God you aren't like her. I'd disappear into the bush for ever.'

'You do that often enough,' I reminded him, laughing. 'You did it in Uganda and Kenya, and here's no different.

This time I'll keep you to your word and join you. I like wild living.'

'So I've noticed,' my husband said, tongue-in-cheek. 'I'll send for you as soon as it's safe to do so. It's bandit country, you know.

'Then it's dangerous for you,' I said concerned. 'I hope you don't take foolish chances, Harry. I've heard it's where they grow opium poppies and that gangs of armed men control it by force. You don't come into contact with those people, do you?'

'I've been with Thai Army patrols that have exchanged shots with some of them,' he admitted. 'Don't worry, it was cowboy stuff, firing wildly into the trees to scare them off. I've mixed it with Panzer troops, remember?' he kidded. 'Anyway, our hope is that we can persuade the peasant farmers to grow cash crops instead of poppies. They'd make more money, actually, and eat better. The drug gangs pay them peanuts.'

'Would they be allowed to do that?' I asked.

'That's the big question,' Harry said. 'The gangs are run by war lords, and they in turn are operated by international drug-dealers, probably the Mafia. My job is to make the people up there see that farming regular crops and keeping more pigs and cattle would improve their lifestyle, so I'm giving them clean water from wells, teaching irrigation and using my team to help all we can. Some are really very primitive tribes, keen to improve village life. Of course the gangs use muscle to dissuade them from anything but growing the poppies.'

'It sounds just the kind of area Magnolia would appreciate – I don't think,' I said laughing. 'But it wouldn't stop me joining you there.'

'So you will, I promise,' Harry said. 'As soon as we get a

safe compound I'll fetch you, Di. The jungle is beautiful, there are still tigers. Give me a few weeks and you will see for yourself. We'll live on Thai cooking and love.'

So I was by myself when Magnolia returned; this time I met her at the airport. On Howard's absence she kept a stony silence. Howard junior, she reported, was now settled in a school in Atlanta. She was still incensed that her boy had been accused of sexual misbehaviour at the military academy.

'With an adult woman too,' she said in disbelief. 'I'm considering suing.'

I suggested that this might not be wise and would only cause a scandal. In the rear of the car sat Howard's twin sister Nicola, smirking all over her pretty face, making me wonder what her brother had told her about me and how she would use that information. The sooner Harry sent for me the better, I decided.

Inevitably, I suppose, it was because of Nicola that I next found myself in hot water. For once I had spent an evening at home and was writing a letter to Harry when the doorbell rang. I found Magnolia looking very grim. The time was almost ten o'clock.

'Nicola has not returned home,' she stated, trying to maintain her usual calm but it was obvious she was worried. 'She was at school all day, I've checked that, but where she has been since and where she is now none of her friends can tell me. She must be in dire trouble.'

I could only agree, inviting her indoors. She accepted the vodka I put in her hand and I poured one for myself. Nicola, after all, was a pretty teenager with a shapely tempting figure and I too feared the worst. Magnolia had rung her U.S. Embassy and they promised to make enquiries. The local police had no one available who could speak English until morning.

It was almost two in the morning before a call came from the embassy to say Nicola had been traced. She was locked up in the cells of the same police station we had telephoned earlier.

'I cannot believe it,' an anguished Magnolia said, replacing the receiver. We had gone into her apartment in case just such a call came. 'They say Nicola was caught with drugs. She was arrested in some Thai cafe with marijuana on her person. In the morning she is to be moved to the prison outside Bangkok. It's notorious, a den of thieves and prostitutes. Nicola doesn't smoke – she must have been picked on. She's a desirable young girl. There's a sexual motive in this, I'm sure.'

I had already considered that. Before eight the next day I went with Magnolia to give her moral support when we drove to the grim Nonthaburi Prison. We were met below the gate of a watchtower by a bespectacled attaché of the U.S. State Department.

'I'm afraid we won't get to see your daughter today,' he said as Magnolia advanced on him determined to make him work a miracle.

'She's being interrogated by the Bangkok vice squad and the charge had been increased to prostitution as well as possession and supply of drugs. It's ridiculous, of course, half the population of this city sell drugs or are into prostitution.'

'Certainly not my daughter,' Magnolia said angrily. 'What do you intend to do about it? I demand some positive action.'

The man shrugged, saying he would insist on visiting rights and would remain at the prison until they were granted. 'Go home and rest, Mrs Wentzel,' he advised. 'I'll telephone you the moment I get news.'

I must admit Magnolia was made of stern stuff, or appeared

to be. We returned to her apartment, where she gave her cook instructions for lunch, and asked me if her choice was agreeable with me. With Nicola in such trouble, food was the last thing on my mind. Magnolia also complained bitterly about her husband's absence just when he was needed and also about the ineptitude of the State Department lawyer we had met. I was searching my brain to see what I could possibly do to help Nicola and suddenly remembered the last visit I had made to Gretel Mannlicher's massage parlour and the Thai colonel who had been introduced to me as head of the Bangkok vice squad.

I asked if I could use Magnolia's phone, using the business card in my handbag to get Gretel's number. She sounded delighted to hear from me and asked if I had had second thoughts about the offer she had made to find paying sexual partners for me.

I explained why I was calling. A young girl was banged up in the Bangkok slammer for drugs and vice. She was white, still at school, and obviously innocent. She was scarcely seventeen, a mere child—

'In Nonthaburi, is she?' I heard the German woman tut-tut. 'She's in trouble then, Magnolia.' It was a bit of a shock when she called me that, and I recalled that in a moment's fickleness I had given her that name. 'You know, even white schoolgirls of seventeen can be very naughty. I suspect she is your daughter, *jah*, *liebling*? What do you want me to do about it?'

'Your friend, Colonel I-forget-his-name. The chief of the vice squad I met at your place,' I began.

'Colonel San-joi. What about him?' she replied.

'I thought he might help,' I said, squirming on a hook. I swallowed hard and added, 'I'd be glad to do anything to get the charges dropped.'

'*Anything*?' I heard Gretel say, smacking her lips I had no doubt. 'Well, the colonel is a kind man, and with my little transactions and enterprises in Bangkok I have to keep on the right side of him. He'll be delighted to hear you remembered him, Magnolia, as he mentions the beautiful chestnut-haired woman with the fair skin every time we meet. He wants you, that is a fact. To put it in plain English, he surely desires to fuck you. Would you be willing to let him, for your daughter's sake?'

I wasn't going to go into a rigmarole about not being Magnolia or that Nicola was not my daughter. 'Yes,' I said simply. 'He can fuck me all he wants, but only if he guarantees the girl is freed without any complications. Just allowed to walk free.'

'What's the time?' Gretel said, then answered herself. 'It's almost eleven. Be at my home, it's a bungalow on Rama the Sixth Road by the Royal Turf Club, by two o'clock. I'll make sure the colonel is present. He'll be there with temple bells ringing the way he has shown interest in you. I'm sure we will come to a very satisfactory arrangement.'

I replaced the phone to see Magnolia regarding me curiously. 'I couldn't help overhearing, Lady Saxon,' she said in her cool southern accent. 'Did you actually say someone could – *fuck* you? Did I hear you say if the girl is freed? Were you talking about Nicola? Are you offering yourself to free her?'

'You'd better believe it,' I said grimly. 'That call was to a woman who has dealings with the vice squad chief. Don't ask me how I know her. She's got it into her head that Nicola is my daughter and I didn't argue. Who cares as long as your girl goes free today? I've got to be at a bungalow near the Turf Club by two this afternoon. You can have Nicola back by three or four, depending how long Colonel San-joi takes to satisfy himself. Forget it, Magnolia, just don't ever mention it happened. You owe me.'

'She's *my* daughter,' Magnolia said, making me think for a moment that she was going to offer herself instead, but I was wrong. 'I insist on being there with you to make sure these people keep their part of the bargain. If they do, I shall have Nicola on a flight out of here tonight. She'll not stay one moment longer than necessary in this God-forsaken place. Poor dear, I must get her away to her grandmother's in Atlanta. I won't rest until then.'

Thank you very much for considering my part in the negotiations, I almost said. By two o'clock we drew up in my car outside an imposing bungalow with gorgeous flower beds. Gretel came out onto the balcony to greet us, looking over the sophisticated Magnolia in her smart lemon dress and liking what she saw.

'So you've brought your friend to make sure the bargain is kept,' she said when Magnolia launched into a series of demands. 'Don't worry, the colonel is a man of honour. Shall we go in? He's waiting impatiently.'

In a delightful room carpeted with oriental rugs, carved furniture and genuine Thai *objet d'art*, San-joi arose to greet me. Also present was a nervous-looking young American, no more than eighteen or nineteen, I judged, wide-eyed behind thick tortoise-shell glasses. He was obviously ill at ease. He was introduced as Chauncey, visiting Bangkok with his divorced father, who built and owned hotels worldwide. A good enough reason for Gretel to entertain him, I decided. As it was, however, the randy colonel was keen to have me at once and he led me through to an ornate bedroom with a four-poster bed. He unbuckled his belt with its holstered revolver and hung it over a chair. Then he proceeded to unbutton his immaculate uniform shirt decorated with badges and ribbons. His trousers were down to his knees when he looked at me sharply.

'Undress, madam,' he said curtly in good English. 'Undress and then walk about the room. I want to look at you.' Naked, apart from his socks – something I have always detested in a lover – he sat on the chair and lit a long thin cigar. He gazed at me with his hard slit eyes as I pulled off my dress, unhooked my bra and stepped out of my panties in front of him.

'Very nice,' he said, nodding calmly. 'Your breasts are very big, but they do not hang. Thai woman have smaller tits, as you call them. You have larger thighs and buttocks too. Turn around so that I may see behind you. Yes, very good buttocks. Your skin is very fair, smooth, soft. I have noticed such in women with your colour of hair. It is the same colour on your cunt, I see. What do you call it, madam?'

'Auburn,' I said impatiently. 'Are you going to fuck me, Colonel, or analyse my anatomy?' It was not the right approach and he scowled and waved the cigar for me to come closer. I noted he was as muscular as a weight-lifter, broad of chest and thick of thigh, but between his legs drooped a flaccid penis, stubby and no more than three inches long.

He placed his cigar in an ashtray beside him on a small teak table, the legs carved in the shape of an elephant. I admired the workmanship even as his hands reached out to cup my breasts, squeezing them tight. He twisted them in his grasp until I let out a moan, concluding that I was in for a rough ride at the hands of a sadistical bastard. As he continued to give painful pinches to my nipples, smiling as he did so, I determined he would not get a whine or protest from me.

'You are strong woman,' he said, gripping my sensitive tits even harder. 'Too strong. I do not like that. I hurt you and you make no noise. Why is that? Why you make no noise? I like noise.'

If he wanted noise he would get it, I thought, for my own well-being. The more I resisted, obviously, the more he would hurt me. 'Please, *please*,' I immediately beseeched in my best weak female voice. 'You are too strong, sir, your hands are so strong. I feel you are pulling off my breasts. Oh, you are hurting me, I can't stand it, you'll make me cry – ohhh—'

It had the desired effect of making him stop handling me so roughly. A hand went between my legs and rudely curled a finger into my cunt. It probed, flicked and pushed into me, so much so that I let out a loud groan, parting my thighs and bending my knees to accommodate the fingering more easily. Against my will I felt a growing excitement, my flowing juices aiding his titillation, my clit emerging from its hood to stiffen and erect at his touch.

'You like,' he said pointedly. 'I make you like. Not make you come yet. Down on knees, madam. Suck dick for me very much.'

His command of English, the crude terms especially, made me think he had used his position of power to have his fun with European or American women before me. As it was I was too slow in obeying his command to 'suck dick very much' and he pulled me down by my hair until I knelt between his muscular thighs, his still limp prick facing me.

Even with me naked before him, which usually was enough to get any man aroused, his rough handling of my boobs and exploration of my cunt had so far produced no effect. The pig has seen and done it all, I thought. This was no time for conjecture, however, as he was pulling my hair impatiently. There I was, on my knees in complete obeisance to a nasty piece of work using his power over me to the full. It was hardly conducive to making me *want* to suck him off. But there are the occasions when women, and that goes for myself, find it highly arousing to be dominated. It is as if we have surrendered all responsibility for ourselves and we submit, which can prove as erotically stimulating as the strongest aphrodisiac. All the same, as I bent forward with open mouth, I hoped Magnolia and Nicola appreciated what I was doing for them.

His dick was of a darker tan than his belly and thighs, hanging over a large pair of balls and sparsely haired. It was circumcised with a good bulbous knob and a thick ridge of skin below, the whole organ scrupulously clean. I tentatively touched the wide split eye with the tip of my tongue, covered the head with my lips and gave the first few sucks gently. The soft stalk did not in any way respond to my light suction and I heard a disgusted growl from above me. 'You are not good, madam,' he said irately. 'Do you not do this to your husband? What you ask me to do, free your wicked daughter, deserves good blow-job. Do you want beaten into being good, like Thai wife? Stand, you will bend over chair, madam, like obedient woman.'

I thought the way I'd started was what men liked – playful kisses and sucks with my mouth and lips before gobbling and slurping away ravenously. Evidently not in his case. He hauled me up and twisted me around to bend over the seat of the chair. I gripped the carved wooden arms to steady myself. With my bottom thus raised, I awaited his next move with trembling anticipation. I was nervous but my cunt twitched and throbbed as if it were a separate part of me. I dared a glance back and saw he held a short whippy bamboo cane in his hand, swishing it in the air.

I drew in my breath as first he drew the cane up the crease of my buttocks. Then, as the initial thwack struck me across both cheeks, I let out an anguished howl. It was not so much from pain as to let him be aware this fine European woman was being put in her place, bowing to his stronger will. The cane stung, just the same, crisscrossing my rounded cheeks with a good dozen stripes while I blubbered and screamed out that I was not used to such treatment and I would try harder to please him! Satisfied, he threw the cane aside and roughly caught my arm, resuming his sitting position with me on my knees before him again. I noted now he had a good erection, the sadistic beast.

My thrashing had been much less punishing than his brawny arm could have administered, I knew, but at the same time it had been painful enough and my reddened bottom felt as if a thousand bees had stung it. I imagined how San-joi enjoyed interrogating his female victims at his headquarters – caning my bum had raised his thick cock to appreciable proportions. This time I determined to please him, my mind resentful but my lecherous nature urging me on. With my cunt tingling, I remembered that Magnolia and the young American would be sitting in the next room, probably drinking tea, knowing full well I had been led off to be fucked. They would undoubtedly have heard my pleas and cries as I was being beaten. That too, had a strange effect on me and caused an additional flutter in my sex.

I took, San-joi's big balls in a cupped hand, licking them and working my way up to the base of his stem while my other hand massaged it roughly. That is what he wanted, I was sure. As I felt the outer skin move up and down in my grasp I warmed to my task, mystified by the absolute iron hardness of his rigid stalk, a tightly solid bar of stiffened flesh such as I'd never felt before. It neither throbbed or pulsed like other pricks I'd held. It was unbending and cold as marble. I could only surmise it was like this through some drug or potion making it unnaturally rampant. It felt more like ivory than flesh as I began to suck hard at the swollen knob, my cheeks hollowing inwards with the power of my suction, bobbing my head and taking its full length back to my throat. I was rewarded by hearing grunts of satisfaction. He squirmed in his seat thrusting at my mouth.

As his excitement mounted, so did mine. Waves of lewd feelings swept through me as my mouth swallowed the velvety glans, the thick stalk stretching my lips. I wallowed in the base carnality of sucking cock. I pumped him hard, intent on suctioning his load from his heavy balls, my head working like fury to aid the movement. I heard short gasps and felt my head pulled hard to his crotch. Aaaagh! he cried and jerked in a wild flurry, spurting an absolute torrent to the back of my throat. I gulped, choking and swallowing hard as the jets of hot spunk flooded my gullet. But even as his thrusting slowed, his prick remained iron hard. I still had come in my mouth and I continued sucking, my fingers rubbing furiously at the nub of my clit desperate for my own relief. But he pushed me away and dragged me across the thickly carpeted floor and threw me across the bed.

I rolled over on my back, my breasts thrusting up, legs parted to present my agitated cunt to him, as eager to be penetrated by his standing cock as I hoped he was to use it on me. I played the helpless woman made wanton.

'Please, you make me want it so much,' I said as if unable to resist. 'You have made me shameless today. Won't you please fuck me?' I reached out to grasp his incredible cock. 'You're so very hard, so beautifully stiff.' My voice was almost a whine. 'It's like a bar of steel.'

He looked pleased and I expected him to suck on my nipples, feel my cunt and perhaps lick and tongue it before mounting me. But he made a circle in the air with his finger, indicating that he would have me turn over. I complied at once, on forearms and knees, my bottom arched backwards to invite his eyes to the firm moons of my buttocks. To increase his lust I lay with my face turned on the bedcover, my hands going back to draw my cheeks apart and reveal the down-hanging hairy bulge of my pussy with the pink flesh now glistening from my arousal. 'Do you see how wet I am there? You have made me so,' I whimpered. 'Made me forget I have a loving husband and want another man's prick to fuck me. Feel me.'

His fingers probed my sex momentarily, then withdrew to stroke the serrated ring of my bottom hole with more interest, the tip of one digit entering and making me jerk my bum and gasp. 'Your cunt is very wet, madam,' he agreed. 'Too wet. I like dry fuck.'

'Won't you lick it for me, please?' I dared say. 'Clean it for me, make it dryer for you to fuck me, sir?'

His answer was to give me a hard smack across my naked bottom, making me shout out in pain. 'I do not lick,' he said sternly, turning to walk away and returning with a small phial of colourless oil. He had obviously come prepared I thought, as he dripped some drops directly between my bum cheeks. It felt cool and tingly as it ran down the cleft, then with the fingers of one hand he began smoothing the oil into my flesh, lubricating the area around my back passage, sliding a finger into the ring of that orifice and moving it back and forth its full length. I squirmed my tormented bum and moaned.

His intention was obvious as he continued manipulating his thick finger in the oil-coated hole of my tight anal passage. No matter how I gripped it by tensing my buttock cheeks and contracting my ring, the slippery sliding went on, bringing whines and moans from my lips as I squirmed feeling both arousal and resentment at his arrogant treatment. The swine did not want an obliging woman, merely an accommodating hole on his own terms. My groans pleased him and I heard a short vicious snarl of triumph from his thin lips as my gyrations increased, my abused bum giving little agitated jerks as the nerve-ends tingled with increasing erotic sensations.

'Have you ever had it there, madam?' he asked derisively. 'Man's big cock in little behind? You like, you do it?'

I wasn't admitting that. 'What?' I said. 'No, no, it's not possible! It is too big to go there.' As if to tempt him I tilted up my plump split mound. 'There, sir, put it in there. I want you to.'

'Your husband, madam, has he never had you here?' he taunted, his finger working away. 'Anyone? Then you will learn new trick.'

The forefinger twisted around and around inside me. 'Go on if you must,' I complained in a whine. 'It feels so, so—' Rump raised, head down on the pillow, I reached back again to draw my buttocks apart for his better access. 'What you want me to do,' I told him, 'is disgusting. Yet I want you to do it to me. You make me feel utterly lewd, like a whore in any Bangkok brothel. Take me there, please,' I begged, still with an eye to pleasing him but now desiring that he continue for my own sake. That I was using him as much as he was about to use me increased my secret pleasure too. Let the fool think it was all one-sided if he liked.

I tried to make my excitement less obvious but could not suppress a sigh of pleasure as he applied the fat knob of his abnormally rigid prick to the entrance of my arsehole and forced a thick inch or two inside. My groan was heartfelt as I eased my rump back to his flat belly and took his whole length up the oiled passage. I felt delightfully filled and gave a soft cry of complete surrender as he began shunting the unyielding cylinder of flesh up and down inside my arse. I felt completely possessed, uncaring now who was having me so, only knowing the unrelenting stalk filling me with its mass was producing vibrations that burned and throbbed throughout my whole body. I cried out loud and bucked my rear to his thrusts. I felt him curl over my back for deeper penetration, his hands reaching down to grasp my breasts as his heaves quickened. I came most violently, helpless in my throes, shaking and vibrating in a long series of intense spasms.

'You beast!' I screamed out. 'Fucking me there, fucking my bum! You animal!' I turned my head to share the lewdness of our coupling, seeing the wild-eyed look on his flushed features. I also saw Gretel Mannlicher at the open door with Magnolia and the young American Chauncey watching the show, the German woman smiling at the sight of my obvious pleasure. Beside her, Magnolia's face was a florid pink, her eyes fixed on our hectic coupling. The American boy stared as if mesmerised. It increased my lust to know that I was being observed. I jogged my backside harder and faster until I was screaming I was coming once again, then I collapsed on my face as my partner finished using my bottom. He groaned loudly as he inundated me with his spurts, withdrawing from my stretched hole to rest on his knees.

I felt as if his prick was still inside me. My back passage was as hot as a furnace, sticky with oil and semen, pulsing like a heartbeat, the aperture contracting and opening like a mouth gasping for breath. To tell the truth, although I lay silent on the bed as if in mortal shame for the benefit of the audience, I felt marvellous. My body was glowing, sexually sated and languidly at ease. A glance showed me that Sanjoi's cock had at last subsided, shrunk to its flaccid proportions as he picked up his uniform to start dressing. 'She was good,' he said casually to Gretel Mannlicher. 'I was glad to have her. Good to fuck—'

'So we couldn't help noticing,' Gretel laughed.

'He was buggering her!' Magnolia said aghast. 'My God, is there nothing you people won't do? Will word now be sent at once that my daughter be released from confinement? We have an agreement.'

'I keep my word,' San-joi said unctuously, buttoning his shirt. 'A telephone call from me will allow the girl to walk free. By the time you arrive at the prison with your car I assure you that she will be waiting for you to collect her. She is a lucky young person. Better that she leaves the country before more trouble.'

On the bed I decided that would be a good idea for all concerned. I intended to ask that all leave the room so that I could rise and get dressed. As if reading my mind, Gretel looked from Magnolia to me with wicked intent.

'We have had a trick played on us, Herr San-joi,' she said teasingly. 'Did you hear what this other woman said: *she* wanted *her* daughter released? It seems you had your pleasure with the wrong person. That she allowed her friend to take her place. She admitted this while in the other room.'

'You fool, Magnolia,' I said, rising from the bed now and going to get into my clothes, not caring that they all saw me naked. 'Why couldn't you keep your mouth shut about it?'

'It is all the same to me,' San-joi said easily. 'I had the woman I wanted, not this other one. Why do you care?'

'Because I know this kind of woman,' Gretel said maliciously, turning to a fearful Magnolia. 'You see them in the best places in Bangkok, looking down on the rest of us. I won't allow her to get away with this. So she's too refined to be fucked to save her own daughter? She allows another woman to do it for her. The agreement was that the mother would be the one and that has not been the case here. I want to see *her* fucked. I insist upon it.'

I saw Magnolia turn ashen, her mouth open but struck dumb at the indignity of what Gretel suggested. 'I don't want her, this other woman was enough,' San-joi said cheerfully, 'but if you have something in mind for her, I shall see it before I telephone the prison. I will take tea also to refresh myself—'

'You shall have tea and lemon rice cakes,' promised Gretel, 'and watch a little amusement I shall arrange for this woman. We will do as we please with her if she wants her daughter returned today. She will obey without argument.' She turned to me with a gracious smile. 'Do not dress yet, Diana Lady Saxon, as I have learned who you are from your so-called friend Magnolia. She allowed you to stand in for her, so now she should be made to pay you back in some kind. Let us all go back into my lounge and discover what I have in mind for us.'

Chapter Sixteen
ENGLAND

My visits to the hospital over the next few days followed the same pattern. I'd lock the door of Harry's room as I entered and he'd lie with a sublime smile of anticipation as I undressed before him. It's the best way to go about it and he never tired of seeing me get naked for him. Aroused at the sight of me, he'd draw back the sheet to reveal his lovely upstanding cock. Then I'd straddle his hips and impale myself on his brute, my breasts swinging like bells in my agitation, the pair of us coming off with muffled cries and gasps in case we should be overheard.

One morning after several days of mounting him like this, I arrived to find he'd been moved to a general ward and now shared with three other men. Harry welcomed me with a rueful grin, hands extended helplessly, so I had to content myself with sitting at his bedside and chatting instead of fucking. Into each life a little rain must fall, we agreed. It was time to return to London for me, anyway, where our son Peter was being cared for by Clara and Richard Long. I had telephoned daily to ensure all was well and been informed that he'd been a good little boy but was now missing his mummy. I caught the night train from Inverness, not sure when I'd see Harry again. Whether I had been made pregnant by my sojourn in the Scottish town was still uncertain. Always one to enjoy rude health, I felt wonderfully well after the relaxing stay in a luxurious hotel and the good twice-daily work-out with Harry.

I settled happily in our flat in the Longs' house, but our fortunes took a blow when I received a letter enclosed with Harry's monthly pay check from his firm. It stated that, as legal proceedings would undoubtedly be instituted against the firm for compensation following Harry's accident, he was no longer considered as employed by them as that would constitute admitting liability. It meant that the cheque I held in my hand was to be the last. Until compensation was paid or Harry was well enough to start work again our total income would be weekly sickness benefit paid by the state. I showed the letter to the Longs, who advised me to consult their solicitor right away after informing Harry, so that legal proceedings could start. It could be a year or two before any compensation was paid, so I was informed. Whatever the outcome, I made up my mind that not one of my family would suffer hardship in the meanwhile.

I had to seek work, being fortunate in discovering a good nursery for infant children nearby. Peter settled in right away, the other children's company delighting him. The care was expensive, but it allowed me to start again at the newsagent's shop where I'd worked before, on longer hours and for more pay as the owner, Sybil Paterson, had branched out and opened a second shop. Wayne was no longer the paperboy, I learned, having gained a place in a ballet company and he was now on tour in Canada. I was almost as sorry about that as Sybil, as several weeks had gone by with no husband to satisfy me and I was growing increasingly frustrated. At night I masturbated for relief, conjuring up lewd fantasies as I built myself to a climax. What wild thoughts come as sex thrills take over! I thought of Harry fucking me, big black Wayne, suave Charles Groves, even at times, my burly landlord and sometimes all of them together.

I was able to pop home at lunchtime to make a sandwich and prepare a proper evening meal for when I collected Peter from his nursery. One day I was peeling potatoes at my kitchen sink when I heard Clara Long calling me from the garden below. She stood by her garage, about to get out her van and drive off in search of what she called antiques for her market stall. I opened the window over the sink and leaned out to hear her better, my breasts almost on the window ledge and the taps against my belly. 'I'll be away all day, Di,' she called up to me. 'I've heard of an old mansion at Kenilworth selling up its contents by auction. Will you give my old man his dinner tonight as I don't expect to be back before midnight? I'm sending him up to you with a leg of lamb.'

I was about to say that wouldn't be necessary when her husband tapped on the kitchen door and entered, placing a large leg of lamb on the table. 'God, but your lovely arse looks tempting in that position, girl,' he said, coming up behind me. 'I've been a good boy, haven't I? Respecting your marital state and all with you looking so bloody enticing about the place. A man can only stand so much.'

I turned my head to smile with amusement at his words, taking no offence as I knew him well enough. 'Then you'll just have to keep standing, Richard,' I teased him. 'Run cold water over it.'

'Dick,' he insisted. 'Everyone calls me Dick. Dick Long, by name as well as nature. Long in length as well as staying power too. Want me to prove it?'

'Is that Dick you're talking to?' his wife called up from the garden. 'Brought the lamb, has he? You make a good

meal of it, my dear.' As I nodded out of the window I felt
hands on my bum.

'I could make a lovely meal of you, young Mrs Saxon,'
my landlord whispered lustfully into my neck, out of sight of
his wife as he clawed my skirt up to my waist. It stayed up,
rucked against the edge of the sink, while a hand plunged
between my thighs, the cupped palm curving directly over
the gusset of my panties, gently squeezing the bulge within
the thin cotton. I gulped, instant arousal pulsating through
my sex. I gave an involuntary shudder as the pressure
gradually increased, my insides fluttering and my hungry
pussy lubricating. 'It's wet there already,' the soft whisper at
my neck continued, a note of triumph in the tone. 'You're
drenched, girl. You want it badly, don't you?'

His wife was meanwhile staring up at me. 'Are you feeling
all right, Di?' she enquired. 'Your face has turned quite red.
Don't lean out so far, it must be a strain.'

I tried to nod and smile down at Clara Long while her
husband drew my panties over my raised bottom. Firm hands
parted both cheeks, making me stifle a groan at the thought
of what was revealed to his eyes: the tightly puckered ring of
my anus and, beneath, the hanging bulge of my cunt with its
crisp hair and outer lips pouting and parted, glistening with
my juices.

'What nectar,' I heard Dick say reverently from between
my legs as his tongue licked up my groove and tasted me. A
glance back showed me Dick Long was on his knees, his face
buried in my crotch.

I pushed my feet apart, tilting my buttocks back to get
more of his probing tongue, too aroused to do anything else
and wishing his wife would hurry up and drive off so that I
could squirm and groan my appreciation of a thorough tongue-
fucking. The thought that she was smiling up at me, unaware

of the salacious act her husband was performing on me, made the whole thing twice as arousing. I had to contain myself, my lips silently forming pleas for him to lap and lick harder, deeper, to reem and clean out every nook and cranny of my cunt while I stiffened my body to prevent shuddering in my anguish in front of the watcher below.

'Goodbye, Clara, have a successful day at the auction,' I shouted down, hoping that would make her start to leave, trusting my voice did not sound too strange. By then both my hands were gripping tightly to the sink's taps, my head and shoulders held still, but my agitated arse circling and jerking as the waves and surges convulsed my lower region.

I sensed Dick getting to his feet and allowed myself a little sigh as his tongue was withdrawn from my unsatisfied cunt, where it had been probing so delightfully. My right hand was drawn back and I felt it curled about a rigid stalk, a hot and throbbing bar of flesh that reared several long inches above my grip as I turned to look at what I held. The plum head glistened a purplish-red on top of a thick veiny stem; below hung heavy-set balls.

'Give me that, I want it,' I heard myself say plaintively. 'Go on, use it. That's what you've been after, isn't it?'

'Only when you begged for it,' Dick said, his breath hot on my cheek. 'I've always wanted to, but I've waited until it wasn't just me who was hot for it. Go on, say it if you mean it.'

His glans was poised at the very entrance to my cunt. 'Fuck me then,' I told him, still whispering. 'Fuck me all you want to. Make me come. I want to be fucked – just make it good.'

'I'll do that alright,' he began delightedly, 'as much and as long as you can stand. What a lovely quim,' I heard him mutter as his whole length entered me. 'What a fabulous cunt! Turn your head, love, raise your arse so I can get it all in. God, this has been worth waiting for.'

'We shouldn't, we shouldn't,' I was whining as I felt his belly hard against my bottom, his warm balls slapping my parted cheeks as he thrust mightily. Talking lewdly always heightened my excitement. That it pleased male partners, and even predatory female ones, I had discovered long ago. Looking down from my position bent over the sink, I saw Clara Long had taken her van out of the garage and was in the act of opening the gate to allow her to drive out. She waved to me cheerily and I waved back, her husband's prick shunting inside me as I did so. 'You're fucking me,' I said, 'and your wife is giving me a wave. We must be beasts to behave like this.'

'And you love every minute of it,' I was told crudely. 'What a nice soft arse you've got. What a delicious cunt. Tell me you love it, tell me what it feels like.'

'It's heaven,' I groaned, watching his wife getting in behind the wheel of her van, bursting to really let myself go and jerk my bottom back to meet his deep thrusts. I longed to throw back my head and cry out in my pleasure. 'Go on, shove it all up me! Fuck it in me to the balls. Make me come!'

'What a randy little slut you are with a cock up you,' my lover grunted out, interspersing his words meaningfully with each thrust. 'Missing that husband of yours, are you, love? Don't worry, I'll fill in for him while he's away.'

His mention of Harry, my infidelity, the lewdness of the act in which we were engaged, only served to increase my base feelings. 'Yes, yes, you can fuck me when ever you want to,' I heard myself blurting out as the big shaft pistoned into my cunt. The unstoppable tremors of what seemed like a continuing climax shook me violently from head to toe, my bottom buffeting back wildly as the surges rippled through my insides.

'Go on!' I shouted urgently, not wanting the ecstasy to end. I heard him panting in short savage grunts and his thrusts increased. I felt the hard shaft penetrate me to its full length, giving a series of quivering leaps as it spurted its full load inside me.

I could only lie bent over the sink and shudder in my final throes, coming to at last with a gasp and a long intake of breath, aware I had been mightily fucked and had loved every single moment of it – though already I was regretting I had allowed it, particularly as he had injected me with his sperm. If I was not already pregnant, I thought ruefully, I surely would be after that.

'Go, Dick, please,' I said. 'I'm not blaming you, I was just as bad to let you but you did take an unfair advantage coming up behind me like that. It musn't happen again.'

'Maybe not until next time,' Dick said, drawing up his trousers while regarding me fondly. 'Look, I know you're a nice lass, but you wanted it, I wanted it, and no one will be the wiser. So why not?'

He stood awaiting my answer. 'Go,' I repeated, shaking my head at his philosophy, realising my knickers were still around my feet. 'You are a randy old thing and should consider yourself lucky. Be satisfied with that.'

'That's impossible,' he said grinning wickedly. 'After having a lovely fresh young thing like you it can only make me want more. Give it a day or two and I hope you'll feel the same. We were good, weren't we?'

'Too good,' I had to laugh with him.

His wife was at home for the following three days and I welcomed her presence, feeling that the interval acted as a cooling-off period. Now Dick had had me perhaps he'd be satisfied to leave it at that. On the following Friday I got up early as usual to make breakfast and take Peter to nursery before getting to work in the newsagents by nine. As usual on that morning I went into Dick's office and left the money for the rent along with the rent book. No one was there as the Longs were having a lie-in. Later, in the shop, Clara looked in to buy her paper and pipe tobacco for her husband. I noted her van was parked outside so I knew she was off on one of her buying trips.

'Would you take these home for my old man, Di,' she said, referring to her purchases. 'It's the first time I've known him to say he's not feeling well and is having a day in bed. Drop these in to him when you have your lunch break. He must be getting old, staying in bed like that. Seeing you will cheer him up, he thinks there's nobody like you.'

With good reason, I thought, hoping my blush did not show, my mind going back to our heated session at the kitchen sink. On my way home at lunch I bought a few groceries and went straight up to my flat to put them away, deciding to take a cup of tea down to Dick when I looked in with his newspaper and tobacco. As I put out the cups on the table I saw my rent book with the money I'd left in his office placed beside it. There was also a flattish box in gift-wrap paper and tied with ribbon. First of all I inspected the rent book, opening it to see that the weekly rent had been marked off as paid for a month in advance. The cunning devil is bribing me now to try for another fuck, I thought, amused. He'd be out of luck, but I wouldn't say no to a month rent free.

The mysterious box intrigued me and I opened it up to find the most exquisite set of black silk lingerie inside. The lacy bra and briefs were completely see-through, and an added touch was a matching suspender-belt of the same gossamer material. To complete the ensemble a pair of sheer black silk stockings were enclosed. It was undoubtedly an expensive gift and very acceptable bait. Good try, Dick, I thought and smiled again at his deviousness, it's a pity it won't do you any good. I went down to the Long's bedroom bearing a cup of tea for him, finding him laid back in bed regarding me with a look of anticipation. To make it quite clear he drew back the bedcovers, revealing that he was completely naked and displaying his large straining upright prick rearing over his belly.

'You fraud,' I told him, laughing. 'You're not unwell at all, you've been lying in wait for me. It won't do you any good and neither will the present you left on my table as a bribe. Shame on you.'

'Did you like the underwear?' he appealed. 'Sexy stuff, eh?'

'It's beautiful,' I said. 'I shall wear it for my husband when he gets home soon. Black lace, he'll love seeing me in that.'

'The idea was that I'd see you in them,' my randy landlord teased. I noted that his splendidly endowed cock still reared unwaveringly rigid, attracting my interested stare whether I wanted it or not. What young woman in the absence of her regular partner could not but admire such a sight? It made me feel momentarily weak at the knees and a spontaneous surge of arousal churned my belly.

'Cover that thing up,' I told him, reaching out to pull the blanket over it. He caught my hand and pressed it against his big stander. As ever, a hot and throbbing prick felt wonderfully good to hold. I rubbed it and felt the outer skin moving over the iron-hard inner column of flesh. I wanted it, there was no doubt. Only by a great effort of will, reminding myself that one lapse with him was more than enough, did I find the strength to release it.

'No, Dick,' I said throatily. 'Thank you for marking up a month's rent and the lovely underwear, but I can't. I can't.'

'I think you can, girl,' he said in a hard flat voice. 'Don't deny your feelings. The way you held my prick for a moment or two there, I knew you wanted more of it. I want to fuck, and so do you – and what's so wrong with that?'

'I've got a husband,' I said, feeling like a hypocrite to brace myself with that excuse. 'You have a wife.'

'And they aren't here,' I heard him shout after me as I almost ran from the room. 'Come back and do us both a favour – you want to, I know bloody well you do!'

I went upstairs trembling, highly aroused. My hand still retained the impression of the warm rigidness it had grasped. On the kitchen table lay the opened box with the expensive lingerie beside it. It was a kind gesture to make a gift like that, even if there was an ulterior motive behind it. Maybe he did deserve some show of gratitude.

That was my excuse anyhow as I found myself taking the garments to my bedroom and undressing to try them on. There was little enough to cover me, I saw in the long mirror on the wardrobe door: the rounds of my breasts were barely contained in the neat bra, the panties were so brief and lacily transparent that my mound bulged enticingly prominent and the outline of my pubic bush showed clearly.

I went back downstairs and entered Dick's bedroom wordlessly, standing before him at what I considered a safe distance from temptation. He was still lying back with his head on the pillows, the bedcovers drawn aside to reveal his naked body. In his right hand he clasped the long rigid stalk of his immense prick, idly stroking it as if in invitation to me to come and do something about it.

'It's such a lovely present that I thought you at least

deserved to see me wearing it,' I said. I turned to show him the back view, the cheeks of my bottom barely covered by the briefs and, on an impulse, I waggled my rear at him. Like a striptease dancer I hooked my thumbs in the waistband of the tiny knickers and lowered them just enough to bare the divide of my bum before drawing them back up quickly.

'Take them off,' I heard him say sharply from the bed. I find authoritative men hard to disobey, particularly when I'm in such a state of excitement. 'Drop them!' he roared.

I stood facing the patterned wallpaper, honestly trying to prevent myself doing as he ordered. I knew full well that no normal male, already fully aroused, would accept my display and not want more. 'I just wanted to show you how I looked in these nice things you bought me,' I said weakly.

'And nothing else?' Dick said in the same terse voice. 'Come off it, young woman, I didn't come up the Thames yesterday. You're as randy as a bucket of frogs standing there. I can see you trembling. You want Dick's big cock, don't you? Stay facing that wall and take down those knickers. Your arse is almost bare as it is. What kind of a man do you think I am, settling for just a show of fancy underwear, both of us knowing what it's meant for? Get them off like I said. Now!'

'Please!' I begged, only increasing my own excitement. 'You shouldn't make me do this.' Facing the wall, hands trembling, I complied by lowering and stepping out of the lacy scrap of material, presenting him with the view of my naked buttock cheeks framed by the suspender belt above and the tops of sheer black silk stockings below. 'There,' I pouted, sounding grudgingly offended. 'Do you see it all?'

'Not quite,' Dick said, knowing he would have his way with me. 'I want you to part your legs, put your feet wide apart, girl. That's right. Now, bend over from your waist, steady yourself with your hands against the wall. Let's see you like that.'

'You're disgusting,' I complained, doing as he told me and growing increasingly wanton at the thought of what he could see of me. 'It's not fair. I feel like a prize cow on show.'

'Stay as you are,' I was ordered curtly as he got out of his bed and crossed the floor towards me, seeing me attempt to straighten up. I got a warning slap on my bottom to make me resume my position, then felt probing fingers exploring my cunt, two at least sliding up easily in my moistness. I jerked and my clitty tingled ecstatically at his touch. Moans and sighs escaped my lips involuntarily. 'Oh yes,' Dick said with grim satisfaction. 'I *knew* you would. I knew you were on heat after trying Dick's big dick the other day. You're a horny little female, Mrs Saxon, admit it. Just built to fuck.'

How many had told me that, I thought cringing at the truth, my cunt positively aching for his prick. 'You shouldn't take so much for granted,' I sobbed out in a last futile protest even as my bottom tilted back for what I now desperately wanted. 'I'm really not like that. You men make me so.'

'Oh sure,' he said, almost a note of scorn in his tone. 'That's why you're so juiced up. I can feel your quim beating like a pulse. Do you want it, girl? Ask for it nicely—'

'You're going to do me anyway,' I grunted. 'Get on with it!' The broad head of his cock nudged in, forcing my outer lips apart and then, as I pushed back against him, I felt the whole sliding up inside me. 'You know I can't help it,' I moaned. 'Fuck it up me, Dick. Give me a good come, fuck me like you did before.' His shafting increased in pace, his belly and balls bouncing against me as the intense poking proceeded. 'More! Harder!' I urged him wildly.

I knew he would fuck me to the finish, until his last gasps

and the jetting of hot sperm flooded me. My hands were pressed palms inward to the wall as his pounding continued, my bottom lifting and meeting the thrust of his muscular flanks, my cunt rammed repeatedly with his rigid girth and length. I heard myself babbling in my delirium and I climaxed wildly, my body gyrating and jerking, neck stretched and head thrown back.

Level with my eyes was a large old mirror in a big wooden frame, hung there slightly tilted forward and allowing me the sight of Dick curled over my back as he manfully fucked away. I also saw beyond him the open bedroom door and, with a shock to my already convulsing system, the figure of Clara, Dick's wife, standing there watching it all. For a moment before she turned and moved out of sight, I thought I detected a nod and a brief smile, as if she knew I had seen her reflection in the mirror.

Her husband was withdrawing after satisfying his lust, blissfully ignorant of our being observed. I hastily picked up my discarded briefs and fled the room, praying that Clara would not be waiting to scream abuse at me in the passageway. I dressed in my flat, dreading going downstairs to return to work. As I passed the door of the Longs' apartment I heard no sounds of a row from inside.

After work I collected my son and went back home expecting to be thrown out. I cursed my foolish weakness in allowing the sex sessions with the landlord. I made the evening meal, bathed Peter and put him through to his bed with a story, waiting all the time for the axe to fall on me. I wondered how I would explain to Harry why we had been made homeless on top of everything else and wished Clara would get it over with. Then a knock sounded at my door and I feared the worst.

She stood there, smiling what could almost be called a

wicked smile and holding in her hand a bottle of sherry. 'Fetch two glasses, Di,' she said cheerily on entering. 'We must celebrate – I think you're pregnant.'

'Whatever makes you think that?' I gasped, as shocked and surprised by her words as her friendly manner after seeing her husband and me fucking like a dog and bitch in heat. 'I don't think so,' I said. 'How could you know?'

'Your face and your figure are a little rounder,' Clara said smiling. We went through to the armchairs in front of the living room fire with our glasses. 'I was a midwife before I got married and I've seen enough expectant mothers in my time. It's not my husband's work, is it?'

'I had sex with Harry at the hospital in Scotland,' I said, hanging my head. 'I feel terrible about this – you seeing what happened today. My husband was in a private room and we did it many times when I visited. If I am pregnant I'm sure it's his.'

'Who cares whose it is?' Clara said sensibly, sounding relieved. 'Just as long as your Harry thinks it's his. As for seeing you and my old man going at it, I blame him, so don't worry your pretty head. You were a lonely girl and I knew the randy sod would be sniffing about you, so forget it. Drink up. He's a very good fuck with that big prick he's got, isn't he?'

'Yes,' I had to agree smiling back at her frankness. 'And you really don't mind that I've tried it? I shouldn't have, I know, but these things happen. I'm shameful, too easy with men.'

'With your looks I don't blame you,' Clara said. 'I knew you were too tempting for my old chap from day one. He's happy and you weren't complaining when I saw you, so what the hell? I'm no angel myself, Di. For the past year or two I've been meeting an auctioneer I got to know on my trips.'

She laughed wickedly. 'Half the trips I've made aren't what they seem. We meet at hotels and fuck like it was just invented. He's a good few years younger than me too.'

'You naughty thing,' I said, laughing. 'It seems we're both as bad as each other. Don't you worry about getting pregnant?'

'It would be a miracle,' Clara said. 'I had my hysterectomy some years ago, so I can do as I like. You can't. Have you had no signs? Tender, swollen breasts? Not that they could get much bigger. What about morning sickness?'

'My tits are always sensitive,' I said shyly. 'That's half the trouble, it makes me want sex. I haven't been sick yet, but then it didn't bother me with Peter. I'm just a healthy peasant, never anything but in fine fettle. It's my normal condition.'

'Not in my estimation,' she said, eyeing me shrewdly. 'I'd lay a bet you were in the club right now, my girl. If my Dick has been at you as well as your Harry, there's twice the chance with two of them at you.'

'Three,' I admitted, seeing as how Clara had revealed her own infidelity so honestly. 'Do you remember the man who came to drive me to Scotland? You let him in the house yourself.'

'You never!' she giggled delightedly. 'You are one for it! I remember what a handsome devil *he* was all right. Never mind, it's a wise father that knows his own child.'

I only hoped that was so!

Chapter Seventeen
THAILAND

Gretel's ornate lounge assumed the menace of an oriental torture chamber as Magnolia and I were led through to whatever fate awaited us. I knew it seemed so to her as well as she looked about anxiously, no doubt furious with herself for revealing she was Nicola's mother. I was immodestly exposed as I had been ordered to remain naked, yet I sensed I was to be a mere bit player in some callous scenario the devious German matron was stage-managing to humiliate the haughty American woman.

First tea and a selection of small sweet cakes were served, the young Thai manservant's eyes boring into my big tits as he served me. The imposed wait increased Magnolia's agitation, no doubt as intended. Impatient and exasperated, she at last demanded sharply that we be allowed to leave, and word be sent at once for her innocent daughter's release.

'This will be reported to my embassy, have no doubt,' she threatened. The words, delivered with a tremor in her voice, brought a scornful laugh from Gretel, who then spoke rapidly in fluent Thai to Colonel San-joi. He grinned and nodded eagerly at whatever she'd told him, looking in turn from Magnolia to the young visitor, Chauncey. The youth sat uncomfortably on the edge of his seat, aroused at the sight of my nudity perhaps from the bulge showing in the front of his trousers, yet nervous about what was expected of him. He was left in no doubt moments later.

'Chauncey,' Gretel said to the young man, 'your father sent you to me to provide a little fun and excitement. He's *such* a dear friend of mine. The time has come for you to discover the pleasures of the flesh. Your father insisted, being a man of the world himself and a regular visitor to Bangkok. I know you don't wish to disappoint him. You must not look so anxious.'

'What does my father know?' Chauncey said, sweating but trying to appear cool. 'The things I've done back in the States with girls at college and on Las Vegas weekends—' He looked at the mesmerised Magnolia apologetically as he made this boast, as if unable to help himself in such company. His eyes tried to avoid all contact with me. After all, we looked like respectable women, embarrassingly so to him no doubt. 'I've been there,' he added lamely to Gretel. 'My old man has nothing to worry about concerning me.'

'Then that is good,' she said soothingly. 'You'll want me to make a good report to him, won't you? Now I want you to undress, Chauncey, and we can begin the little entertainment I have in mind. Don't be a shy young fellow,' she rebuked, seeing his hesitation. 'Since you've had such experiences at college and Las Vegas. Diana is already naked as you can see and Magnolia is going to take off all her clothes for you. That is so, *ja*, Magnolia?'

'I said I want to leave *now*,' Magnolia insisted, unable to control the high pitch in which the words came out. 'Allow Lady Saxon to dress and we will not stay here a moment longer.'

'As you wish,' Gretel said casually. 'No one is stopping you. There is, of course, the small matter of a telephone call to where your daughter is held on serious charges. Have you forgotten that?'

'This is blackmail,' Magnolia shouted. 'It's outrageous!'

'Quite outrageous,' Gretel agreed. 'Now get up and stand by that table in the centre of the room so we can all see you take off that chic lemon dress, please. That's the last time I shall say "please" to you. Now strip.'

I watched Magnolia's reaction. She rose to her feet with her back straight, head erect, defiant to the last. With the fingers of her right hand she nervously twisted her wedding ring around and around, giving away her inner apprehension. 'Strip,' Gretel barked at her again and she drew off the dress as if in utter mortification, then she removed a peach-coloured silk slip, revealing herself in yet more peach, an obviously expensive bra and briefs set with a frilly suspender belt holding up sheer stockings. Her breasts were neatly pear-shaped, I noted, and of a good size contained in the half-cups of the bra. Flat of belly, curved of hip, long of leg, Magnolia was blessed with a lovely figure. Between her thighs her love mount made a delightfully curved bulge in the brief panties, the blur of her pubic hair visible through the material.

'Take it off, you have nothing to be ashamed of,' Gretel said, impressed by Magnolia's figure. 'Such a fuss about a little thing like getting in the nude. Do it, or I'll have Chauncey do it for you.'

'I don't want to,' Magnolia whined. 'I won't!'

'Look here,' Chauncey piped up in protest, 'This lady is an American and obviously in distress. She's being coerced against her will to do these things.' He blinked at Gretel from behind his large round spectacles, appealing to her. 'Can't you see she doesn't want to?'

'Then *you* make her want to,' Gretel said severely. 'Or perhaps, as your father suspects, you'd prefer I got a nice boy for you, eh Chauncey? Surely not? Your father would delight in these proceedings. Out of your clothes *now* and dear Magnolia will finish undressing too.' I saw her eyes narrow as she brought out a length of short whippy bamboo cane from behind the plump cushion of her chair, cracking it threateningly against the palm of her hand. 'Or do I have to use this on you both?'

Magnolia gulped but finished disrobing by the low oval table, standing with one hand covering her breasts and the other held to her heavily bushed cunt as if to protect it. Chauncey stripped beside his chair, red in the face, his body rather over-fed and startlingly white from the neck down for a Californian college boy. He had lost his erection under Gretel's bullying and his prick hung thickly curved over large tight balls.

'Very promising,' Gretel said, lifting his cock with the bamboo cane and then letting it droop again. 'We will see how it compares with your father's once it is excited. Magnolia will give it a nice suck for you, won't you, *liebling*? Sit on the edge of the table and Chauncey will come to you.'

'I'll do no such thing,' Magnolia began, but changed her mind when Gretel advanced on her with the cane. So Magnolia sat, her eyes on me sorrowfully as I gave her what I hoped was a brave smile of encouragement. After all, I could have told her, you're only going to suck a nicely formed clean dick and if you've never done that before at your age, well, it's about time you did.

Slow in shuffling forward to position himself, Chauncey let out a howl of pain and indignant surprise as Gretel urged him on with a sharp crack on his fat bum with her cane. Then she herself held his prick up for Magnolia.

I wondered just when my part in the action would come. I felt my excitement growing as is my nature when in a sexually charged atmosphere surrounded by naked and attractive bodies. Anything other than that wouldn't be normal, would it? I sat with my legs crossed, my thighs involuntarily squeezing my cunt, a fluttering in my lower tummy and my nipples swollen.

Magnolia had opened her mouth to cover the plum helmet of Chauncey's stalk which Gretel was holding to her lips. I wished it were me. Her mouth closed over the knob distastefully and she made loud sucking sounds as if to get the task completed, only to be told sharply by Gretel to suck harder. As her head began to bob and the whole penis disappeared into her mouth, I suspected that she was beginning to enjoy it, even against her will. Chauncey's knees trembled and buckled, groans and whimpers issuing from his lips. Then Gretel roughly pulled Magnolia's head back and Chauncey's now staunchly erect prick emerged from her mouth with a definite plop and sprung up stiff as a pole.

It was obvious Gretel had more in mind for the pair than a straightforward gobble. I noted that Magnolia was frowning when made to cease. Whether she was disappointed at not finishing off the job or because she was aroused by the act and wanted to continue, I was not certain.

'Get onto the table,' Gretel commanded her. 'Grip the edges with your hands, part your legs and raise your buttocks.' I had to admit the oval shape was exactly right for someone to assume that position, but Magnolia was having none of it, having guessed the outcome. Her protest was forming in her mouth when Gretel held her down and delivered two sharp cracks with the cane across Magnolia's buttock cheeks to make her comply.

'You bitch!' screamed the sophisticated Magnolia, obviously never having been in such a situation before –

unlike me. Her loud protests only made Gretel thrash her
until her shrieks turned to squeals and she began to plead for
mercy while her bottom turned red. She squirmed her fleshy
rump from side to side, still whimpering at the hurt and
indignity. Sitting across from her I saw it all, her bare-arsed
flanks quivering, the pale white skin of her globes criss-
crossed with the marks of the cane. Magnolia's long shapely
legs were parted and fully stretched out revealing the white
rounded cheeks and, in the deep cleave between, the mysteries
of her most intimate parts. Standing over her, with Gretel
still holding his rigid cock, Chauncey could see all too: the
puckered ring of her arsehole and, an inch or so below, the
hairy split-bulge of her cunt, the full nether lips invitingly on
offer.

'Just look, Chauncey,' said Gretel. 'Isn't that a most
tempting sight? She's begging for a prick and you musn't be
shy. Come closer, you can't do it from there. Here, I'll direct
it in for you. I know she'll love it, you're so big and stiff.'

I heard Magnolia give a low moan. 'No, no, you musn't,'
she begged. 'Not that! Please.' The next moment she groaned
almost as if in disbelief as Gretel pushed Chauncey forward,
directly between the ivory buttocks, guiding the red knob to
her cleft. The young American muttered as if in the most
awkward dilemma, then gave up the fight, grasping
Magnolia's cheeks and forcing them apart. His hips thrust as
he was lost to all but the great pleasure of being embedded in
a receptive cunt, going up on his tiptoes in his forward
heaves to gain full penetration.

His aroused state was patently obvious and he fucked
away strenuously at Magnolia as his lech increased. Her
reaction was of more interest to me and I observed that,
despite her protests and her head bowed to hide her shame,
her buttocks were raised to accommodate the shunting bar of

flesh. I detected a jerking of her bottom each time Chauncey plunged into her, his balls slapping noisily against her divide.

Gretel was aware of it too, watching every sticky thrust with lustful eyes. 'See how eagerly she takes him now!' she exulted. 'The high and mighty lady fucks like any other woman.'

Poor Magnolia, I thought, she was embarrassed to the core. However, she was moaning softly, helpless to stop her arse buffeting back to devour his cock until she came off with a series of loud cries.

Chauncey was in his last throes too, convulsing and shouting as he emptied his balls up her. At once he was pulled aside by Colonel San-joi who had approached wearing only his military shirt, his prick rearing from his loins.

Gretel laughed. 'So you want her now? Go on then, I'm sure we'd all like to see that. I thought that watching them might give you the urge, Colonel.'

Magnolia turned her face and saw San-joi's thick cock as he moved between her parted legs. Her swollen sex lips were on full pout and revealing to us the glistening pink inner folds. 'No, please, no!' she implored. 'Enough is enough, I don't want to again.'

'Do be quiet, Magnolia,' snapped Gretel. 'Colonel, smack her bottom if she is obstinate. She must learn.' She watched San-joi bring out his little bottle of sweet oil and nodding. 'I know what you want,' she said. 'She won't forget this day, will she?'

I was certain Magnolia wouldn't, hearing her wail of despair as the lecherous Thai poured a little oil into her buttock cleft and rubbed it into her rear orifice. He pushed in a finger to the first knuckle. Her sudden twitch in response to the penetration of her back passage was followed by an unbelieving stare at the perpetrator of this ignominy. 'You can't! You mustn't!' she screeched in alarm. 'It-it is surely not possible! You are too big and I am too small.'

'Madam, be quiet,' San-joi threatened. 'Would you prefer I brought your daughter in and fucked her? No? Then ease your bottom for me.'

Magnolia relaxed her exposed buttocks, lying limply across the oval table, drawing in her breath, knowing she must accept this further outrage. I saw the bulbous knob nosing against the serrated rim, both his hands pulling her cheeks apart, hips pressing forward. There was a low moan from Magnolia as the ring yielded and she took several thick inches of the throbbing stalk. From my seat I saw half of his prick embedded up her rear portal. She clenched and received a quick slap to make her loosen up. Heart-rending sighs were expelled from between her clenched teeth as Magnolia was fully impaled and stuffed with his rigid cock. I well knew feeling the throbbings and palpitations in her passage that would be caused by that rude intruder.

'She grips tightly,' San-joi announced happily. 'Very nice and clinging. Now she is ready for me, I think.' With that he began his first movements, pistoning slowly into her and withdrawing halfway only to slide forward again. After several minutes of this I watched Magnolia begin to respond, her bum circling, lifting, pressing back to meet the thick penis in her tight rear hole. Now her moans of despair had turned to cries of pleasure. Her head was raised, back dutifully dipped, rear gyrating as the erotic feeling generated in her arse and cunt made her wanton. 'Good, good,' said San-joi, his cock sliding in a velvet grip, lodged to his balls on each thrust. She reared to him, on her hands and knees, her pear-shaped tits swaying at each buffet. Magnolia, I thought lewdly, you are getting a right buggering and loving every inch up your tight little arse. Gretel must have been thinking the same thought, that her victim was now in a state of lust that would permit anything.

'Diana,' Gretel said to me sharply. 'You must play your part. Stand by her head, I want to see her eat your cunt. Go on!'

I was happy to obey, seeing Magnolia's flushed face and wild-eyed look as she observed the closeness of my sex thrust out to her. To my joy she gripped my thighs for support as the jolting of her buttocks continued apace, small husky sobs coming from her lips as she shifted forward to kiss my mound, her tongue seeking my slit. I parted the lips for her, steadying myself with feet apart as she licked greedily, her tongue now probing me deliciously, lapping at my clitty.

'Yes-yes-yes!' I cried. 'Come in her bottom, Colonel!' Magnolia was jerking and bucking wilder each moment and suddenly I was spending gloriously in her wide mouth. Then with a loud 'Aaaaaah!' and a furious churning of her bottom she climaxed violently as San-joi's root flooded her innards. I saw Chauncey looking on with mouth agape as we sagged apart, breasts heaving with the exertion, sated and quite exhausted. Gretel beamed at us delightedly.

Shown into a bedroom with an adjoining bathroom, Magnolia and I showered and dressed. Her face was set and her silence was annoying. Obviously the old Magnolia was back to her former, stuffy self. 'Don't say you didn't enjoy any of that,' I said as we prepared to return to Gretel's lounge. 'We were both carried away. Just forget it, if it worries you.'

'I was forced,' she said determinedly. 'You weren't. At least, you needed no encouragement when you were told to come to me for – what I had to do to you!'

'I didn't notice you finding it so awful,' I replied. 'You ate me out like you were greedy to get more, and all the time with that prick up your behind driving you crazy. What the devil are we going on about, anyway? It was all to get your daughter off the hook.'

'It was a deliberate ploy for them to vent their filthy lust on me,' she said, as if she were accusing me of enjoying the whole scene if not actually part of the conspiracy. I was about to deny this, or at least the part of it that hinted I was in on the plot, and remind her that I'd volunteered to take her place, when the door opened and Nicola burst into the room. She hugged her mother frantically as her saviour. All the same, standing behind them as the girl looked at me over her mother's shoulder I suspected I saw a glimpse of her old devilry directed at me even through tear-filled eyes.

It was an Academy Award performance, I decided, as Nicola blubbered her complete innocence out in sobs to Magnolia. 'We know, we know, dear,' her relieved mother repeated, patting her solicitously. 'Now I intend to get you on a flight out of this awful place this very evening. You'll go to your grandmother's in Atlanta and we'll join you as soon as I get your father to resign his post here.'

Gretel stood in the doorway while this poignant reunion was taking place, smiling as if delighted with the happy outcome. 'You see, Mrs Wentzel,' she said benignly. 'We even sent for your daughter to be delivered safely to you. I'm only sorry to hear you will be leaving Bangkok yourself before long. I felt we were just getting to know each other and that you would enjoy visiting my home again.'

If ever a look of loathing could be put into an expression, that was what Magnolia gave the plump German woman as she swept past her holding tightly to her daughter. I drove them back to our apartment in silence and helped Nicola assist her mother to her bed.

'You must drive her to the airport once Nicola has packed,'

she said to me feebly, refusing the smelling salts I offered and asking for something stronger. I placed a glass of vodka in her trembling hand. 'This whole day has been a nightmare for me, I must lie here with the curtains drawn and try to recover. God, what we were made to endure. I can't bear thinking about it.' She covered her eyes with her hands, groaning. 'The bastards,' she swore, making me think that perhaps her old superior attitude was returning after downing the vodka. 'To think that obnoxious little cocksucker Chauncey had the downright impudence to fuck me. Me! You saw him.'

'He did get carried away once he was up you,' I had to agree, stifling a smile, leaving the vodka bottle at her bedside table. 'I'll see how Nicola is getting on with her packing. There isn't much time before her flight leaves, is there?' Her hand gave me a feeble squeeze of thanks as I turned to go. As ever, I thought, how do I find myself in these situations? Never a dull moment, I chuckled.

I found Nicola sitting on her bed smiling wickedly as I entered. 'I guess it's all been too much for mommy,' she said. 'I can just imagine how she'd go on, thinking of me thrown into that jail with all the thieves, junkies and whores of Bangkok.'

'Yes,' I said, not taken in by her schoolgirl smile. 'I just hope you didn't corrupt them too much while you were there. On your feet, we're going to the airport and your loss is Bangkok's gain. Go and kiss your mother goodbye. Make it quick, we all want you on that plane.'

While she was gone, I regarded the teenage mess left behind in her bedroom: discarded jeans and tee-shirts, records of the latest pop hits, her school uniform and gym-slip piled on the bed as if of no further use. On her dressing table were coins and used tubes of make-up, and one solitary earring of

Thai workmanship that I knew I could match, its partner having been found under my bed while the maid was tidying up. 'The little bitch!' I swore, pocketing it as a souvenir, a memento of her seducing my husband as well as myself. Despite all, I grinned at the thought, but I had no intention of letting her have the pleasure of knowing I knew.

'What did you and my mother have to do to get me released?' she asked cheerily as I drove her to Bangkok airport. 'I was guilty of those charges, you know, so it must have been payment of some kind. I bet you were both fucked by customers of that German woman. I can't imagine mommy on the job!' she laughed. 'You'd do it though. We had a good time together, didn't we? My brother fucked you too, I know, because he told me. He said how good you were. We said we'd like to have you in bed together.' She smiled at the thought. 'I think I'm just like you. Don't you agree?'

Whether I did or not, she had made a good start and I was glad to see her disappear through the customs barrier with one last knowing wave in my direction. I went back into Magnolia's apartment on my return and found her fast asleep on her bed with the vodka bottle almost empty by her side. Drawing the bedcover over her, I went into my own apartment, deciding it had been quite a day even for me. I was preparing for bed when the doorbell sounded. I found Magnolia standing there swaying, her hair for once around her cheeks.

'I can't stay in there by myself tonight, Diana,' she said. 'My mind is too full of everything that's happened. Let me stay with you. I need to be with someone who knows what I've been through.' I led her through to the spare bedroom, helping her undress and get into bed. Five minutes later, in my own bed and settling down for the night, she appeared and wordlessly got in beside me, cuddling up, her body smooth and warm against mine.

'Try to sleep,' I told her, easing my body slightly away; the feel of her naked skin was arousing and I was unsure of her need apart from human company. 'Nicola's off safely to America and you've nothing else to worry you now. Sleep is the best thing.'

'What about the things that took place this afternoon?' she said. 'How can I explain that to Howard? How can you explain that to *your* husband?'

'Why explain?' I said. 'Forget it. Put it out of mind.'

'But you know they made me climax,' she admitted suddenly. 'How can a woman come like I did, and have such strong orgasms, if they don't like what's happening to them?' She gave a long sigh. 'The truth is it aroused a strong feeling in me, one that I've never had. I loved the fucking, even the buggering.'

'Then make sure you get Howard to keep giving you that nice feeling when he's with you,' I said, thinking how he would love that proposition. 'Forget the guilt, anyone can be tempted temporarily. I was made to come myself.'

'Yes, I made you,' Magnolia recalled. 'I wanted to. It wasn't my first time with another woman either. At college it was quite the thing. I liked it and, after all these years, I wanted to do it again.' I felt her hand slide over me, clasp a breast, squeeze it tenderly, her palm slowly circling over the hardening nipple. 'Have you ever been with another woman Diana?'

'It's been known,' I admitted, 'and if you continue playing with my breasts like that I shall want to again. You're making me want to now.' Further words were silenced as her lips met mine and I returned the kiss, our mouths crushing together, tongues probing. My hands sought the firmness of her breasts, then she was guiding my head down to suckle them. Her hands held each one in turn to my lips, my hand sliding down to the fork of her legs to seek her cunt, her legs parting for my access. Then Magnolia gave a loud sigh and rolled over on top of me, working her furred mound to mine, the pair of us lost in the delightful joining of our bodies. With soft female lips to kiss, breasts to fondle and suck, other more lewd and imaginative acts to indulge ourselves in, it was hours before we fell asleep tight in each other's arms.

I was awakened by the ringing of the telephone and lifted the receiver to hear Harry on the other end of the line. 'Good news, my love,' he began. 'You can set off and join me any day now. I've found a bungalow for us.'

I listened excitedly as Harry described the arrangements, delighted by the knowledge that I'd be joining him. But a large part of that excitement was brought on by the woman in bed beside me sitting up to press kisses to my shoulders and neck. I felt her hand infiltrate between my bottom cheeks, stroking my cunt sensuously as I eased myself up to allow her that pleasure.

'So what's the news at your end, Di?' he enquired finally. 'Nothing much, I suppose. I'm sorry if it's been terribly dull for you, my darling.'

'Terribly dull,' I agreed, saying goodbye for now and replacing the receiver. I turned to Magnolia with a mischievous smile, our lips brushing lightly. 'I just don't know what we would do without men, do you?' I said.

'Let me show you,' she replied, drawing back the cover and lowering her face between my spread thighs. 'How about this?'

'Wonderful,' I moaned in appreciation as her soft lips surrounded my sex and I arched my back to get more of her long tongue exploring inwards. 'That will do nicely!'

Lustful Liaisons

EROTIC ADVENTURES IN THE CAPITAL CITY
OF LOVE!

Anonymous

PARIS 1912 – a city alive with the pursuit of pleasure,
from the promenade of the Folies Bergère to the high-
class brothels of the Left Bank. Everywhere business is
booming in the oldest trade of all – the trade of love!

But now there is a new and flourishing activity to
absorb the efforts of go-ahead men-about-town: the
business of manufacturing motor cars. Men like Robert
and Bertrand Laforge are pioneers in this field but their
new automobile has a design defect that can only be
rectified by some cunning industrial espionage. Which
is where the new trade marries with the old, for the
most reliable way of discovering information is to enlist
the help of a lovely and compliant woman. A woman,
for example, like the voluptuous Nellie Lebérigot
whose soft creamy flesh and generous nature are
guaranteed to uncover a man's most closely guarded
secrets . . .

FICTION / EROTICA 0 7472 3710 7

Headline Delta Erotic Survey

In order to provide the kind of books you like to read – and to qualify for a free erotic novel of the Editor's choice – we would appreciate it if you would complete the following survey and send your answers, together with any further comments, to:

Headline Book Publishing
FREEPOST (WD 4984)
London
NW1 0YR

1. Are you male or female?
2. Age? Under 20 / 20 to 30 / 30 to 40 / 40 to 50 / 50 to 60 / 60 to 70 / over
3. At what age did you leave full-time education?
4. Where do you live? (Main geographical area)
5. Are you a regular erotic book buyer / a regular book buyer in general / both?
6. How much approximately do you spend a year on erotic books / on books in general?
7. How did you come by this book?
7a. If you bought it, did you purchase from: a national bookchain / a high street store / a newsagent / a motorway station / an airport / a railway station / other . . .
8. Do you find erotic books easy / hard to come by?
8a. Do you find Headline Delta erotic books easy / hard to come by?
9. Which are the best / worst erotic books you have ever read?
9a. Which are the best / worst Headline Delta erotic books you have ever read?
10. Within the erotic genre there are many periods, subjects and literary styles. Which of the following do you prefer:
10a. (period) historical / Victorian / C20th /contemporary / future?
10b. (subject) nuns / whores & whorehouses / Continental frolics / s&m / vampires / modern realism / escapist fantasy / science fiction?

10c. (styles) hardboiled / humorous / hardcore / ironic / romantic / realistic?

10d. Are there any other ingredients that particularly appeal to you?

11. We try to create a cover appearance that is suitable for each title. Do you consider them to be successful?

12. Would you prefer them to be less explicit / more explicit?

13. We would be interested to hear of your other reading habits. What other types of books do you read?

14. Who are your favourite authors?

15. Which newspapers do you read?

16. Which magazines?

17 Do you have any other comments or suggestions to make?

If you would like to receive a free erotic novel of the Editor's choice (available only to UK residents), together with an up-to-date listing of Headline Delta titles, please supply your name and address. Please allow 28 days for delivery.

Name ....

Address ....

....

....

A selection of Erotica from Headline